Gertie Milk

& the Great Keeper Rescue

Featuring . . .

Robot Rabbit Boy
as
Robot Rabbit Boy

SIMON VAN BOOY

RAZORBILL

RAZORBILL

An Imprint of Penguin Random House LLC
Penguin.com

RAZORBILL & colophon is a registered trademark
of Penguin Random House LLC.

First published in the United States of America by Razorbill,
an imprint of Penguin Random House LLC, 2018

LIBRARY OF CONGRESS CATALOGING-IN-PUBLICATION DATA
Names: Van Booy, Simon, author.
Title: Gertie Milk and the great Keeper rescue / Simon Van Booy.
Description: New York, NY : Razorbill, [2018] | Series: Gertie Milk ; 2 | Sequel to: *Gertie Milk & the Keeper of Lost Things*. | Summary: Gertie, Kolt, and Robot Rabbit Boy continue to return missing objects throughout history while trying to find out what happened to the imprisoned Keepers of Lost Things.
Identifiers: LCCN 2018026457 | ISBN 9780448494616 (hardback)
Subjects: | CYAC: Lost and found possessions—Fiction. | Time travel—Fiction. | Rescues—Fiction. | BISAC: JUVENILE FICTION / Fantasy & Magic. | JUVENILE FICTION / Historical / General.
Classification: LCC PZ7.1.V3623 Geg 2018 | DDC [Fic]—dc23
LC record available at https://lccn.loc.gov/2018026457

Printed in the United States of America

1 3 5 7 9 10 8 6 4 2

Interior Design by Jessica Jenkins

I've never felt completely at home anywhere in this world, which is why I searched so long for the Island of Lost Things. This book is dedicated to the people who live there with me or sometimes visit, especially Christina and Madeleine, but also the creatures who share our lives (known and unknown), including but not limited to: Tuesday, Little, Rhubarb, Max the sheep, Lester, Yolk, Big Bear, Megatronus, Ellie, Simple Bear, Pastry, Saturday, Phyllis, Jig, Coconut, George the mouse, and Robot Rabbit Boy (yes, he's real).

Part
1

1

The Crisis of Lost Keepers

THE HEAVY CLOCK ON the mantelpiece chimed as two hands joined to announce the hour. Gertie was studying a map of Japan. In particular, a dark forest clustered at the base of Mount Fuji. It was said to be haunted by the screams of people who'd never found their way out, and so, Gertie thought, it was *exactly* the sort of place where those despicable Losers might have chosen to dump a Keeper of Lost Things.

The map was dark green, with shadowy peaks rising up to the snowcapped tip of Japan's tallest volcano. A crimson patch bloomed where the Pacific Ocean touched land, reminding Gertie of the birthmark that covered one side of her face.

A fly landed on the white tip of Mount Fuji, rubbed its stringy black legs together, then flew off in search of peach cake crumbs.

Gertie looked down at the map, and knew full well the only way to find out if there were lost Keepers wandering the haunted forest at the base of Mount Fuji was to go there and explore it.

But that was impossible.

The clock over the fireplace continued its even ticking, a flicking away of each second as the moment passed. Gertie sat back in her chair with a sigh. It was impossible to travel to any one of these places she had looked up over the past few weeks. For the truth was that she, Kolt, and Robot Rabbit Boy could only get off the island of Skuldark when the Big Dusty Book Upstairs (also known as the B.D.B.U.) sent them somewhere to return an object lost from time. She had appeared on the island not long ago herself—washing up on the beach with no memory of who she was, or where she had come from.

Gertie's only thought back then had been to solve the mystery of her identity. But now that she had more or less figured *that* out—all she wanted was to find a way to free her fellow Keepers, who were being marooned in the most terrible places throughout history, instead of coming to Skuldark as fate had once intended.

But the chances of going to Mount Fuji to look for them were slim at best. Even if Gertie and her Keeper gang were sent to Japan in their time-traveling car, the Time Cat—the B.D.B.U. only gave them eleven hours to complete each mission. If they didn't return to Skuldark before then, using the time machine, they would get "snatched" home by the

B.D.B.U., which was like walking thirty miles in wet clothes with stones in both shoes—though it had never happened to Gertie (yet).

Anyway, eleven hours was hardly enough time to return some vital object *and* search for missing Keepers, not to mention they'd have to be very lucky indeed to land in the same time period as one of the kidnapped Keepers.

Gertie had spent a lot of time at the top of the lighthouse where the B.D.B.U. lived, going on and on to the enormous book about how vital it was to start rescuing Keepers. Surely the grumpy old encyclopedia could choose things for them to return to the world that were within shouting distance of a lost Keeper? But Gertie had received not even a single page flutter in response. She was thinking about dragging a sleeping bag into the tower and camping out until she could get some response from the stubborn book. Until then, all she had were her maps of history's scariest places, like the haunted forest in Japan, or the Black Hole of Calcutta. Gertie couldn't help imagining what dangers the kidnapped Keepers must be facing.

Suddenly there was a silver flash as something darted from under the bookcase and zoomed across the floor toward a cabinet of rocks and fossils. Gertie jumped back in her seat as she always did when one popped out.

"Kolt!" she cried. "Kolt!" But he was outside with Robot Rabbit Boy. She had found one just yesterday in the bathtub, scratching the sides to get out. She had used a marshmallow toasting fork to put it in a bucket. The rogue robot hands had been infesting the cottage for weeks. It was creepy how they were getting into *everything*. Gertie even had to check her bed at night, in case one lay in wait under the covers.

Kolt stored the ones he caught in glass jars so he could study them. And last week Robot Rabbit Boy had blasted one with his nose laser after it had lunged for a baby Slug Lamp.

Gertie considered getting up and poking under the cabinet with a broom. But what was the use? Until Kolt found out which bedroom under the cottage the robot hands were escaping from, catching one wouldn't make any difference. There was always another to replace it.

She listened for the metallic shuffling of its fingers under the cabinet, but all was quiet. She let her mind sink like a stone in water, down and down to the 945 bedrooms in the cliff underneath the cottage. It was a sort of never-ending basement, with long dark corridors, and Cave Sprites to lead the way. Each room had been carved into the rock and was filled with different items lost from the world.

The ancient mission of the Keepers was to return certain things that were lost, so Gertie was becoming familiar with the dim passageways, rope bridges, and underground rivers inside the cliff. There were more things in those rooms, she often thought, than fish in the sea, or even stars in the galaxy.

Although some items seemed boring and unimportant to human progress, it was impossible to tell when a stick might be the key to discovering the size of planet Earth—as it had been on their mission to North Africa.

The objects Keepers returned led to new inventions or cures, or inspired people to do their best. Sometimes they even helped people to feel less afraid—which made them kinder. Gertie had seen this herself from the return missions she had been on, as Skuldark's newest official Keeper of Lost Things.

Literally any object Gertie could imagine was in the maze of rooms under the cliff. From the annoying robot hands that were loose in the cottage, to rooms packed with toys, shrunken heads, strange weapons, photograph albums, lost packages, comic books, and masks for breathing underwater—Gertie always managed to find something new when she went downstairs.

She wondered if she could figure out which rooms to look in for items from Japan. Then she could go to the top of the lighthouse and dangle something from Mount Fuji before the B.D.B.U. Would that convince the eccentric book to send them there on a mission?

Gertie was still staring at her map, daydreaming, when the ear-piercing screech of Kolt's high-powered electric drill came from the Garden of Lost Things. He was working on his latest project with Robot Rabbit Boy—restoring an aircraft for Gertie to fly.

For the past few weeks—when not traveling through time, or harvesting moonberries, or watching a television dragged up from one of the rooms below—Kolt had been in the garden banging around on the fighter plane.

Gertie considered peeking out to see what exactly they

were doing. But she couldn't be bothered. It was cozy and warm at the kitchen table, hunched over her map.

During the big mission to ancient China over a month ago, when they rescued the B.D.B.U. after it was stolen by Losers, Gertie had discovered her brother, Gareth, was one of the Losers—and that she herself had been a Loser too. Gareth had tried to convince her to stay with him, but Gertie had chosen Kolt and Robot Rabbit Boy over her own family. Blood was not thicker than water, but it was definitely more colorful.

While she was trapped underground with Gareth Milk in the snake-filled Crown of Triangles, she'd also found out about the Losers' plot to kidnap young Keepers, hiding them in gruesome places throughout history. She could hardly believe her brother was a part of something so dastardly.

Gertie spent most of *her* free time between missions trying to find out exactly *where* in history the Losers might have hidden the children. In addition to her map of Mount Fuji, she had already filled a wooden box with other maps, pictures, keys, old books of legends—even photographs of weird and scary places where Keepers could be trapped.

She thought back to her sleeping bag, folded up in the closet. There really was no other way; she would have to sleep up there in the tower until the B.D.B.U. gave her a sign it understood her plight. Kolt had told her to keep looking, continue collecting information—just in case they *were* lucky enough to return an object to one of the places on Gertie's list.

But what were the odds?

Slim to none, Gertie thought. She was tired of relying on chance. It made her feel helpless, and reminded her that Gareth was still with the Losers, determined to carry out whatever heartless plan they came up with next.

The guilt she felt about leaving her brother behind was like an anchor attached to her thoughts. Whenever she started to feel happy about something, the anchor would tug, reminding her of all the things she had to feel bad about.

It wasn't fair that trying to do the right thing had caused just as much misery as doing the wrong thing.

Then from outside came a clanging as though a giant bell were bouncing down a hill. Gertie plugged her ears until it stopped. A moment later it was metal plates being smashed up against each other. Then grinding. Then drilling, which ended with an explosion that made the cottage windows rattle. A moment later the front door was flung open and Kolt appeared, flushed and out of breath. There was engine oil on his cheeks, and a perfectly round hole in his Fair Isle sweater-vest.

Gertie pointed toward the cabinet of rocks and fossils. "Another robot hand. It's under there if you want to look."

Kolt was glowing with excitement. "Forget about that! We've finished, Gertie! Ready to fly a restored fighter aircraft?"

"It sounds like you just blew it up."

"Oh, that was just one of my slippers exploding." Kolt lifted his leg to reveal a gray sock with scorch marks.

Gertie put the lid on her box of maps and old books.

"Fear not," he reassured her, "no Slug Lamps were harmed during the blowing-up of my slipper. You know how Robot Rabbit Boy feels about their squishy little faces? He made sure they were safely tucked into their leaf beds on the other side of the golden moonberry statue."

"What is Robot Rabbit Boy doing?" she said, changing the subject.

"Sitting on the grass squeezing leftover moonberries."

"Leftover from what?"

"You'll see!"

The repair and restoration of a World War II Spitfire Supermarine aircraft had taken Kolt the better part of a month. They had discovered some dusty instruction manuals in one of the bedrooms under the cottage, along with tools, spare parts, training videos, and an electronic box called a television, which Kolt said had once been very popular before interactive virtual reality.

The fully sized fighter sitting outside the cottage was enormous. Apart from the landing gear, black rubber tires, and a few metal parts, it was covered in camouflage paint. Kolt said it must have gone missing during a midair battle, as Robot Rabbit Boy had found several machine-gun bullets in the tail section during the early days of restoration.

Gertie rose from the table and followed Kolt into the garden. It was bright with late afternoon sunshine. The sun felt warm on her cheeks, though a cool wind was blowing off the sea beyond the cliff.

Robot Rabbit Boy was lying in the shade of the aircraft's wing, popping the juice from moonberries into his mouth— but missing, so that his fur was stained with purple and red blotches. His eyes glowed pink when he saw Gertie. The restored Spitfire fighter plane boasted many new or restored parts. The propeller was silver steel and dazzling. But a flower-patterned seat bolted into the cockpit didn't seem to fit.

"Um, isn't that the rose armchair from the kitchen?" Gertie asked.

Kolt nodded. "It was the only cushioned seat to pass the bounce test, which Robot Rabbit Boy and I discovered after an afternoon of test-bouncing. The original eject mechanism was broken, so bouncing off a springy cushion seemed like the best chance at survival if things go wrong."

Gertie stared at the massive hunk of metal and imagined it crashing. "Think I can really fly it?"

"Well, if you can't, you can certainly learn," Kolt said. "We have all the manuals, and you can watch those training videos again if you need to."

But Gertie did not feel confident. "It's a lot bigger than the one I flew in London, and it has machine guns. Remember what happened to your cauliflowers when I accidentally nudged the firing button on the control ring?"

"I'm glad you asked about those, because we modified them to shoot frozen moonberries—about twenty a second to be exact. We also installed an 'interrupter' so you'll never hit the propeller and juice yourself."

"The guns shoot moonberries instead of bullets?"

Kolt looked pleased with himself. "Why kill someone when you can soak them in juice?"

"Lavender," said Robot Rabbit Boy from under a camouflage wing.

Gertie sighed and looked around at all the tools and debris laid out on the grass. Next to the vintage war-bird was a dented space rocket. A few of the Spitfire's spare parts leaned against it. Gertie couldn't imagine how such a heap of junk could ever have made it into Earth's outer space (or inner space for that matter).

Kolt saw her looking. "I've seen garden sheds that would fly better than this heap," he said, eyeballing the rusty space rocket, as though for his next project. He knocked on the hollow shell and listened.

"Useless . . . I've seen less rust on sunken ships."

Then he turned proudly to the Spitfire.

"So, ready to test-fly your restored fighter plane?"

Gertie felt her legs tremble—then a rising lightness in her stomach. But before she could answer, several flashes of lightning lit the sky, followed by an almighty crackle of thunder. A strong wind kicked up and blew them back toward the old space rocket.

The B.D.B.U. was calling. Something had to be returned. The Spitfire's maiden flight would mercifully have to wait.

2

It Glows in the Dark

GERTIE'S FIRST THOUGHT WAS, *This is it*—the Big Dusty Book Upstairs had finally recognized her longing to locate the missing Keepers. She dashed through the kitchen, pulled out *The History of Chickens* to reveal the secret passage, then took the tower steps two at a time.

Kolt followed at half the speed. "You're like a mosquito, Gertie! Wait for me!"

Once they reached the apex of the tower, both Keepers uttered the secret Keeper motto, and the guard doors opened.

The giant book was shaking and there was faint smoke curling about its gnarled edges. Gertie went up the stone steps and peered down into the pages. One showed a moving picture of cauldrons of black liquid. Another, horse-drawn wagons plodding along, loaded with sacks of rock.

13

Then into the frame with the bubbling cauldrons came a woman in a long coat.

She was holding glass tubes with purple smoke pouring out of them.

Gertie could smell the faint aroma of whatever the woman was cooking.

"What's she doing?"

"I believe that's Marie Curie," Kolt said, "the world-famous scientist."

"Are you sure?" asked Gertie, her voice full of disappointment. "I was hoping it would be one of the missing Keepers."

The old book was still shaking as one of its giant pages began to turn. Now displayed were bustling streets, with women in long dresses and men with shiny top hats. In a small picture at the bottom of the page was the object that had to be returned.

"There," Kolt said. "It's some kind of bowl with something inside." They both leaned in to read the fine print. "One tenth of a gram of radium salts."

"A bowl of salt?"

"Yes, but not ordinary salt, Gertie, radium salt! A highly radioactive substance."

"What does 'radio active' mean? Something to do with music?"

"A substance is radioactive when it gives off energy as rays that are powerful and potentially harmful. Everything around us—except energy itself—is made up of atoms. You and me, Robot Rabbit Boy, the B.D.B.U., the tower we're standing in, all the lost things from the world under the cottage, even the air. Each atom, Gertie, is a cluster of what humans call protons and neutrons, which are tightly packed into a center that's called the nucleus. Tiny electrons dance around this nucleus in a pattern. Between the nucleus and electrons is just empty space."

"Have you ever seen one of these atoms?"

"No I have not, and neither did Marie Curie. They're rather small. . . . A scientist I once met called Doctor Feynman said that if an apple were magnified to the size of the Earth, then the atoms in the apple would be approximately the size of the original apple. The nucleus is even smaller, and when one is going bad, it gives off energy."

"Like when it's dying?" Gertie asked.

"Well, things don't really die in the way humans think. Energy simply changes form and keeps going. It cannot be created or destroyed, only changed."

Gertie nodded. Kolt seemed to know everything, which sometimes she found slightly annoying.

The old Keeper smiled as though reading her mind. "Don't forget that before you came to Skuldark, I was alone for a hundred years without a television, so I did a lot of reading."

Back downstairs in the kitchen, they found Robot Rabbit Boy waiting dutifully.

"Eggcup?"

"That's right," said Gertie, "an immediate return."

"Lavender!"

"Paris, France, at the beginning of the 1900s," Kolt said, putting on his bowler hat. Then he swept away the rug that covered the trapdoor. Outside the cottage, tiny pieces of hail smacked against the windows. Robot Rabbit Boy pointed with a grubby paw toward the glass.

"Dollops mush?"

Gertie looked. "I think he's worried about Slug Lamps getting pummeled by the hailstones," she said. Robot Rabbit Boy's eyes were glowing raspberry, which meant danger.

"Well then, he should go check on them while we're under the cottage."

"Are Slug Lamps made of atoms?"

"Oh, for sure . . ." Kolt said, taking the first cold step to the basement, "they're mostly water molecules. And before you ask, a molecule is when two or more atoms hold hands. Water is two hydrogen atoms and one oxygen atom—hence its chemical symbol H_2O."

When they arrived at the main level under the cottage, they saw the familiar sight of all the different vehicles, machines, and devices for getting around the cliff. Then a Cave Sprite appeared. It was moving slowly, and had much less glow than the others.

"Hello, Sunday," Gertie said. Kolt had named all seven Cave Sprites after days of the week. "We're here for some weird salt that gives off energy rays."

Sunday hovered for a few seconds as though thinking, then floated off down one of the many rock wall corridors, each lined with dozens and dozens of numbered doors.

As they followed, Kolt took out two pairs of thick green gloves for them to put on.

Gertie grimaced. "What are these for?"

"I'm afraid this salt is rather nasty stuff."

"It didn't look nasty, just small and harmless."

"Well, it's not. Wear these gloves, Gertie, and don't get too close to it. If we spill any in the Time Cat, it's going to have to be decontaminated, which is a nightmare, basically—like going through a car wash five thousand times."

Just then they arrived at bedroom 91. The door was made of lead, and so heavy, Kolt was only able to open it partway. Gertie squeezed to get through. Kolt had to leave his bowler hat outside on the ground.

They didn't need Sunday to light their way because all the objects in the room were glowing in different colors.

"It's magic!" Gertie said.

"No," said Kolt, "it's radiation. Remember, when atoms decay, they leak energy in the form of short but powerful rays that can penetrate almost anything."

"It's cool that it glows though. Why is the room so small?"

"Because lost items that are radioactive are dangerous, Gertie. For safety, Mrs. Pumble—who you know was the Keeper here when I arrived—had to construct ten-foot walls of concrete around this bedroom, with lead plates, because those rays I told you about can destroy the human body."

"Shouldn't we be wearing more than gloves then?"

Kolt bit his lip. "You mean like safety goggles?"

"Er, I mean like full-on lead suits with concrete helmets!"

"Probably," Kolt said. "But it's a tiny amount, and we'll have it such a short time, we should be okay."

In a corner, Sunday was hovering over a small dish. Gertie put her green gloves on and went over to it.

"It's empty!"

"No it isn't," Kolt said, peering over her shoulder and pointing to a white flake the size of a rice grain.

Gertie picked up the bowl. "You're right. It is small. Are you sure it's dangerous?" To Gertie it seemed just an innocent flake.

"I'm afraid so—but there are different kinds of radiation. Some types can power space stations, while other kinds kill cancer cells. Which is why Marie Curie's discovery of radium was such an important step for human progress. Doctor Curie was the first woman to ever be awarded the Nobel Prize, and the first person to win it twice. But don't mention that to her."

"Why? Seems like she'd be proud."

"Because *we've* got her radium sample, so she hasn't won it yet."

GERTIE CARRIED THE BOWL carefully with her green gloves all the way back upstairs—where a soaking wet Robot Rabbit Boy was pawing his ears, sore from the barrage of hailstones.

"Save any Slug Lamps?" she asked him.

"Mashed potato."

Kolt whistled. "That bad, eh?"

"Are hailstones made of atoms, Kolt?"

"Yes, Gertie—everything is."

The water dripping from Robot Rabbit Boy's fur had formed a pool at his grubby feet.

Gertie set the dish of radium salt on the kitchen table, worried what would happen if Robot Rabbit Boy accidentally swallowed the contents. Even if he didn't die, the Series 7 might glow for the rest of his life.

"Stay here for this mission," Gertie told him gently, "because if the hail gets worse, you might have to rescue more Slug Lamps."

"Eggcup?"

"She's right," Kolt agreed. "And we won't be long, Paris in the winter of 1901 is not dangerous at all. We'll be back in a jiffy with rhubarb jam, fresh croissants, and a little absinthe for me."

WHILE GERTIE WAS IN the Sock Drawer choosing which dress to wear, Kolt started a fire in the kitchen for Robot Rabbit Boy to dry out. Then, before leaving, they plonked him in a cozy chair with his favorite snack: a jar of lemon curd.

Gertie had chosen a long, wine-colored dress that hung an inch off the floor. The tiny floral pattern on it was from Liberty of London, and very fashionable in its time, according to Kolt. It had white silk-covered buttons from the bottom of the skirt all the way to the blouse. An attached white lace collar covered Gertie's neck. There was also floral embroidery at the hemline, and riding up the long cotton sleeves.

Kolt opted for a gray lounge suit with his black bowler hat, which had been popular back then.

With the morsel of radium still giving off a bluish glow, Gertie attached a handkerchief tightly over the top to stop the flake from falling out and getting lost. She wondered if she should find something heavy to block the radiation, but hopefully they'd be rid of the item quickly. She placed the wrapped dish in a Bon Marché wicker picnic basket, which would have been a normal thing to carry in Paris of 1901.

With Robot Rabbit Boy snoozing away in the armchair, Kolt and Gertie braved the hard pellets of hailstones and raced to the Time Cat. After fiddling with the door lock, Gertie slid past Kolt into the driver's seat.

"I'll drive!" she said.

"Fine," Kolt said, going around to the passenger side and getting in. "Just remember the clutch trick I showed you."

He set the time clocks on the dashboard, then checked the emergency peach cake and moonberry juice situation. Gertie removed the actual time machine (a small wooden box) from the glove box and readied her key.

"So it's Marie Curie, and Paris?"

"That's right," Kolt said. "The B.D.B.U. should get us within shouting distance of her Shed of Discovery."

"Her what?"

"Where she worked with her husband, Pierre, another brilliant scientist, who sadly will be . . ."

"What?"

"Er, it doesn't matter, Gertie, our job is to help the world by returning vital things, nothing more, I'm afraid."

Gertie shrugged and slotted her Keepers' key into the time machine. With an intense flash of green light and the usual fizzing, they were soon on their way. A split second before crossing the graviton bridge, however, the steering wheel came off in her hands.

3

The Radioactive Woman

"SORRY," KOLT SAID, AFTER a moment's panic getting the steering wheel back on. "I'd been meaning to fix that."

But Gertie was too busy looking around. Her first impression of Paris during La Belle Epoque was that it reminded her of London in the 1920s—where she had tried to return a watch to the champion swimmer Mercedes Gleitze.

All around them, horses, carts, and people in dark clothes with bamboo-handled umbrellas rushed about. The men sported large mustaches, while the women Gertie could see had on giant floppy hats and long dresses like the one she was wearing. A few pedestrians stopped to stare at the Time Cat. Kolt waved nervously.

"I'm afraid they'll have to wait another sixty years or so to get their hands on this beauty."

"Let's drive somewhere quieter," Gertie said, "before

anyone gets suspicious—maybe we should have come on foot? I don't see any other cars."

"Well, they existed. Peugeot had something called a Bébé, unveiled at the Paris Salon earlier this year. It had a top speed of about twenty-eight mph, which is actually the top speed of a Slug Lamp in panic mode."

Gertie put the Jaguar in first gear and they crawled through the Paris streets. Kolt said he'd been to Paris quite a few times, and from his memory, they were close to where the famous scientist worked. Soon she pulled into a narrow road with crumbling white buildings on either side. The windows of the buildings had closed wooden shutters, and the street was made of cobblestones that caused the car to creak as they bounced along. Then a group of street dogs bounded past. They were chasing a cat with a fish bone in its mouth.

"Let's cloak it," Gertie said, reaching for the button with a question mark on it. This turned on the Narcissus paint, which enabled the Time Cat to reflect its surroundings perfectly, making the car disappear from sight. Standing outside in the wintery Paris street, Gertie kicked an invisible tire with a thump. "What if someone walks into it?"

Kolt laughed. "Then he or she will get a shock, but this return shouldn't take too long—that street there is Rue Lhomond—do you have the time machine, your key, and the item?"

Gertie held up the wicker basket. "What language does she speak, French?"

"Polish and Russian too, but remember that Skuldarkian adapts to whatever language is being spoken around us."

Their destination was shielded by an ivy-coated wall with a door in it. But as they were crossing the road, a bicycle came hurtling around a corner and collided with them. Everyone, including the cyclist, went sprawling on the cobblestone street with a clatter.

Kolt was the first to jump up, but then tripped on his bowler hat and went flying again. Gertie stood and rushed over to the woman to see if she was hurt.

"Are you okay?"

"It's all my fault!" the woman cried. "Please forgive me." Gertie scanned her dress for any sign of blood.

A few yards away, Kolt had picked up his bowler hat and was muttering to it angrily.

The woman looked over. "I think there's something wrong with your friend."

"Oh no, he's always like that."

Kolt saw he was being watched and discreetly put the dented hat on his head. Then he hurried over to check on everyone.

Gertie collected the picnic basket and raised a flap.

"Any damage to the . . . muffin?" Kolt asked, trying to be subtle while raising the woman's heavy bicycle.

"No, it's fine," Gertie said, thankful for the handkerchief she'd wrapped around the dish.

She could feel it vibrating, which meant they were close to finding its rightful owner.

"I'm sorry about our frightful collision," the woman said. "Please come in for some tea; I live very close by."

"Don't worry, we're not injured," Gertie told her, "and we're sort of in a hurry."

Kolt smiled awkwardly. "But tea might be nice?"

The woman grinned. "You could meet my daughter, Irène, and my husband, Pierre, and it would make me feel better to give you some refreshment. I love cycling so much, I sometimes forget how fast I'm going."

Gertie nodded, wondering how the woman was able to pedal in such a long dress.

"When my scientific work becomes too much, I really need to breathe, so I go racing around the Paris streets."

"Sounds like fun! But we have to locate someone here in Paris and return this very, very important *muffin* to them," Gertie said winking at Kolt.

"I see," said the woman thoughtfully. "I live here, so perhaps I can help? Ah, where are my manners! My name is Madame Curie. It's a pleasure to meet you both."

Gertie tried not to look surprised. This was the person they had come to see. The B.D.B.U. had done it again. Placed them exactly where they needed to be—even if it meant getting run over.

"Actually, tea sounds great!" Gertie said.

Kolt nodded vigorously. "Yes it does, and one of those small madeleine cakes to go with it would be a dream!"

They followed the young scientist through the white

door in the wall, and found themselves in a courtyard with three different fires going.

Gertie sniffed. The air smelled heavy and sulfurous.

Kolt chuckled. "I can see why you like clearing your head with fast bicycle rides."

The scientist agreed. "Yes, the smell is terrible, truly— but work comes first in our household. When I got married, I even chose a dress that I could also use for lab work."

Over each courtyard fire was an iron cauldron like the ones Gertie had seen in the B.D.B.U. Passing one, she could see a heavy black liquid with black rocks floating in it. Madame Curie put on thick gloves and stirred the contents with a metal rod.

"As you know, metal and water conduct heat, so if I were to touch the metal with my bare hands, I'd get burned."

As they approached what Madame Curie called her Shed of Discovery, Gertie noticed burn marks on the scientist's arms, and remembered Kolt's warnings about the rays given off by the decaying nucleus of an atom.

Kolt nudged Gertie and leaned in. "This whole place," he whispered, "even those children's toys—all dangerous! All . . ."

"I remember," Gertie said, "radioactive."

The woman overheard and looked around in surprise.

"You've read my work, child?"

"Um, what?"

"Radioactive! That's the term I came up with! For when an element is giving off radiation. I'm glad you're interested, because we need more women in science. I was only one of twenty girls in a group of two thousand students, but I came first in my class! Remember that nothing is impossible."

Before going inside, Madame Curie said she had to top up the cauldrons with a black rock called pitchblende. She led Kolt and Gertie over to where at least two hundred sacks were piled up.

"It comes all the way from an Austrian forest by horse and wagon—the uranium has already been extracted for glass making, so it's my job and my husband's to isolate the other elements in it."

Then her face darkened. "It's such a long process—first I have to pick off all the pine needles from when it was dumped in the forest. Then I boil and crystalize it—trying to isolate something called radium. But a few days ago the dish with the purest sample we have ever collected went missing."

"I wouldn't worry," Kolt said buoyantly. "These things have a habit of bobbing up."

"Well, if it doesn't, I shall keep working," she told them. "Nothing in this world has been able to dampen my curiosity and passion . . . yet."

Just as Madame Curie opened up a fresh sack of pitchblende, Kolt cleared his throat. "It was so kind of you to invite us in for tea," he said.

"The tea! Yes, of course!"

She led them inside her laboratory, which she told them was a former animal-dissection shed. On every possible countertop were glass tubes, flasks of green and yellow liquid, open flames, and the strangest smells. The floor was caked in dirt, and there were buckets where the roof leaked.

"We're in need of funds for our research," she admitted, "but that's always been the case. We're poor in money, but rich in ideas."

As she went off to fill a copper kettle from an outside faucet, Kolt told Gertie not to drink anything if she could help it.

"This whole lab is glowing with radiation," he reminded her. "And radiation kills living tissue, which is why at one point it was an effective treatment for cancer."

"But if radiation is so bad, why isn't she sick?" Gertie asked.

"She is! Didn't you see the red marks on her arms?"

"Well, shouldn't we warn her? What about her daughter?"

"Her daughter grows up to be rather clever herself actually, but the B.D.B.U. is crystal clear, Gertie—we can return things, but we cannot interfere in a person's fate. Now get that bowl out of the picnic basket and put it down somewhere, before we start glowing in the dark ourselves."

"She's very serious, isn't she?" Gertie said, unwrapping the protective handkerchief.

"Marie Curie? Oh, she had to be, Gertie—she lived in a time when women's views were not taken seriously at all."

"That's so stupid."

"Typical history, really, but in the end she succeeded, breaking countless barriers for women in the sciences and proving women were capable of genius—quick! Put that bowl down before she gets back."

"Think she might know about where our missing Keepers could be?"

Kolt blinked a few times and stared at her. "Of course not! Why would she?"

"She just seems so clever, I thought . . ."

"You're obsessed, you really are."

"No, I'm just focused, and determined—like Marie Curie."

Kolt shook his head. "Rescuing Keepers the way you want to is probably going to be impossible."

"Nothing is impossible if you work hard enough," Gertie said, remembering the great scientist's advice.

"That's right!" said Madame Curie, returning with a full kettle of water.

Gertie quickly placed the bowl down and pretended to inspect the contents: a tenth of a gram of radium salt.

"I'm so sorry for keeping you waiting," Madame Curie said, putting the kettle onto an iron stovetop, "and it seems Irène is out with her father."

"This is *so* interesting," Gertie exclaimed, pointing to the grain-shaped sample of radium salt in the dish.

Madame Curie dropped the kettle with a clang. Water spilled out all over the concrete floor and onto Kolt's shoes.

"That's it!" she cried.

Gertie tried to appear surprised. "This little bowl is what you've been looking for?"

"Yes! That's our radium salt!"

"And my feet are soaked," Kolt muttered.

Madame Curie rushed over to the dish with the tiny rock at the bottom.

"This *is* it!" she cried. "The sample that dear Pierre and I have spent years on! It was just sitting there?"

"Hmmm, I suppose, yes, um . . ." Gertie stammered.

"Well, isn't that nice?" said Kolt loudly, stepping toward the door with a squelch. "Sometimes, what you're looking for is right under your nose all along. . . . Well, we must be going, I don't have any spare socks, so . . ."

"But what about your tea?"

Kolt raised his dented bowler hat to say goodbye, and they shuffled over to the door. "Not thirsty anymore!"

"Good luck with your experiments!" Gertie said.

"Thank you, child. I am one of those who think that humanity will draw more good than evil from new discoveries. But are you sure you don't want tea? Or some bread and cheese?"

"Sorry, we have to go, bye! We love you!"

THEY CLIMBED BACK INTO the invisible Time Cat, then uncloaked it.

"We 'love' you?" Kolt said.

Gertie blushed.

"You must have really liked her," he went on, "to blurt out something like that."

"Well, didn't you like her?" said Gertie.

"Of course, I respect her enormously; she's a genius with a kind heart, a rare combination."

Kolt then explained to Gertie that Madame and Monsieur Curie, like many scientists of their time, could have patented their ideas and become very rich from selling the information, but instead they chose to struggle and share their knowledge freely with people everywhere, in the hopes it might make the world a better place.

Listening to this reminded Gertie how important it was to keep going in *her* quest to rescue Keepers and maybe even her Loser brother. Like Madame Curie, she would persevere—even when it felt like everything was against her, including that stubborn old encyclopedia—the B.D.B.U.

4

A Show of Keeper Loyalty

WHEN THEY GOT BACK to Skuldark, Robot Rabbit Boy was snoring away in his bed. It was dark, and all the things in the garden were cold and still dripping wet from the hailstorm. Kolt made some tea and they sat before the warm, glowing fireplace, not speaking.

After a long night of deep sleep and dreams that were lost just moments after waking, Gertie cut herself a slice of breakfast cake and sat down. Kolt and Robot Rabbit Boy were outside checking that the hailstorm hadn't damaged the Spitfire. Gertie looked at the wall where the secret passage to the tower was. What could she do to make the B.D.B.U. take her Keeper quest seriously this time? She was about to take a bite of peach cake when she heard knocking on the window. Kolt's face appeared through a parted moonberry bush.

"There's no damage! She's ready to fly when you are."

Gertie grunted. Another distraction. And one she was not enthusiastic about. A month ago, the aircraft had been just a hunk of rusting metal in the garden, with flat tires and weeds growing in the cockpit. She had only flown an aircraft once before—and that was in the excitement of a mission.

Outside Robot Rabbit Boy was popping moonberries again under the wing. When he heard the cottage door open, he jumped up and scuttled over.

"Lavender mush?" he said, pointing to the cockpit with a juice-stained paw. Although he had learned one or two new words since becoming part of the Keeper family, he still relied on the ones he had known when they found him in the abandoned city.

"I suppose," Gertie said, realizing that she had to focus on the things she *could* do, rather than the things she couldn't. And if there was a way to save these lost Keepers and her brother, it wasn't by wallowing in self-pity. She took a deep breath and turned to Kolt and Robot Rabbit Boy, who seemed concerned at her lack of interest in the aircraft.

"I'm grateful for all the work you've both done so that I can practice flying—I am just a teeny bit afraid, that's all."

Kolt couldn't believe it. "I'm the one who should be concerned! *You've* got absolutely nothing to worry about, apart from dying in a horrible, blazing fireball as you slam into the sea trapped in the cockpit, burning alive."

Gertie made a pained face.

"You'll be fine! Don't forget you have a rescue cushion!"

Kolt went on. "Officially certified by the bounce commission of Skuldark, which is myself, Robot Rabbit Boy, and a few energetic Slug Lamps that got on the seat and jumped with us."

"Slug Lamps can jump?"

"Well, it's more a sort of uncontrolled flop."

Kolt was normally cautious about any dangerous feat, and so Gertie couldn't figure out why he had gone to great lengths to enable such a mad experiment. Maybe his lack of safety measures with the radium salt now extended to daring feats of aviation?

Kolt glanced up at some drifting clouds. "C'mon, Gertie, the weather is perfect—apart from that morning wind blowing off the sea."

"What if the B.D.B.U. wants us to return something while I'm in the air?"

"Hmm, I suppose that could be a problem," said Kolt, thinking aloud, "especially if there's lightning—but you're such a good pilot, Gertie, you'll figure it out once you're up there."

"Well, okay," she said. "But where's the runway?"

"Don't you see?" said Kolt, waving his arms around, "Robot Rabbit Boy and I have cleared a path to the edge of the cliff!"

"The edge of the cliff! No way!"

Gertie felt there was something else he was planning, which he hadn't told her about. Then it dawned on her why Kolt was so eager to get the old aircraft flying again.

In addition to reading the Spitfire manuals, she noticed he'd been poring over old plans from when he'd turned the Jaguar racing car into the Time Cat.

"You want to convert this old aircraft into another Time Cat! That's why you're so eager to get it going!"

"Well, the thought had crossed my mind," Kolt admitted. "You *are* a pilot, Gertie, after all—and with the Losers more determined than ever to destroy us, it might be nice to have a flying machine in addition to a motorcar. And you'd get to drive all the time!"

"You mean fly . . ."

"It might be the edge we need to pull off a daring rescue."

"You mean my brother?"

"If he's ready to join us . . . and if you can fly this, Gertie—we can actually chase the Losers' ship, *Doll Head.*"

"That's true, I suppose. But a cliff-edge runway?"

"Just imagine what could be possible with a time-traveling aircraft."

"Well, don't we need gas? How much of that do we have under the cottage?"

Kolt looked suddenly pleased with himself. "I've converted the engine to drink Skuldarkian seawater."

"What about history?" asked Gertie sensibly.

"What about it?"

"Won't history be affected if the Aztecs are worshipping their sun god, and then we pop out of a cloud waving?"

"Well," Kolt said, thinking on his feet, "you could say the same for the Time Cat. I'm not sure the ancient people of

Mexico had British sports cars—we'll just have to be discreet, try and go unnoticed."

"But this is a fighter plane that fires fruit!"

"Come on, Gertie, stop putting it off—climb up into the cockpit and let's see if this heap will fly."

Nervously, Gertie clambered into the cockpit and strapped herself into the kitchen chair with the bounciest cushion on Skuldark.

Despite the faded black paint and a few cracked instrument panels, Kolt assured Gertie that the modified Rolls-Royce Merlin engines were even *more* powerful with Skuldarkian seawater pouring through them.

Kolt and Robot Rabbit Boy walked around the aircraft one final time, checking the elevators, the rudder and hinge blade, the tires, and finally the propeller.

When they gave Gertie the thumbs-up, she pulled on her flying gloves, which were thin enough to operate the controls but thick enough to give some protection in the event of a cockpit fire. She set the throttle half an inch open, then pushed the fuel-gauge button. Thirty-seven gallons of Skuldarkian seawater in the lower tank. Then she shut and latched the pilot's door, set the elevator trim with half-fuel, one division—nose down. After pressurizing the fuel lines, Gertie double-checked the hood was locked for takeoff, then set the speed control fully forward.

So far so good.

But when it came time to flick the magneto ignition

switches in preparation for the engine starting, Kolt seemed to get nervous.

"Think we should measure the runway?" he shouted through the cockpit glass.

Gertie opened a little window in the hatch.

"What?"

"The manual said the runway should be four hundred yards, and I thought two hundred would be enough with the faster propeller and fuel modification, but now I'm not sure...."

Gertie stared straight ahead through her flying goggles at the dots of birds drifting at the cliff edge. She could feel her hands sweating inside the gloves.

"It'll be fine," she said, not because she believed it, but because she didn't feel like getting out and going through the whole thing again. And Kolt was right. If she *could* fly it, having a fighter plane would give them a massive advantage over *Doll Head*—which Gertie imagined she could blind by firing a barrage of frozen moonberries into its giant eye sockets.

She was strapped in now, and ready to go. A part of her wanted to rip off the harness, jump down from the cockpit, and run back into the cottage. But she had to try. She knew that. The increased chance to rescue her brother was worth the risk, especially if Kolt could convert the aircraft to travel through time.

And there were *some* safety measures in place. Kolt had insisted that Gertie strap Russian Fire Whistles to her legs, which he had dug out (with the help of a gravely concerned Cave Sprite, Sunday) from one of the 945 bedrooms under the cottage. These thick copper tubes (which Gertie thought looked like the inside of toilet rolls painted gold) allowed a person to hover in midair for about five minutes, while having the ability to move around.

When it came to landing her "kite" (pilot slang for a fighter aircraft), Kolt had said if she didn't feel comfortable coming back down over the mashed gooseberries and chopped spinach of the vegetable patch, she could set down on the open, grassy part of Turweston Passage, just beyond the western gate to the Garden of Lost Things. This would allow her to get used to the landing gear and the wind currents that might make landing British war-birds slightly tricky.

With Kolt and Robot Rabbit Boy staring at her through the cockpit window, Gertie started the engine, then immediately grabbed her earmuffs. The plane made the loudest, most deafening sound she had ever heard—like five hundred angry lawn mowers coughing. Even with ear protection, Gertie decided she would be stone deaf if she survived the flight.

For the first few seconds, the engine wasn't firing evenly, and sputtered green smoke from the burning Skuldarkian seawater. But when Gertie checked the oil pressure and adjusted the fuel pump, it soon cleared. Kolt stepped back and gave a second thumbs-up through the dissipating green mist. Then he scrambled beneath the wings to remove the wedges from under the tires. Gertie adjusted the flaps to account for the pull to one side with rapid ground acceleration.

But then, just as she was about to attempt takeoff, a frantic Robot Rabbit Boy hopped up on the wing, his cute little robot eyes glowing bright red and his fur mouth moving in the shape of the words *mashed potato*. Gertie shook her head sternly. But his face was one of grave determination. Gertie knew if she turned the engine off now, she might be too scared to start it again. She and Kolt had told Robot Rabbit Boy, over and over, that the first flight in the Spitfire had to be Gertie by herself. But no matter how many times they said it, he kept clamping himself to the fuselage with a Magnetic Bond Feature in his tool mode settings. While it was true that magnets were a Keepers' worst enemy (other than the Losers of course), Robot Rabbit Boy was able to switch off the magnets in his paws most of the time.

But there was no telling him. Their robot rabbit refused to get off the wing. Gertie suspected he was still hurt from being left behind when they went to visit Marie Curie in Paris. And so she gave in, motioning with her gloved hands for him to clamp on to the fuselage behind the cockpit.

With the engine roaring, they tore over the grass runway toward the cliff.

One hundred yards passed in a flash, then another fifty—then suddenly they were at the cliff edge. Gertie's eyes moved frantically between her instrument gauges and the blue horizon as a ferocious gust of headwind lowered their ground speed and the old aircraft simply dropped off the edge of the cliff, its engine screaming. Gertie's stomach turned inside out. They were now plummeting toward the sea in a straight dive. She imagined Kolt screaming at her to bail out. Faster and faster they fell to the dark waves. But Gertie would not abandon her fluffy friend clamped behind, and so—trusting the instinct all pilots have—she stayed calm in her gloves and goggles, knowing that if she timed it right, the momentum of her dive could be used to gather the speed they needed. A second later she pulled back on the control ring with all her strength. They were only yards now from splashing into the sea, but somehow the Spitfire responded and Gertie felt them skimming the white-capped waves—giving Robot Rabbit Boy a saltwater bath.

Within moments they were roaring over the grassy meadows, dark forests, and monstrous cliffs of Skuldark. It was the most exciting thing Gertie had ever done. The sheer speed of the aircraft was terrifying, but Gertie felt fully in control as she flew over the cottage several times, just low enough to see Kolt jumping up and down in the garden.

Robot Rabbit Boy looked determined too. The rushing air parted his fur, but his neon eyes glowed lemon yellow.

The power of the aircraft was astounding to Gertie, but she had to keep her mind on what she was doing, and not get distracted by the sights. She also had to be careful not to run out of fuel.

Gertie soared over the beach where she'd washed up. Johnny the Guard Worm was sitting on a rock out at sea while the white dodo birds panicked and ran at the sound of the Spitfire's engine. The rocky shore looked smaller than she remembered. But the cliffs were very high. She felt proud then, of how she had so bravely made it through the cliff when she first arrived.

In the distance, the Skuldarkian Mountains rose majestically as if to beckon her. The highest, Ravens' Peak, was tall, dark, and snow-capped. Gertie didn't want to get too close on her first flight in case the drop in temperature affected the seawater in her fuel lines.

As she turned back toward the cottage, something on the ground caught her eye. Gertie pushed forward on the control ring, and went down for a closer look. Not only were there ruins of old buildings, but there was also a bright light coming out of the earth, a dazzling orange glow a little bigger than a Cave Sprite. Some kind of signal perhaps? A warning of danger?

Whatever it was, Robot Rabbit Boy saw it too. They would have to ask Kolt—though so much of the island remained a mystery, even to him.

5

Insects and Pirates

GERTIE'S LANDING IN A meadow just outside the Garden of Lost Things was close to perfect. Despite gusting crosswinds, she handled the Spitfire with the ease of a veteran pilot.

She knew Kolt had been watching from the ground as they rocketed through the sky, banking and sweeping in arcs over the tall trees of Fern Valley, and it made her feel good to think of how impressed he was.

The old Keeper had some cakes and cold bottles of ginger beer waiting in a wicker basket, but Gertie was too excited to eat.

"We saw something! A glowing light!"

"In the sky?"

"Lavender," nodded Robot Rabbit Boy, hopping down.

"It was on the ground, a glowing light . . ."

"Probably nothing," Kolt said casually, "a reflection from one of those robot hands that keep appearing?"

But Gertie was convinced the bright light was more. "I think we should go investigate, it could be something big."

"Well, where was it?"

"Near some ruined buildings."

"The Ruined Village," said Kolt carefully, as though realizing it could be something after all.

"Should we go down there?"

Kolt rubbed his chin. "Let me think about it," he said. "It'll be dark soon, we can't go today."

At dusk, they carried the plates and empty bottles inside, then cleaned up from the day's excitement. Kolt was hungry for something sweet, and put a tray of Darren's double-Dutch-chunk chocolate cookies in the oven to warm. They had bought them on a recent return to Amsterdam, where they'd met a young, cheerful painter called Rembrandt, who was missing a brush.

"So we'll check out what that light was tomorrow?" Gertie said. "I think it means something."

"The Ruined Village is miles from here, Gertie. Let's talk about it in the morning over breakfast."

With all the excitement of the Spitfire's maiden flight over Skuldark, and the dazzling light Gertie had seen emanating from the earth, they had forgotten something very important.

"Mashed potato, lavender eggcup room?"

"That's right," Gertie realized, checking to see if the chocolate cookies were ready, "it's movie night!"

After bathing and getting into their nightclothes, the three Keepers settled into a nest of blankets on the velvet couch to watch a film about insects on pirate ships. The kitchen smelled of baking and the fire crackled.

Halfway through the movie, Robot Rabbit Boy yawned. "Maaasssshhhhed doooollllllloops . . ." he said, lifting a paw to the flickering screen. There were still a few moonberry stains on his fur.

"Someone seems to have lost interest in the moving picture," Kolt chuckled. "I won't say who."

Gertie peeled her eyes off the screen to see what Robot Rabbit Boy was doing. "This always happens when there's too much talking," she said.

Gertie reached over and patted him. The fur was soft but mottled from years of neglect in the abandoned city.

"There has to be *some* storyline . . ." Gertie explained gently, "it can't all be explosions and sword-fighting."

There was a cookie crumb on the floor, and Robot Rabbit Boy brought his foot down on it. "Mush," he said quietly.

The insect pirates were now swinging between ships.

They had dragged the television up from bedroom 771 some time ago, for a weekly movie night, after Kolt had tried to explain the concept of moving pictures with stories. He said it was also a way for Gertie to learn about different parts of the world before they went there. All you had to do was find the silver disk of the program you wanted to watch, then slot it into the TV.

However, Gertie found it boring to watch for a long time, and so the television was enjoyed mostly by Robot Rabbit Boy very early in the morning for cartoons, and by Kolt very late at night when everyone else was in bed. He enjoyed flickering black-and-white films that Gertie found more boring than watching moonberries ripen.

"Mush mashed potato?" said Robot Rabbit Boy, more interested now in being petted than anything taking place on the screen.

Gertie was still trying to follow along with the story.

"Let's listen," she said, as the chief insect pirate drew his sword (a toothpick).

Then she reached for a cookie, but felt only crumbs. "If you're not watching the film anymore," Gertie said, "would you get another plate of cakes and cookies from the kitchen?"

Robot Rabbit Boy slumped down off the couch, his metal legs clanking.

"Eggcups?"

"Not eggcups, double-Dutch-chunk chocolate cookies," Kolt said, "and hurry up or you'll miss the grasshoppers taking over the pirate ship to rescue Big Skinny."

"Lavender?"

"The grasshopper king," Kolt explained, "who was kidnapped at the beginning of the film, remember?"

But Robot Rabbit Boy, their Series 7 Artificial Intelligence Forever Friend, wasn't listening.

The empty kitchen was far more interesting with all its dark corners and little passageways that only a rabbit could fit through.

"C'mon!" cried Gertie at the flashing screen. "Use your cannons!" Then she turned to Kolt. "If we had cannons like that we could blast *Doll Head* into oblivion."

"What about the cannons on the Spitfire?" Kolt said, not taking his eyes off the screen. "Didn't you fire a few frozen moonberries on the test flight?"

"Er, I was too busy watching the fuel level," Gertie said, but the truth was she had forgotten.

Movie night was when they tried to forget their problems and lose themselves in whatever story was playing out on the screen.

Gertie only really liked watching films when it was very cold outside. Then they could snuggle under their own blankets with things to eat and mugs of hot chocolate. Sometimes, Gertie and Robot Rabbit Boy built a fort from all the couch cushions, and used the blankets to form a giant roof. They would watch from underneath.

"Mush, mush, mush!" Robot Rabbit Boy said from the kitchen, peering over at Kolt and Gertie, who were still mesmerized by the flickering glow and mumble of voices.

"I hope he hasn't found one of those horrible robot hands," Kolt said.

Gertie thought about the one she'd seen dart across the kitchen yesterday afternoon—and the one she found in her bathtub. Not even the Cave Sprites seemed to know where they were coming from.

Robot Rabbit Boy scrambled up the ladder Kolt had built for him and walked along the countertop toward a stack of cooling double-Dutch-chunk chocolate cookies.

"Hurry up! You're missing the best part!" Gertie called out.

Kolt turned his head toward the kitchen, but kept his eyes glued to the screen. "The grasshoppers are about to do martial arts—like in China when we rescued the B.D.B.U.—only it's insects doing it this time."

"Dollops?" Robot Rabbit Boy said dreamily, more interested in a pair of Slug Lamps suctioned to the kitchen window, snuggling against the cold wind. Their slug-baby faces were pinched, and they glowed bright green. Robot Rabbit Boy stuck one grubby paw on the glass, while balancing the plate of cookies on his other. But when they noticed a pair of glowing robot rabbit eyes, they got scared and squelched along the glass back to their moonberry leaf beds, leaving a trail of neon slime.

Robot Rabbit Boy followed them with his eyes until the last squashy bit of Slug Lamp had disappeared altogether.

Then he skipped across the counter, went down the steps of his ladder, and stood there in the dim, cool kitchen light, still balancing the plate of cookies. On the floor beside him, a petrified crocodile head sat with its jaws wide open.

"A dollop?" he said, bending down to inspect the razor-sharp teeth. "Ooh, eggcup, mush . . ."

"I don't believe it!" Gertie shouted at the film. "Why doesn't he try and escape?"

"I don't get it," Kolt said. "He knows they left the ship's cabin door unlocked, it's obvious. Just walk through it!"

Robot Rabbit Boy looked around and saw the front door of the cottage happened to be open too. He went toward it and just stood there.

"Just walk through it!" Gertie pleaded with the confused insect on the screen.

"C'mon, walk through it please!" came Kolt's voice from the couch. And so Robot Rabbit Boy did. He walked through it.

There was a trail of Slug Lamp slime on the step. He followed it, which took him into the garden. Then another slime trail caught his eye. He followed that one all the way to the treasure chests.

Back in the cottage, Kolt and Gertie were on the edge of the velvet sofa, awaiting the big rescue.

"Hurry up with those cookies!" Kolt said, without turning around.

"Yeah, come on!" Gertie cried. "You're missing the best bits."

6

A Lost Rabbit

AN HOUR LATER, THE film ended. The pirates had been defeated by the insects. Big Skinny, the grasshopper king, was safe. Gertie and Kolt lounged on the couch under heavy sheep's-wool blankets.

"Wish we had some insects warriors to round up those robotic hands," Gertie said. "I always get a shock when one darts out from its hiding place."

But Kolt appeared to be lost in his own thoughts.

Gerte's mind wandered to her box of maps, which she hoped might lead her to where the trapped Keepers had been hidden.

The fire was low now.

Logs had burned down to red embers that radiated a deep warmth Gertie could feel in her bones.

Her eyelids were heavy with sleep. The cushions were

like a warm nest. She was about to drag her body off the couch and down the corridor to her bedroom when she noticed cookie crumbs all over the floor.

She looked around. "Where's Robot Rabbit Boy?"

Kolt rose with a yawn from the cozy bliss of blankets and cushions. He scanned the kitchen counters. "Wasn't he getting more double-Dutch-chunk chocolate cookies?"

"Yes, but that was ages ago." Gertie wrapped herself in the blanket and stood up. "Robot Rabbit Boy!" she called. "Where are you? Eggcup! Lavender!"

"I'm sure he's around somewhere," Kolt said. "Good film, wasn't it? I'm so glad I dragged that television up from the basement." He leaned over and collected cookie crumbs from the cushion by pushing on them with his finger. "The little chap probably went to sleep somewhere."

Gertie laughed, but couldn't shake the feeling that something was wrong. Still wrapped in her blanket, she took small steps toward the kitchen so as not to trip. She checked under the main table, in the big velvet chairs, in cupboards, behind doors, even under the sink. She *even* looked in some of the boxes that said DO NOT OPEN THIS BOX, EVER, which were mostly full of Kolt's powders and potions, including newly discovered rhyming spice from a strange land where people communicated through songs.

But the fluffy mechanical rabbit who loved moonberry jam and Slug Lamps was nowhere to be found. Gertie checked his bed several times, but found only empty blankets, a few of his toys (chewed), and a few tufts of fur he must have pulled off during a bad dream.

Then she noticed the front door to the cottage.

"Kolt!" she said, with mild alarm. "The front door is open!"

Kolt was now slumbering lightly on the couch.

"Sorry? What? Who?" he said with his eyes still closed.

"The front door is open!"

"The front what . . . door?"

"It's open!" Gertie repeated, an edge of urgency in her voice.

Kolt's eyes gradually widened. He seemed surprised to find himself on the couch and not snug in his bed. "The door?" he said. "Open? Ah yes! I needed a draft for the chimney when the film was on . . . got smoky in here if you remember . . . I had to open it. Is it too cold?"

"I think Robot Rabbit Boy went outside."

"Well," Kolt said, sitting up now, "he is a curious little fellow."

They both stared toward the open door, at the strip of darkness that led into the night.

"He's been out alone before," Kolt said.

"But never at night!"

"That's true."

"I know he's a clever, self-powering, independent robot child with a high-powered deadly nose laser—but he's also just a rabbit who likes lemon curd and moon-berry jam."

Gertie suddenly remembered the Spitfire, but it would be useless at night in the darkness.

Kolt had begun to search now too—even pulling out *The History of Chickens* and slipping through the secret door to peer up the tower where the B.D.B.U. lived.

"I don't think he's up there," Gertie shouted, feeling a draft of frigid air, "because he can't pull out the chicken book that opens the secret door."

Kolt's voice echoed from the dark stairwell. "Ah yes, good point."

They flopped back down on the couch, now certain that Robot Rabbit Boy had gone outside and both feeling guilty for being too engrossed in the film to notice him slip away.

"We have to go after him," Gertie said. "We must."

"The garden is one thing, Gertie, but if—"

"Then we load up on Slug Lamps!"

"Yes, of course, but if he's unlucky enough to have left the garden and stumbled into Fern Valley—or ventured beyond the Line of Stones, then we may have to take precautions."

"I thought you said there were no millipedes in Fern Valley? That you made the story up?"

"I did, but there are still Attercoppe hives and Orispian Tunnelers who might find our little friend interesting enough to carry underground."

"Would they eat him?" Gertie said, horrified at the thought.

"The Tunnelers? No, no, nothing like that—they collect things they find interesting and store them away deep in the Tunnels of Bodwin."

"What do they look like?"

"Imagine a dog with very strong, short legs, and the long head of a horse, and bright red eyes, and a tongue like a shoelace. They can live for hundreds of years down there, feeding on tree roots and coal. They're more a nuisance than anything else, like those robotic hands. Sometimes they'll steal things from the garden and take them underground."

"What were those other things you said, that live in hives?"

"Attercoppes?"

Gertie nodded.

"Nothing to worry about, just your average giant flying spider."

Gertie reeled in disgust. "Flying spiders! Eek. Do they sting?"

"Absolutely not. No Keeper in the history of Skuldark has ever been stung by an Attercoppe."

"Phew, that's a relief."

"But they do have a nasty bite," Kolt went on. "Don't get bitten, or you'll die in agony or turn into one yourself, depending on whether you have any Attercoppian DNA."

Gertie felt sick and dizzy at the thought of Robot Rabbit Boy buzzing around with eight bulbous eyes after getting stung by an Attercoppe. She dropped her blanket, and hurried toward her bedroom in search of warm clothes.

"Where are you going?"

"I'm summoning myself for a rescue mission!"

With Attercoppes flying about, Gertie also decided she

would bring her new ax, just in case. It had been presented to her on a mission as a token of thanks by a young Viking named Leif Erikson. Gertie had returned his lost map by signaling to his fleet of ships from the top of an iceberg off the coast of Greenland.

"It's pitch-black out there tonight," Kolt said when she returned—bundled up and armed. He had put on three woolly sweaters, a woolly tie, gloves, and his usual bowler hat, which still had the dent in it from when Marie Curie had knocked them down.

"We'll carry two Slug Lamps in each hand!" Gertie instructed. "We can't leave Robot Rabbit Boy outside all night with these flying spiders."

"Well, I suppose you're right," Kolt said, looking at the poor creature's empty bed. "We might even be able to investigate the glowing light you saw from the Spitfire . . . though I doubt he's wandered that far."

Gertie felt a sudden wave of impatience. "How are we supposed to find the trapped Keepers if we can't even keep an eye on Robot Rabbit Boy when he's in the same room?"

"Faith," Kolt said, "has always seen me through."

"Well, it's time for action now," replied Gertie, gripping the handle of her ax.

7

Silent Flight

It WAS VERY DARK. The air was cold and damp. With two Slug Lamps in each hand, a Viking ax on her belt, and a tweed deerstalker hat with flaps to keep baby flying spiders out of her ears, Gertie set off around the garden with Kolt in tow.

First they checked the tree of scarves, an ancient oak that towered over the cottage. From its long dark branches dangled hundreds of lost scarves. They searched in the rowing boats, life rafts, red telephone boxes, and intergalactic escape pods (which Kolt used for growing tomatoes). Gertie wriggled under the massive heap of tangled bicycles, barely breathing in case the mass shifted and she was trapped.

They searched high and low, calling out Robot Rabbit Boy's name in whispery voices and peering into any nook or cranny where he might have fallen asleep.

Finally, after checking the cracked mummies' tombs of

ancient Egypt, and the empty zoo cages from Hungary, they were back to where they had started. Kolt and Gertie sat down at Napoleon's banquet table, and stared at the bone china plates and soup bowls, which had filled over time with a swampy mix of leaves and rainwater.

"It's no use," Gertie said breathlessly. "We've searched the whole garden, and there's no sign of him."

She felt a bit more used to the dark now, but still kept one hand on the ax handle—just in case they met an Attercoppe or two.

Kolt shone his Slug Lamps under the banquet table, just to be sure. Then they looked at each other, a silent knowing stare, eyes lit up just enough by the glow of eight Slug Lamps to know what the other was thinking.

"There are risks if we leave the garden at night," Kolt said, "but nothing we can't handle."

"The flying spiders?"

"Attercoppes, yes, but there are other creatures too. Skuldark has many legends about what goes on here. My favorite is 'Music of the Guardians,' which I should tell you about someday in case there's an emergency."

"What is it?"

"A distress call when the island of Skuldark is in grave danger. Do you have your key with you?"

Gertie took it out.

"On second thought," Kolt said, "I'll show you later. Let's concentrate now on finding Robot Rabbit Boy."

Gertie was relieved to finally hear determination in

Kolt's voice. Keepers not only had a duty to the world, but to one another. And besides, the fluffy little Series 7 was their friend. Gertie put her key away and adjusted the handle of the Viking ax on her utility belt.

"I see someone is prepared for the wild woods of Fern Valley."

"Actually," Gertie said, "I think he would have avoided Fern Valley, considering how little he is—remember how we had to lift him over all the low bushes on the Chinese mountain?"

Kolt pulled down the stiff brim of his bowler hat. "Well, if he took Olde Path to Turweston Passage past where you parked the Spitfire, then followed it, he might eventually reach the Line of Stones."

Its name sounded innocent enough, Gertie thought—but Kolt had never explained exactly what the Line of Stones was.

"Should we be worried about the stones?"

"Oh no, it's just a boundary of rocks that goes on for miles across the prairie, marking the entrance to the Ruined Village, once the center of Keeper life on Skuldark."

"I saw it from the Spitfire," Gertie said.

"The ruins? Well, they're many miles from here."

"Can we take the Time Cat? If it can drive through the North African desert, how bad could a meadow be?"

"I'm sorry, Gertie, but even for a 1960s Jaguar racing coupe—the prairie grass is too high this time of year."

"Well, we can't fly," Gertie said, "obviously."

Kolt rubbed his chin as though in deep thought. "We might not catch him on foot, but with a pair of Golden Helpers..."

"What are they?"

"Danish army off-road bicycles with self-powering electric motors and giant spotlights."

"Time kittens!" Gertie said. "Why didn't you tell me about these before?"

"I just remembered myself. I came across them when searching for things to repair the Spitfire."

"Are they under the cottage?"

"No, I keep them in the rusted-out hull of an old ship at the far end of the garden. They appeared some time ago from Denmark according to writing on the frame, from the year 2020."

"Can we go right now?"

"We might want to pack some supplies first."

Gertie thought about what she might want to eat or drink on the way, but then an image of Robot Rabbit Boy getting carried off by flying spiders buzzed through her mind.

"No time," Gertie said, glancing down at her ax. "We'll have to take a chance."

They hurried to the eastern edge of the garden, where sat a rusted-out old boat with a massive hole in the hull. Kolt went in through the hole and appeared a moment later wheeling two Golden Helper bicycles.

Gertie shined the Slug Lamps so that Kolt could adjust the seats. Each bicycle was matte black with a small, gold cartridge attached to the frame that Kolt said was the actual Golden Helper motor.

The handlebars were short. And instead of spokes in the wheels, there were five carbon-fiber blades. The tires were thick and even spiked to maintain grip on loose earth and ice.

The best part, Gertie thought, was the headlamp, which was the size of a soccer ball, with a flat front of toughened glass to protect high-powered halogen bulbs. The spongy seat had sides and even a backrest with a Kevlar belt to strap the rider in.

"Whatever you do," Kolt said, "don't look into the headlamp directly, as it will burn the corneas in your eyes."

"They're not radioactive, are they?"

"No, electrified phosphorous."

"And that's safe?"

"Phosphorous? Oh sure. In the 1600s, a German alchemist, Hennig Brand, was convinced you could make gold from pee. He had his son collect hundreds of buckets of it from neighbors, with the promise of gold in return."

"There's gold in pee?"

"Of course not, but after a while all the equipment in his lab began to glow. He had accidentally discovered phosphorous, an element found in pee."

When Gertie climbed onto her bicycle, it stood upright without her having to place her feet on the ground.

"Wow," she said. "It knows I'm sitting on it!"

"It knows a lot more than that," Kolt said. "Ready?"

"How do I move it forward?"

But Kolt had already taken off. He called back over his shoulder, "Just push the pedal like a normal bicycle! The harder you push, the faster you go."

Gertie pressed hard into the top pedal and the Golden Helper search-and-rescue vehicle lurched forward, its front wheel rising in the air with the speed of her takeoff. For a few seconds she felt she would fly off the back, but then the front wheel touched earth, and she was right up against Kolt's back tire, as they dodged various objects in their path.

"I forgot to open the eastern gate!" Kolt shouted, his hair blowing back. "But there's a mound of earth we can use as a ramp."

"We're going to jump the gate?" Gertie said in surprise. "But it's taller than me!"

Kolt had already increased his speed and was disappearing from view. Gertie swallowed and pushed harder on the pedals as her Golden Helper motor whirred, and she sped toward the small mound of earth. But as they got closer, the two Keepers noticed young pear trees growing on the other side of the eastern gate. Their jump would have to be enormous—over the gate and over the pear trees.

"More speed!" Kolt cried. "Push as hard as you can!"

Nothing, Gertie thought, *could be scarier than yesterday's near-death plunge in the Spitfire.* She drove her feet into both pedals, reaching such a dangerous speed her bike was shaking as she hit the ramp a few seconds after Kolt. The takeoff came with a sudden rushing of wind, and she was soaring through the darkness as she gripped the handlebars for dear life. She managed to sail over the spiked metal gate with *just* enough height to clear the trees growing beyond.

When she felt herself descending, Gertie leaned back in the seat, and upon touching down in the field with a hard bump, she pulled on the back brake, skidding to one side in a shower of mud and grass.

A few yards away, Kolt and his Golden Helper were on the ground in a mangled heap. The old Keeper seemed to be fine, but his pants were ripped and there was a tuft of grass where his bowler hat was supposed to be. It took every ounce of Gertie's strength not to start laughing.

"I misjudged the landing," he explained, "as you can see."

"Your pants are ripped. Pretty badly."

"Yes, Gertie. Thanks for reminding me."

Gertie bit her lip, trying not to explode with laughter. "There's, um, also some mud on your head?"

"Yes, I know that too, Gertie, thank you. Have you seen my hat anywhere?"

ONCE KOLT WAS BACK in the seat and strapped in, they discovered his headlamp had smashed in the fall.

"Not only have I lost my hat, but I'm riding blind. You're going to have to lead. Let's go this way," he said, pointing. "You're probably right about Fern Valley; Robot Rabbit Boy would never have been able to get over the low hedges."

Gertie pushed down on the pedal, and they were off

again, past the dark shadow of her Spitfire, and zipping down the grassy slope of Olde Path, which then narrowed into Turweston Passage, and curled around toward the eastern edge of the Fern Valley woodland.

Gertie's headlamp was so bright that it lit up the entire area in a white glow. She hoped it would be enough to scare away anything dangerous.

After ten minutes of careful searching, Gertie noticed the deep, wild woodland of Fern Valley on their right side. She was glad she'd brought the ax, and hoped the hairy, buzzing creatures were slumbering in their hives.

The night was chilly and they moved through clouds of their own breath. When Turweston Passage took them right up alongside the dark edges of Fern Valley, Gertie felt branches whip against her arms. With exposed tree roots up ahead, she undid her safety belt and stood a few inches out of the seat. When she heard a cry from behind, she turned to see Kolt bouncing up and down as his tires thumped the protruding roots. He seemed to be staying on his machine, though a series of ripping sounds suggested more trouble with his pants.

Fern Valley was so thickly forested, it fascinated her. She had flown over it in the Spitfire, but to truly explore this vast woodland, she'd need lamps, a good supply of food and water, and perhaps even ropes in case there were valleys cut deep into the earth.

Small lights in the trees and bushes twinkled. Kolt had told her they were the eyes of dangerous creatures, but by now she was all too familiar with the glow of wild moonberries, a little sour but harmless.

After a particularly steep descent, Gertie thought she might go over the handlebars after hitting a hard clump of earth, but the tire smashed right through it. Then the ground evened out and she stopped to say something to Kolt.

"We need some kind of h—" But before she could get the word out, a gigantic white bird with a furry back appeared from a dark cluster of trees. Gertie stared in disbelief as it circled noiselessly over their heads. Kolt tipped his bike to one side and jumped off.

"What kind of bird is that?" Gertie said, marveling at the thick fur on its body.

"It's not a bird, Gertie, it's an insect—a spotted Moondrop Moth. I've never actually seen one before!"

"It's so big!"

"That's only a baby," Kolt explained. "An adult moth is so large it could carry a human on its back."

"I think it wants us to follow," Gertie said, pushing down on her pedal. "Maybe it's seen Robot Rabbit Boy!"

Kolt jumped back on his machine.

"Is this insect one of those Skuldark Guardians you were telling me about?"

"Every species has one Guardian member, Gertie, but this is just a baby."

"You said Guardians protect Skuldark when there's an emergency?"

"Yes, in the event of some terrible calamity, Keepers can summon the Guardians by playing the 'Music of the Guardians.'"

"Great! Can they help us find Robot Rabbit Boy?"

"You can only call them in a true emergency, I'm afraid."

"But this is a true emergency!"

"Sorry, Gertie, the whole island of Skuldark has to be in peril, not just a single Keeper."

"Even if it's a rabbit?"

"Yes, even then."

Soon they were moving too quickly to speak, the baby moth gliding just ahead of them with an occasional powdery snap of its wings.

But then after some time, the strange insect went so high, Kolt and Gertie lost sight of it in the darkness. They stopped their bikes. They were in open country now, far off Turweston Passage. A freezing night wind bit into their faces.

"That's it?" Gertie said. "It leads us into the middle of a field?"

The ground was so waterlogged that Gertie wondered if they were on the edge of a swamp. She feared that if it got any wetter, the thick tires of their Golden Helpers might get stuck.

But with the absence of trees and Attercoppe hives, she felt comfortable lifting the flaps of her deerstalker hat and getting off her bike. For some moments, she took in her surroundings, getting used to standing instead of riding. Kolt climbed off his bicycle too. Then they stood, listening to the distant bark and whistle of wild night creatures—hoping for a sound that might give some clue as to the whereabouts of a little rabbit they loved so much.

8

Stampede!

"MAYBE ROBOT RABBIT BOY is asleep somewhere in this tall grass?" Kolt said, looking around.

Kolt and Gertie took the Slug Lamps from their pockets and began to search.

"Can't believe I've got wet feet again!" Kolt said, squelching along.

"Again?" said Gertie, but then she remembered. "Oh, that's right, Marie Curie dropped the kettle of water."

They stepped over the tall plants, pointing their Slug Lamps down in the hope of seeing a furry bundle. Gertie felt like she was climbing around on the hairy scalp of a giant head. Then, in the distance, at the top of the hill, the blue sky of night darkened to starless black. It was as though a giant wave were coming toward them.

Kolt seemed alarmed. "Oh, what's that? Up ahead? Shine your bike lamp on it, Gertie."

Gertie put the Slug Lamps back in her pocket and returned to her Golden Helper, turning the handlebars so her lamp was shining in the direction of the shadow.

"It's too far away," she said as the white light lit up the tall prairie grass, "though there is *something*," she added, noticing a rocky lump farther up the hill. "A giant boulder."

"Yes, I know about that . . . it's a very special rock, but listen! Do you hear that?"

"Not really," said Gertie. "What are we listening for?"

"You don't hear that low hissing?"

"No . . ." Gertie said, but then she *did* hear something, though to her it was more like a drumming.

"Sounds more like a drumming."

"No, it's definitely hissing," Kolt said.

"Really? Because I've heard hissing when I was trapped with that giant snake, and this is more of a light drumming."

Kolt thought for a moment. "I suppose it could be a tapping along with the hissing, but there's definitely no drumming."

"It's too low for tapping," Gertie insisted, "but I will admit there is a hum."

Gertie dropped the bike and went back over to Kolt. The hissing-drumming-tapping-humming was now a low and constant rumble. It was as though something very big and very heavy were coming toward them down the hill.

"Could it be the Line of Stones?"

"The Line of Stones is not dangerous," Kolt explained, "it just marks an entrance."

"An entrance to what?"

"I told you, the Ruined Village. Long ago there were dozens of Keepers living down there. Shops, bakeries, even a cinema."

"If it's abandoned, what was that golden shimmering light I saw from the Spitfire?"

"It was most likely a ground-to-air reflection," Kolt said dismissively.

But Gertie wondered if the dazzling glow had something to do with what was going on now. She found it hard to imagine that an entire community of people had once been living in a village on Skuldark. Having friends, being able to play, explore the valley and forests with children her own age was something she longed for, something she thought about in bed, her first dream in a chain of dreams that would pull her through the night.

Just then, the drumming-hissing-tapping-humming-rumbling got much louder, and Gertie felt trembling in the ground.

"Back to the bikes!" Kolt said. "Quick as you can!"

"What is it?"

There were now heavy, thumping vibrations in the wet earth.

As they reached their Golden Helpers, the ground seemed to break apart as the shaking grew more intense and the dark cloud on the horizon reared up, almost swallowing the sky.

"Drop your bike!" Kolt shouted. "The ground is too unsteady. We're going to have to make a run for it."

Gertie looked around in a panic. "But where to?"

"That giant boulder you saw . . . RUN TO IT NOW!"

Gertie felt her blood freeze with fear as she scrambled after Kolt up the soggy slope through the tall wet grass.

"But we're running toward the shadow!" she cried. "How is that a good idea?"

"That rock is our only hope to survive!" shouted Kolt, his ripped pants flapping as they scrambled up the hill.

"Survive what?"

"Skuldarkian Tapirs!"

"What!?"

"Megatapirus augustus—PREHISTORIC RHINOS!"

"On Skuldark?" Gertie was now moving her legs as quickly as she could—but the ground was squelching and sucking at her shoes.

Kolt was still trying to explain, but Gertie could only hear bits of what he was saying, over the hissing-drumming-tapping-humming-rumbling-thumping-shaking. "I brought them here . . . just a few . . . many years ago . . . B.D.B.U. . . . allowed it . . . meteor . . . flash . . . wiping out . . . grown into a herd . . . now stampeding . . . apparently . . . make for the boulder . . . trampled . . . horrible . . . squish . . . QUICK!"

Then the most awful thought occurred to Gertie. What if Robot Rabbit Boy had been trampled? Part of her wanted to stop running, face the titanic creatures that were lashing furiously toward them, and shout: *WHAT HAVE YOU DONE WITH ROBOT RABBIT BOY?!*

But her legs just kept on squelching over the sopping field toward the rock. Just as the galloping mountain of tapirs bore down upon them, Gertie and Kolt reached the boulder—but instead of crouching for shelter in front of it, Kolt fumbled for his Keepers' key, and drove it into a small hole in the stone. A doorway appeared. Kolt pulled Gertie through the opening and they tumbled down a flight of wooden stairs as the thunder of prehistoric hooves passed over them.

For a moment, Gertie and Kolt were just a wheezing tangle of Keepers at the bottom of a long, dark staircase.

When they were able to stand and catch their breath without the threat of being trampled, they freed the Slug Lamps from their pockets and used what light was left from their squishy bodies to check themselves for injuries. No one spoke, as though sensing the worst for their little friend.

"You hurt, Gertie?"

"No, you?"

"Just bruised, and my, er, pants . . ."

They sat down on the step and shone their Slug Lamps into the room.

"Series 8 Forever Friends had a flying package," Gertie remembered wistfully. "Kevlar-drone blades that could lift them twenty feet into the air."

"But Robot Rabbit Boy is a Series 7," Kolt pointed out.

"Yes, I know . . . which means he doesn't have it and

there would have been no way for him to escape a stampede, without knowing about the secret door in the rock. What is this place anyway? Where are we?"

Gertie lifted her Slug Lamps, but their glow had started to wane, and they squirmed to be set free. Kolt stood, then took a box of matches from his pocket and shook it a few times.

"What are you doing?"

He said nothing and stepped through the darkness. Gertie heard the rough strike of a match. A moment later, several candles on a long wooden table flickered to life. She could see clearly now in the shadowy glow. They were deep underground in a large, furnished chamber that seemed to be abandoned.

"How did you know there were candles on that table?" Gertie asked.

"Because I put them there," Kolt said. "With no one living here anymore, I had to shut the generator down and turn off the water to stop the pipes from freezing."

"Why?"

"Because when water freezes it expands, so it would have cracked the pipes in the winter, flooding the room when the ice defrosted in springtime."

"No," Gertie said, "I meant why is there no one living here, and why is the entrance hidden?"

"It has always been hidden, and it's empty because there aren't enough Keepers to man the Gate Keepers' Lodge."

"Or woman," Gertie said. "Not enough Keepers to *woman* the Gate Keepers' Lodge."

"Or *rabbit* . . ." added Kolt, getting technical.

Gertie stared at what had once been someone's home. There was a table, comfortable armchairs, an early piano (which Kolt said was called a harpsichord), a bookcase, a mantelpiece, cupboards, a narrow wooden bed, and something called a billiards table. There was even a large chiming clock, not moving and, like everything else, coated in thick layers of dust. When Gertie got up to look around, the floor was covered with broken pieces of pottery and knives and forks that had been twisted into weird shapes—clearly not by human hands. Every mirror in the room had also been broken, as though whatever had caused the destruction wished not to look at itself.

To make the room even more frightening, the stone fireplace whistled. A cold draft was blowing down the chimney that smelled faintly of wet fur.

"Something has gotten in . . ." Kolt said, "something not particularly nice."

Although Gertie had a sort of morbid curiosity at the idea of discovering the source of the destruction, she felt the pull of something more urgent. "When will it be safe to go back outside and keep looking?"

"I'm afraid we're trapped down here until the main herd passes," Kolt said. The ceiling was still shaking with heavy galloping hooves.

"What if Robot Rabbit Boy's injured?"

"We'll leave as soon as we can."

Gertie sighed impatiently and rubbed thick dust off a tabletop.

"Why do you think all the mirrors are smashed?"

"I was afraid you'd ask that," he said. "Let's hope it was moisture that froze when winter came—same for the bowls."

"But the knives and forks?" Gertie said, picking one up. "That can't have been moisture."

Kolt's face looked dark and old in the candlelight. "Something has been going on down here we didn't know about."

Gertie was now on the other side of the room, looking at a giant rug hung on the wall. People had been sewn into the fabric with different colored thread. Kolt said it was the Turweston Tapestry, which told the ancient stories of Keepers. Gertie noticed several of the panels showed people with Keepers' keys running from a giant tornado—which had been expertly spun into the cloth using white thread.

"You didn't tell me about this place," she said. "Did you ever meet the Gate Keeper?"

"They had gone before I appeared on the island. Mrs. Pumble, the Keeper who taught me everything, might have known who it was, but I didn't."

"But you've been down here before?"

"A long time ago to visit someone."

"But I thought it was abandoned?"

Kolt hesitated. "Not exactly. Most Gate Keepers had a

little helper, who kept them company on long, cold nights, when blizzards could trap them down here for a week or two."

Gertie looked into the dark corners of the room. "What kinds of little helpers?"

"Creatures, Gertie—the kind that probably wouldn't stick around in all this mess."

"I wish you'd told me about this place before. How many more secret entrances are there hidden in rocks?"

"There's a lot you don't know about this island, but finding things out gradually is a normal part of life on Skuldark."

"Huh," she scoffed. "There's nothing normal about this place."

Then Gertie noticed a steel door at the very back of the room. It was marked EXIT ONLY. The door stood out because almost everything else in the Gate Keepers' Lodge was made of wood, and this was shiny, bright, steel. Gertie was going to ask Kolt what it was when something zipped out from a hole in the wall and hopped up onto the table in front of them.

9

George's Battle to Save the Lodge

KOLT CLAPPED HIS HANDS in front of his mouth.

A large white mouse was standing on the table looking at them. It had a long pink tail and a fluffy white coat, and was wearing a black mask with two holes cut out for its eyes.

"George!" cried Kolt. "I haven't seen you in years. Can't believe you're still here—you don't look a day over two hundred, seriously."

The Lodge mouse stuck out her mouse tongue three or four times.

Kolt seemed surprised. "It's been that bad, has it? Is that why you're wearing the crudely improvised superhero mask?"

The mouse looked down as though embarrassed.

Kolt turned to Gertie. "She's been having a tough time down here apparently."

"George is a she?" Gertie said, staring at the creature.

"Well, her full name is Georgina, but she always preferred George."

The mouse confirmed this with a nod. Then she picked up her tail and pointed it at Gertie.

"Oh, this is Gertie Milk," Kolt said, "the newest Keeper."

The mouse scampered over to Gertie and began to sniff.

"No, I'm sorry, George, Gertie *isn't* the new Gate Keeper, we just literally dropped in by accident, trying to avoid a grisly trampling death."

Then the animal made a small squeaking sound, which Gertie thought sounded like the rubber duck in her bathroom.

"I *know*, George," Kolt said. "You haven't had a Keeper for eighty-eight years—I would feel abandoned too, I really would."

Then the mouse looked Kolt up and down with a single squeak.

Kolt blushed. "What happened to my pants? Never you mind!"

"You understand Mouse?" Gertie said.

"Well, I'm not fluent, but . . ."

Then Gertie had a thought. "Maybe she knows where Robot Rabbit Boy is?"

Kolt nodded. But before he could open his mouth, the mouse had jumped down and skipped over to the steel door that said EXIT ONLY. George was now squeaking up a storm.

Gertie followed the creature, noticing what George must have wanted them to see. It was a robot hand. The sort that had been showing up in the cottage for the last few weeks.

Gertie was disgusted. "They're here too!" This one was blackened near the fingers as though it had been set on fire.

Kolt dashed over and picked up the robot hand by the wrist. It wriggled for a second or two, then gave off a puff of smoke and went limp.

"It must have come from under the steel exit door," Kolt said, as George let loose a series of passionate squeaks. Kolt listened, then translated for Gertie. "George says the hands keep appearing and she's been fighting them off with silverware for weeks."

"That must be what caused the damage!" Gertie thought out loud.

The mouse nodded.

"What's on the other side of that Exit Only door?"

"A long staircase leading to an enormous storage room deep underground."

"Like the ones under the cottage?"

"Exactly, but this room is not directly under us in the cliff; it's much farther away, for practical reasons."

"Because it's radioactive?"

"Mmmm, yes and no."

"I thought the most dangerous things were at the very bottom of the cliff at sea level, or surrounded in concrete?"

"They are, but the items in *this* room are not so much dangerous as completely unpredictable."

"What are they?"

"Machines," Kolt said, "from the twenty-second century and beyond."

"Is that all?"

"No," said Kolt, "there are devices related to artificial intelligence, like Robot Rabbit Boy—but much more advanced."

"Though probably not cuter . . ." Gertie added, glancing up at the ceiling and wondering if the tapir herd had passed so they could resume the search.

"The B.D.B.U. likes to keep these A.I. rooms pretty much off-limits," Kolt explained, "which is why they're hard to reach—even for Keepers."

"Could Robot Rabbit Boy be down there?"

Kolt turned to George.

"Have you seen any robot rabbits?"

George squeaked twice, then straightened the (clearly homemade) mask she was wearing.

"*No*, she says, it's just been hands, no rabbits." Then he looked down at the mouse again. "How long have they been bothering you?"

George raised both paws and wagged her ear.

"Three weeks?"

The mouse nodded.

"It must be lonely for her down here," Gertie said.

The white mouse picked up her tail. Then she pointed it at the messy room, and let out a long, sad squeak.

"She says we can't imagine how awful it's been with the

robot hands crawling around trying to destroy things, and that she's been rather depressed without a Gate Keeper companion, which is why all her cleaning duties have come to a halt."

"Yes, I can tell," Gertie said, looking around. "But can you ask about Robot Rabbit Boy again? Maybe she heard something?"

The mouse scurried toward Gertie, then ran up her body to perch on her shoulder.

"What's she doing?"

"You'll see, just keep still."

The big mouse fluttered her eyes behind the mask, as though in a trance, and stretched her front paws out in front of her.

"What's happening?"

"She's trying to find Robot Rabbit Boy for us."

"By doing yoga on my shoulder?"

"George is a Turweston Long Tail," Kolt explained, "a species that has a special connection to all the places where it's been to the bathroom."

"Is she going to the bathroom on me?" Gertie said, not daring to move, but willing to go along with anything that might help find Robot Rabbit Boy.

"Don't be silly. Wherever George has peed in the past, she is able to connect with that area and sense what's there. It's why Turweston Long Tails make great Lodge companions, because they know when something is approaching."

"But how?"

"Don't ask me," Kolt said. "I'm not a mouse living in a secret lodge on a strange island with a superhero mask and magical pee."

Just then, George's eyes opened very wide, and she nodded at Kolt, then waved her tail several times in a looping motion.

"He passed through!" Kolt said. "But many hours ago."

George pulled down the lower eyelid of one eye, to reveal a red squishy part.

"Urgh," Gertie said, "what does that mean?"

"No, that's good!" Kolt explained. "It means Robot Rabbit Boy was not on the plain when the tapir stampede began, and he's not on the plain now, as we feared."

"So where is he?"

"George believes he most likely made it to the Ruined Village."

"Then let's go!" Gertie said, now certain the bright light they had seen from the Spitfire had somehow drawn Robot Rabbit Boy from the cottage.

The mouse jumped down and scooted toward the staircase with them.

By now the thudding of the animals over the room had stopped. The old timber beams were no longer shaking.

"Oh dear . . ." Kolt said. "Our Slug Lamps are too exhausted to be any help, but hopefully it will be light soon."

Gertie had put hers on the long table next to Kolt's, and they all squirmed weakly with their tongues out.

"They're hungry," Gertie said, feeling a pang of guilt.

"We should have filled our pockets with moonberries."

George jumped up on the table and poked one.

"She wants us to leave them here," Kolt said, "so she can take them to the nearest moonberry bush to feed."

"But what about their Slug Lamp family outside the cottage?"

"Slug Lamps are one giant family, Gertie, all cousins, and so as long as they've got moonberries to chomp on, they're blissful anywhere."

As they climbed the stairs, Gertie asked if the tapirs would stampede again.

"They'll more than likely settle somewhere on the low ground to graze, then wander back up in the afternoon—unless we spook them again."

"I bet it was that moth . . ." Gertie said. "The furry pest." Then she glanced back at the Gate Keeper's little helper to say goodbye.

"Don't worry, George," Gertie said, "we're going to find you a new Gate Keeper, I assure you."

"And get rid of these annoying robot hands!" Kolt added.

The white mouse squeaked and raised a paw to her cheek.

"That's nice," Kolt said. "George thinks your birthmark is pretty."

"Thanks," Gertie said, "but how come I can't understand Mouse with my Skuldarkian?"

"Because it's not a language. Animals can communicate, but they don't have language the way humans do."

"Will you teach me Mouse after we've found Robot Rabbit Boy?" Gertie asked as they went up the stairs to ground level.

"Yes," Kolt said, then shouted down into the room, "Don't forget to blow the candles out, George, and try and run a broom through the place from time to time, eh?"

They heard a faint squeak as the stone door closed behind them.

"We should come back and visit," Gertie said, cheerful since the mouse was certain Robot Rabbit Boy had escaped the tapir stampede.

"We're many miles from the cottage, Gertie. It would be a whole day's excursion back here, unless I find more of those Golden Helper bicycles."

"I'm fine with that," Gertie said, thinking she might fly over in the Spitfire and drop a block of cheese through the sliding hatch. "How long has the Lodge been empty?"

"Well, apart from mice and robot hands, it's been eighty-eight years since there were feet going up and down these steps regularly."

"And was it tapirs that ruined the village?"

"No, it was the weather—with nobody living in the houses, water rotted the wood roofs and they fell down."

Light was creeping back into the world. It had been a long night.

In the distance, Gertie could see the hairy, cream-colored tapirs chewing on thick prairie grass. One tapir was close. It turned its giant head. White mist unfurled from its black nostrils. The head was big and slow. The curious eyes reminded Gertie of the Chinese water buffalo Robot Rabbit Boy had ridden through the jungle in ancient China.

"For some reason, they've grown hairy coats since coming to Skuldark, which I don't quite understand," Kolt said. "I'll have to ask Charles Darwin, if we ever meet again on a mission to Victorian England."

Gertie stared at the enormous animal, which looked like a cross between a hairy pig and an anteater.

"C'mon," Kolt whispered. "We'd better keep going."

With the door closed, the entrance to the Gate Keepers' Lodge turned back into a giant rock. Without going too far, they could see what remained of their Golden Helper bikes. The frames were broken and twisted, with bits of plastic spread across a wide area.

But Gertie wasn't worried about the bikes. Even though he hadn't been smushed by hairy tapir feet, Robot Rabbit Boy was still lost, and it was their fault for being too engrossed in the film.

As if sensing her despair, Kolt spoke. "If he made it to the Ruined Village, there would have been places to hide, places that protect Keepers from harm. The village is a sanctuary for our kind, Gertie, and also where the enchanted trees used to grow."

"Isn't the B.D.B.U. made from enchanted tree paper?"

"Exactly—from the last tree, which had all the power of the others."

They plodded quickly now through the wet grass. The

sky was growing lighter. Soon they could make out the glistening, snow-capped Ravens' Peak.

"How far to the mountains?" Gertie asked.

"Six more hours walking."

Then Gertie had an idea. "When it gets lighter, maybe I should go back to the cottage and get the Spitfire? I might see more from the air."

"Without Golden Helpers, it'll take us a good day to walk back. We'd best keep searching on foot."

After stepping over a short, moss-covered wall that Gertie couldn't believe was the famous Line of Stones, they stopped to survey the ruins that appeared before them. Gertie sat and rested on a fallen tree trunk. It felt good to not be walking. Her legs ached, and her feet were wet and numb. They had both been awake all night with nothing to eat or drink.

"There's no way Robot Rabbit Boy made it through the village toward Ravens' Peak," Kolt said, "unless he has four-wheel-drive paws we didn't know about."

"So he's here somewhere?" Gertie said, feeling a rush of positive energy through her exhausted body.

"That's what I'm guessing."

The tall grass had now given way to stubby green pasture. Tiny yellow wildflowers and weeds with purple thistles carpeted the ground before them.

The two Keepers walked on in silence toward the ruined buildings, hoping with all the strength they had left that some force in the universe had spared their little friend from a nasty fate.

But then they stopped suddenly.

In the distance was a ball of shimmering golden light hovering several feet above the ground.

"I hope that's not what I think it is!" Kolt cried fearfully. "Robot Rabbit Boy's doomed soul."

"It can't be!" Gertie said, trying to get the words out as quickly as she could. "It's exactly what we saw from the Spitfire, the bright light on the ground!"

"It really is bright, you weren't joking."

"Do you think it's dangerous?"

"I don't know. I've never seen anything like it before on Skuldark."

They crept toward the eerie glow with slow, fearful steps.

"It could be a Loser trap, Gertie."

"But what if Robot Rabbit Boy needs our help?"

"Let's hope he had the good sense to steer clear."

Part
2

10

Outlaws

A HOT WIND BLEW through a small North American town nestled snugly in a mountain valley.

Shard Pinch, a wiry man with a hard face and heavy black eyebrows, moved with deliberate slowness down Main Street. He had on a black wool frock coat, brown buckskin pants, and black riding boots.

For years, Morrisville had bustled with travelers, carpenters, cooks, tailors, saddle makers, coopers, and gentlewoman gamblers.

The busy Main Street shops, built from both wood and bricks, once sold everything from felt hats to hot buttered rolls to playing cards decorated with mythical creatures.

When Shard Pinch took over the town, the people of Morrisville had two choices: either leave with what they could pack on their horses—or stay and live under the rule of the new sheriff, self-elected judge, and mayor, Shard Pinch. He probably knew the law would catch up with him one day, in the form of soldiers sent from the capital, but until that happened, he would enjoy wielding power mercilessly over those townspeople foolhardy enough to remain.

To be despicable in North America in the early 1800s was not terribly hard. Large parts of the country had already been stolen from the native inhabitants, who would never recover their lands or their numbers. There *were* laws, but not everybody had the same freedoms or rights—such as the men, women, and children bought and sold as slaves.

The only business left in Morrisville that Pinch wasn't interested in stealing from was the funeral business—which wasn't really business at all, but simply a matter of measuring the client, getting the body inside a wooden box, then dropping it into a hole with a few words of comfort for whoever was listening (which was usually no one, unless circling turkey vultures count).

The local undertaker was a man named Moses Franks, who lived with his wife, Wendy Franks, and their son, Max, in a log cabin just outside the town.

Max Franks was no ordinary nine-year-old boy. He read complicated books on mathematics, when he could get hold of them. That's not to say arithmetic was easy for Max—it was very hard at first and took a lot of practice. Max tended to mess up simple calculations that ruined his chances with the bigger and more interesting problems. But the unique thing about this boy was that he *enjoyed* doing sums.

He played with them the way most people play with puppies. Algebra didn't make him feel sick like it does for most people, and the major questions of philosophy—such as the meaning of life, or what happens to us after death—occupied his nine-year-old mind for hours and hours.

But for Shard Pinch, Max was nothing more than the stupid, clumsy son of an undertaker.

"Faster, boy!" he snapped as Max Franks's hands smoothed the jet-black polish over the cracked leather riding boots. "Have you forgotten what happens when you're slow?"

Max had not forgotten. There was a scar to prove it.

"That woke you up, didn't it, you little fool?" said Pinch. The last time Max polished his shoes, the evil sheriff had thought it might be funny to snap his leg up and catch Max in the chin with the edge of his heel.

"You got blood all over the boot leather from your stupid face," Pinch went on. "What an idiot you are."

"Sorry, Mr. Pinch."

They were in his office at the town jail. The cells were full of valuable things from oil paintings to silk dresses that Pinch had stolen from the local people of Morrisville.

"It's Sheriff Pinch! Not *Mister*, you complete imbecile. Or should it be Lord Pinch? Or President Pinch? Yes, that sounds important. The whole world, I mean town, will have no choice but to worship me even more than they do!" he snarled as the small boy rubbed his boots furiously with a ragged cloth.

"From now on, I'll be President Pinch. *Remember that!*" he roared. "No need for elections, of course. Anyone who doesn't see how great I am is simply stupid or evil—because I'm always right—even when I'm wrong, which is never, by the way."

"I've finished, Mister—I mean, President Pinch."

"Well then, what are you still doing down there? Go back to your pathetic family and wait for somebody to die!"

"Yes, Mr. President."

The child got up and ran outside into the bright sunshine.

When Max arrived home, his mother was cooking red beans in an iron skillet. There were only three rooms in the house, one for the bodies that came in, one with a pot-bellied stove for cooking and eating, and a tiny room at the back just big enough for a boy's bed. Since Mr. and Mrs. Franks couldn't afford a bigger home or a normal bed for themselves, they slept in the empty coffins beside their customers.

"Hungry, Max?" Mrs. Franks said weakly. She was worn out from another sleepless night. Pinch's drunken gang had been out shooting through people's windows for fun and beating horses.

Max sniffed the air. It was the 168th straight day of beans. He never wanted to see another bean for as long as he lived, but he knew he couldn't blame his parents.

"Sure, ma," he said. "You know how much I love beans."

"Then go get cleaned up and let your father know to come eat."

Max's mother had once been a schoolteacher. But with no children (except her son) left in the town, she had learned to help her husband make the coffins and dig the holes to put them in.

Max pumped some water into a basin and washed the black boot polish from his hands.

"If only the bad parts of people could be washed away," he said, rubbing his fingers under the shimmering stream.

When his hands were free of the black polish, Max went into his tiny bedroom to look inside the little wooden box under his bed. The box was actually a small coffin his father had made for someone's cat, but the old lady who had ordered it died herself before she could pick it up.

Max kept all the objects that were valuable to him in the box. There was a lucky bullet, a spinning top, a spool of silver thread, a wooden horse toy, a dozen different fish skeletons, and a Cherokee arrowhead found in a dry riverbed. A large group of Cherokee lived above the town in the mountains, but unlike other villages, this one kept to itself, and didn't trade with the people of Morrisville.

A recent addition to Max's small coffin box was a large key he had discovered not long ago in his pocket. It didn't look like any key he'd ever seen before, and he didn't remember picking it up. It just appeared in his pocket one day. It had twirls in the handle, and there were four letters engraved on the long barrel: K.O.L.T. He tried to guess what the letters could mean, "Keep Only Little Turtles"? or "Kidnap Old Ladies' Tongues"?

Max had never shown it to anyone—even his parents. But sometimes at night he thought he heard it moving under his bed, scratching against the wood of the box, as if trying to get out, as if trying to get closer to him.

11

Not All Cupcakes Are Innocent

Despite Vispoth (the Losers' evil genius supercomputer) being able to get the Losers to any year in history it pleased (and brew hot chocolate so good anyone who tasted it was instantly addicted), the giant machine found it incredibly tricky (just as the B.D.B.U. did) getting its loyal evildoers anywhere near their intended targets.

After hours of wandering through swarms of mosquitos in the North American woods, the two Losers who had been out searching finally found Morrisville. They had two very important missions in the town. One involved a little boy named Max Franks, and the other was to save the life of their leader, Cava Calla Thrax, who (according to Vispoth) had only three more days to live.

On discovering Morrisville, the Losers made detailed notes about where everything was. Then they returned to their ship, *Doll Head*, to tell their leader they had located the targets, Shard Pinch and the boy.

The Losers spent the afternoon in *Doll Head*, triple-checking the tiny machines hidden inside two red velvet cupcakes.

When the sun began to set and the trees around them darkened, *Doll Head*'s rotted teeth parted, and three figures stepped into the cool evening air.

Leading the group was a fifteen-year-old from the twenty-sixth century, who was part girl and part droid. Her name was Mandy Zilch, and she was one of the most destructive children who had ever been born. Anything she touched, she broke—not out of clumsiness, which can be forgiven and even viewed as charming—but out of sheer spite. The droid part of her had been implanted by her crazed parents, who had wanted a son instead of a daughter. They had foolishly thought that installing aggression circuits from a fighting bot into their daughter's brain might turn her into a feisty boy. But the robot part made Mandy not only want to constantly argue, but destroy anything she encountered that wasn't a robot. The human part of Mandy Zilch was so enraged by her parents' selfish actions that it thought the best thing in the world was to destroy *all* robot life. She was a person of total opposites, united by a single impulse to destroy.

For the Losers, this North American excursion was so important they had dressed for the occasion. Instead of wearing her usual silver overalls and aluminum helmet with yellow visor, Mandy Zilch had put on a tartan day dress along with a matching tartan bonnet, which covered the robotic part of her head (a steel plate of tiny flashing lights and wires).

Cava Calla Thrax told Mandy Zilch never to take her bonnet off in the presence of locals—at least until the second red velvet cupcake had been eaten by the local sheriff known as Shard Pinch. The first would be eaten by Thrax himself.

The second figure to emerge from *Doll Head* (also dressed for the time in brown pants with a tapered navy blue coat with puffed shoulders) was a muscular giant of a man named Roland Tubb. He had once been an ordinary shoe salesman in 1980s Wales—but somehow lost his mind looking at cheap soles all day. The shoddier and more plastic shoes became, the more insane Tubb got. Then, at the height of his rage over mass-market footwear, he was scooped up by *Doll Head* on his morning walk to the dismal shopping center in Swansea where he worked.

Tubb had been a loyal member of the Losers for so long now, he functioned as chief advisor to the third figure, that frail Roman politician Cava Calla Thrax, supreme leader of Losers everywhere.

They had found Morrisville while on the trail of Max Franks—a very dangerous child who would have to be disposed of in the usual way. In a book on Franks's location, Roland Tubb read a few sentences about a local rogue sheriff named Shard Pinch who fancied himself a Roman

Caesar—even going so far as to wear a toga and to eat lying down. Then, after just over one year as a local official, he disappeared without a trace.

This dense volume of history was mostly about how families of the Cherokee Nation had been cheated out of their rights by corrupt government officials in Washington, but the chapter about Shard Pinch really caught Tubb's eye.

Thrax had agreed it was too much of a coincidence for the boy to be living in the same town as an evil villain who behaved like a bona fide Roman leader. Somehow, the man described as Shard Pinch in the book *had* to be Thrax in disguise.

But even the greatest scientist wouldn't be able to explain how a person could be in two places at once.

It was a question for super machine Vispoth, who took a full two days to formulate a response. The answer was then incorporated into the most wicked scheme ever devised by an out-of-control hot chocolate machine. If everything went as planned, not only would Cava Calla Thrax be given a new body so that he could continue living—but the Keepers would be destroyed forever. Completely eradicated from existence. The only difficult part of the plan was keeping the latter part secret from Gareth Milk, brother to that traitorous Keeper child—Gertie Milk.

THREE FIGURES, MANDY ZILCH, Roland Tubb, and their dying leader, moved slowly through the darkness toward the faint lights of Morrisville. Their first target was the self-appointed sheriff himself.

While the innocent slept (or tried to), Shard Pinch and his gang were wide awake in Tara's Tavern, drinking whiskey, playing cards, shouting, not cleaning up after themselves, arguing about who got to use the bathroom first, and trying to start fights (but like all bullies—only with people they knew they could beat). This was how they enjoyed themselves. It simply wasn't a good night without teeth on the floor and the toilet overflowing.

Suddenly the tavern doors flew open. The piano player looked up from his instrument. Not a single person spoke. All eyes turned to Shard Pinch, who stood quickly, hands on his mother-of-pearl-handled dueling pistols, stolen years ago from an English sea captain.

His eyes blazed with delight and menace. "Well, look here! Looks like we got some surprise guests!"

The room erupted with laughter, as the piano player, a waiter, and a waitress slipped away, for fear of being caught in the impending crossfire.

Shard Pinch rolled his shoulders and marched over to the three strangers. On meeting a new person, most people would worry about being liked, or saying something embarrassing, or doing that thing where you accidently spit a tiny piece of food while talking. But Shard was not *most people*, and instead was wondering what he could get out of these three strangers, and how he might inflict the biggest amount of suffering while getting it.

"Your friend . . ." Pinch said, pointing with the barrel of his weapon at the third frail figure, "looks pretty close to dead, so why don't you drop him where you see a space on the floor—and get yourself a drink, ha ha ha, ha ha ha, HA."

His gang laughed too and made mocking sounds.

"Shut up!" roared Pinch. Then he looked at Mandy Zilch, who was holding a beautiful red velvet cupcake on a little plate. Pinch looked at it, then at Zilch. "And who might this nice yun' lady in tartan be?" Pinch said, grabbing the cake and shoveling it into his mouth. "Hmmmmmm, wow, hmmmmmmmmmmmm, oh, hmmmmmmmmmm, hmmmmmmm, hmmmmmmm, heaven, hmmmmmmmmmm," he said, completely unaware of the tiny body-swap-bot hidden in the fluffy sweetness. The first cake had been eaten by Thrax moments before entering the tavern.

"That was the tastiest baked thing I ever had! Now, are you some kind of magic bakers?"

"Yes indeed," said Tubb seriously. "We're master cooks, but definitely not an evil time-traveling gang that wishes to eradicate knowledge by causing as much loss in the world as possible."

Mandy Zilch smiled. "And I'm just a lonesome human hybrid, Mr. Pinch, who needed a home for her cupcake."

Pinch was confused as to how she knew his name, but liked how weak and vulnerable she sounded. The taste of the cupcake was still in his mouth, and the lingering sweetness made him wonder if she had any more.

Then Tubb spoke again. "We have gold for you too, Mr.

Pinch." He emptied out his pockets and heavy coins tumbled to the floor.

Everyone gasped. Pinch's sudden excitement quickly turned to suspicion. "And what do you want in return?"

"For our friend to die with a great outlaw leader such as yourself at his bedside."

"Me? An outlaw?" Pinch said, vanity clouding his judgment. If there was one thing Pinch loved, it was himself. "Why, mister, I'm just a law-abiding sheriff, judge, mayor, and president. Who said I was an outlaw? Who?"

Everyone in the room twitched with nervousness.

"You calling me a criminal of some description?" Pinch said, unwisely eyeballing the frail figure of Cava Calla Thrax. "That's what you think I am, grandpa?"

Then, with the certainty that everyone was under his spell of menace, a corner of Pinch's mouth curled up into a smile.

"Well, I am feeling merciful at the sight of this gold, and so I'll forgive y'all for thinking bad of me, and will allow your dying friend to pass away in my good company, in return for something of course . . ."

Pinch turned sharply to a couple of his men, who were sitting with their legs on an empty chair.

"Take them upstairs to one of the rooms! Then guard the door until I get there," he said, staring down at all the gold coins on the tavern floor. "Your accomplice can die in peace. Then you can tell me where you got those coins—or you'll be joining him sooner than you expected."

Tubb pretended to be nervous. "Y-y-yes, Mr. Pinch," he said, "we'll tell you everything there is about our coins."

"And baking! I want to know about that too!"

Pinch's men escorted the three Losers up the staircase, and into one of the empty rooms on the second floor of the saloon. Pinch watched them disappear, chewing on a slimy cigar end.

While the outlaw's men guarded the door, Tubb and Zilch got their dying leader into bed.

There was a chair in the corner of the room, and Tubb brought it over to be near the thin, sickly figure propped up on pillows. The chair looked small in Tubb's enormous hands. There was no way his massive frame would fit, so Zilch sat there instead.

Suddenly Pinch burst in without knocking and plonked himself down on the bed next to the very old, white-haired Roman under grubby sheets.

With each swig of liquor, Shard Pinch's vanity seemed to get the better of his lingering suspicion. The tiny robot he had swallowed was now working away as it had been programmed, zooming around the brain collecting and downloading data ready to beam over to the other tiny robot now in Thrax's body.

Shard Pinch truly believed that the gray, sickly figure in the bed saw him as a sort of hero outlaw. The truth is that no one had ever admired Pinch before. Even as a baby, he was ignored and despised. No one held him, or kept him safe. Growing up, Pinch had learned that if he couldn't earn love, he could command obedience through fear. And so when a withered hand appeared from under the bedclothes, despite how disgusting and claw-like it was—Shard Pinch felt as though he owed it to the old man to hold it. But as soon as he did the old fellow's eyes opened slowly, and his lips rolled upward into a grin.

Then something very strange happened. Something most peculiar that Pinch did not have any words to explain.

He was suddenly in the bed, holding hands with himself. He watched the grin he had seen on the old man's face appear on his own, and there he was, lying in the bed in the old man's body. He felt the impulse to jump up and scream, but there was no strength in his muscles. Worse than that, his eyes wanted to close.

Pinch tried to let go of the hand (*his* hand), but suddenly wasn't strong enough. He tried to cry out to the members of his gang, but his mouth was old and brittle. With one final heaving gasp, he shouted, "Help me!" But his two men just stared. They had no idea that through some kind of futuristic technology hidden inside cupcakes, their sheriff was now in the body of the old man dying in the bed.

His eyelids got very heavy then, like two lead curtains. He felt a weakness in his body that he'd never known, but which he suspected must be old age. He wanted to grab his pistols, but he couldn't move. And whom would he have shot anyway? Himself?

Everyone stared as Shard Pinch cradled the old, dying man in his arms with a large grin.

"Not everyone gets to die with such honor," said Pinch—who was now Thrax.

Then the old white-haired stranger in the bed croaked, "I'm Shard Pinch!" and everyone laughed as they would laugh at a child pretending to be his hero.

With that, the vicious outlaw took his last breath in the wrong body.

The body-swap-bots had worked.

The new Shard Pinch stood and turned to his men. "Unless you want to die a very slow and painful death—tell me where I can take a bath."

"Er, yessir!"

"And get me some conditioner."

"What's that?"

"Curses," said Pinch. "It hasn't been invented yet."

When the two members of Pinch's gang had left the room, Mandy Zilch stared at the new Shard Pinch, her circuits blazing under the bonnet.

"Is that you, Master Thrax?"

"Of course it's me," Thrax said. "Just be glad you didn't mess up this mission the way Gareth Milk ruined his chance to destroy the B.D.B.U."

"It was his sister's fault," Zilch said, her circuits fizzing with hatred for the disgusting human quality of compassion Gertie Milk had shown in the ruthless Chinese king's palace.

"I don't care," Thrax said. "If Vispoth's plan works, we'll be rid of them both, once and for all."

Thrax then pulled a flat sheet off the bed, which he quickly fashioned into a sort of Roman toga.

"Now get out while I change," he said. "And go draw me a bath! I want bubbles! Lots and lots of bubbles!"

"Where will we find bubbles in Morrisville?" Tubb asked.

"How should I know? Make them if you have to!" Thrax barked. "There are more beans here than a vegan wedding."

Vispoth's plan was running like clockwork. All they had to do now was find some disgusting nine-year-old creature named Max Franks, slap a magnetic cuff on his ankle, and pack him off with a one-way ticket to the Black Hole of Calcutta.

12

The Spirit of Keepers Lost

GERTIE AND KOLT STEPPED cautiously toward the golden glow, still hovering in the distance.

As they got nearer, both Keepers realized it was coming from something buried in the ground.

"Be careful!" shouted Kolt. "Don't get too close until we know what it's going to do!"

"What could it do?" Gertie said.

"I don't know exactly," Kolt said. "Maybe turn us into light balls?"

"Light balls?" Gertie said. "You mean lightbulbs?"

"No! I mean BALLS."

"Like Cave Sprites?"

"Nah, I was thinking more like ball lightning."

Gertie tried to imagine herself as a sphere of electricity. "I think it's going to blind us," she admitted, "though not permanently, but in a weird way where, say, tomorrow we wake up and have some kind of magical power?"

"Oh, I'd love that!" gushed Kolt. "What kind of power do you think?"

Now they were only yards away.

"Maybe we should talk about this later!" Gertie suggested. "In case it's dangerous!"

"Good idea."

"Personally," she went on, "I don't think this is a Loser trap anymore."

"You don't?" Kolt said.

Gertie took out her Viking ax. "I think I know what it is," she went on, now chopping at the ground. Kolt joined her, trying not to look directly into the light.

"Because it's not just a glow," she said, squinting, "there's also a vibration!"

Kolt was squinting too. "What does that mean?"

"It's a key!" Gertie blurted out, remembering the morning she woke up on Skuldark, and her trip through the cliff. "It's a Keepers' key, I'm sure of it!"

Kolt didn't believe her. "This thing in the ground is a Keepers' key, you say?"

"*My* key vibrated when *I* was lost, under the mountain, before you discovered me sleeping at the edge of Fern Valley."

"I've never heard of such a thing," Kolt said. "Vibrating keys?"

"Well, it's true," Gertie told him, trying to think of a

reason why Kolt hadn't experienced this phenomenon before. "Maybe I got a newer model than you?"

Kolt whisked the Keepers' key from the pocket of his shredded, mud-splattered pants and looked at it. "So I got the boring one?"

"This key might even lead us to Robot Rabbit Boy. You did say there were things in the Ruined Village that protected Keepers—maybe this is one of them?" Gertie added, hacking away with her ax.

"I don't see how, and be careful you don't chop your hand off!"

"Then I could get a hook, like the pirate in a book I'm reading..."

"What book?"

"Look, we're almost there, Kolt..."

He tried to look, but the light was still too dazzling. "Let's hope it is a key and not something vicious," Kolt said. "We're wet, hungry, and tired, the last thing we need is a radioactive worm chasing us around."

"Trust me, Kolt, it's not a worm—it's a Keepers' key."

"Well, if it's much deeper, I say we come back after we've found Robot Rabbit Boy."

Gertie agreed. Then the soil became hot and steamy. Gertie reached in and plucked from the ground a glowing Keepers' key.

Kolt was lost for words. As soon as Gertie touched it, the small silver instrument for opening doors and operating time machines ceased glowing and was just a normal piece of metal with twirly bits in the handle. Gertie gave it to Kolt to inspect.

"Yes! This is the real thing all right," he marveled. Then he took a whiff, and turned away quickly. "It smells like rotting fish for some reason."

"What should we do?"

"Wash it, most likely . . ."

"No! With the key!"

"Since it was glowing and shaking before you touched it, I'm thinking we have to return it?"

Gertie's body was shaking with excitement. "To a missing Keeper, you mean?"

It was what she had hoped for, but her excitement was dampened by the fact that they still hadn't found Robot Rabbit Boy.

She slipped the new key into her pocket and got up. She was about to suggest they split up to search the Ruined Village, but then spotted something in the distance. It was something quite small, a gray bundle stirring at the bottom of a half-crumbled wall. Kolt and Gertie exchanged quick glances, then took off running.

When they got there, Robot Rabbit Boy was fast asleep, with one arm still balancing the plate of double-Dutch-chunk chocolate cookies Kolt had asked him to get.

"You're alive!" Gertie screamed, joy gushing from every pore in her body. Rabbit Robot Boy's eyes shot open. They were usually pink in the morning, but now they were bright green. He blinked a few times, then handed Kolt the tray of cookies.

"Marvelous," Kolt said, putting one in his mouth. "I'm starving."

Robot Rabbit Boy yawned and stretched out his paws.

"What happened?" Gertie asked.

"Eggcup?"

Kolt swallowed and reached for another. "What on earth are you doing out here? You were only supposed to cross the kitchen! We've been out all night and were almost killed by prehistoric rhinos."

"Smushed?"

"Yes, exactly," Kolt said. "Like dollops of mashed potato."

"Go easy on him!" said Gertie, scooping the Series 7 into her arms. "He's only a rabbit!"

THEY ARRIVED BACK AT the cottage sometime in the late afternoon. The first thing to do was warm up with long, hot baths as a slab of cheese lasagna bubbled away in the oven.

When it was ready, they ate together at the table, staring at the Keepers' key before them.

"Well, it's not mine," Kolt said.

"And it's not mine," said Gertie. "And Robot Rabbit Boy never had one."

"Lavender?" the Series 7 said, folding his arms.

"I mean," Gertie corrected herself, "Robot Rabbit Boy doesn't need one. So then *who* does it belong to?"

"Mashed potato?"

"I have a theory, Gertie, based on what I said in the Ruined Village, and it has to do with all your research!"

"You think the B.D.B.U. heard about the Keepers trapped somewhere in history? And wants to help?"

"I don't know if it heard us, but something weird is going on."

"I know!" Gertie said triumphantly. "So if we return the key, we find . . ."

"Its owner," said Kolt. "A missing Keeper of Lost Things."

"The island might be jam-packed with buried keys!" Gertie said, looking around. "We found this one because it was glowing. Maybe the others will do the same?"

"Something has certainly changed," said Kolt. "Maybe the B.D.B.U. has decided it's time for us to start finding them—hence the dazzling light you saw from the Spitfire?"

"Oh, I love that crusty old book!" cried Gertie. "It must have figured out what I've been trying to tell it about rescuing lost Keepers!"

"Lavender eggcups!"

"That's right," Gertie said moving the fur from his eyes in a gentle, circular motion. "You led us right to it, you clever little rabbit."

"He really does love getting his eyes swirled," Kolt said.

"Well, he deserves it."

"For running away and almost getting us all killed?"

Robot Rabbit Boy's glowing eyes went dark blue. "Mush," he said quietly.

"Don't listen to Kolt," Gertie told him soothingly, "you helped us find the key. I don't think you going missing with a plate of cookies was an accident, it was part of a plan."

"Hmm," Kolt said, "it does indeed sound like something that overactive comic in the tower would dream up."

"That's right," Gertie added with smirk, "especially the part where you split your pants."

Kolt slurped his hot chocolate loudly. They had made it fresh from cocoa beans they'd picked up in the Aztec empire while returning a ceremonial bowl.

"Why don't we take the key up the tower and see if the B.D.B.U. has anything to say?" Gertie said.

BUT WHEN THEY GOT to the top of the tower half an hour later, everything went wrong. They stood for ages over the B.D.B.U., dangling the key, but nothing happened, not even a flash of light, or a burp. The old, mattress-sized book didn't glow, shake, or emit even the faintest tendril of smoke—and neither did the key. It was just a plain old piece of metal, hanging above an ordinary monster-sized book in a tower.

"This is useless!" Kolt said. "Like drawing a face on a tomato and waiting for it to speak."

"It's as if the B.D.B.U. doesn't want us to return the key and find the missing Keeper," Gertie said with bitter disappointment.

Kolt shrugged. "We'll just have to have faith in the old thing—after all, it did manage to get itself rescued from the evil king who wanted to boil our heads in ancient China, when it got kidnapped."

"By my own brother!" Gertie said ashamedly.

"He'll come round, maybe not for a while, but one day he will, trust me on this."

"I hope so. . . ."

"Always remember the Keeper motto: It could always be worse."

"So what do we do in the meantime?"

"Go searching for more keys in the Spitfire and keep a closer eye on that rabbit!"

13

An Escaped Mushroom

THE NEXT DAY BLACK clouds swarmed over the Garden of Lost Things. Gertie awoke early to the sound of rain lashing her bedroom window. She switched on a lamp and lay there in silence, watching water run down the glass, and hoping the bad weather meant a return of that all-important Keepers' key.

But Gertie knew the B.D.B.U. was unpredictable.

It was Sunday, and so as usual, Kolt was most likely under the cottage. It was a ritual he had, to polish the various modes of transport, from atomic snowmobiles to Santa Cruz zombie-head skateboards with light-up wheels—very useful on twentieth-century city streets.

She pulled a robe over her pajamas, then climbed the spiral staircase to the upper part of her bedroom. The rain was whipping against the large window. Gertie stood looking out at the rough, open sea.

A part of her still wondered how she had gotten to the island, and hoped that one day she might see one of the ships Kolt said got beached occasionally.

There was a book on her desk about pirate ships. She had become interested after seeing the film a few nights ago. Gertie carried it to her couch and sat down, tucking her feet under her. By the intensity of the storm, she knew there wouldn't be long to relax. If Kolt didn't come knocking soon, she'd have to go down to the basement and notify him of a return.

The upstairs of Gertie's bedroom was more like a workshop now that she'd lived there for a while. There were two large desk surfaces, coffee and tea cans full of pencils and markers, brushes, and different-sized pairs of scissors. She also had various reams of paper for drawing, mapmaking, and any other craft she fancied having a go at.

Gertie looked up from her book on pirate ships, and scanned the cubbyholes over her desk—thinking how interesting it would be to draw a map of the basement. List all the things in the different rooms on the various levels. With 945 bedrooms in total, and thousands upon thousands of lost objects—it would take years, but no other Keeper had ever attempted such a feat. The Cave Sprites would be there to help. Gertie relished the idea of getting to know them better. Maybe she could learn to speak Cave Sprite with the same confidence Kolt spoke Mouse.

But of course, all big plans such as these were on hold until she could begin the process of rescuing Keepers. She felt that *this* was her life mission now. Knowing that children, *Keepers* like her, were somewhere in the world living miserable lives kept her awake at night. She would never have said it to Kolt—but she felt deep down that rescuing Keepers was more important than returning lost things, and perhaps even more vital than rescuing her estranged brother.

Gertie looked out to sea again. She hoped the upcoming mission had to do with returning the key to its Keeper. But what would this new Keeper be like? What if she didn't like him or her?

When Kolt finally made it upstairs from the basement through the trapdoor, Gertie was at the kitchen table with Robot Rabbit Boy playing cards. The rain was now coming off the roof like small rivers.

"I had no idea the weather had turned!" he said.

"How's the cleaning going?"

"I was actually trying to find out where those robotic hands have been coming from, but the Cave Sprites haven't got a clue."

Gertie put down a card. Then Robot Rabbit Boy did.

"You should have fetched me!" Kolt said. "It must be an urgent return with this sort of tempest. Have you been up to see the B.D.B.U. yet?"

"We were waiting for you."

But Kolt knew her too well. "Sure you're not just scared of being disappointed again?"

Gertie blushed. "It might be more convincing if the three of us go up there."

"Mashed potato?" said Robot Rabbit Boy, laying down three queens to win the game.

Moonberry bush branches were now rattling fiercely against the windows. Kolt fetched his bowler hat from the shelf and tightened his apron strings. It was time to climb the tower and find out what needed to be returned, where it had to go, and to whom.

"*Please* let it be the key..." Gertie said, as they shuffled toward that fowl volume, *The History of Chickens*. Kolt pulled the book from the shelf, and the secret passage opened to the tower. Just as they were about to start climbing, Gertie noticed the Keepers' key on the table.

"Look, everyone!" she cried. The Keepers' key was glowing again.

Kolt and Robot Rabbit Boy turned quickly.

"This is it, gang!" shouted Kolt.

Gertie was so excited she took the stairs to the tower three at a time.

Gertie told herself that she absolutely *had* to complete this mission. It was probably the most important one she would ever undertake. Not only would another Keeper mean a new friend (hopefully), but it also gave her a better chance of defeating the Losers' next evil plan (whatever that was), which meant the opportunity to rescue her brother.

Soon they were in the tower standing over the B.D.B.U.

As usual, its pages flashed, hummed, and turned by themselves to reveal strange scenes. One picture was of an avalanche, and there was suddenly a mighty tumbling of snow across the page covering several paragraphs. Another was of a meteor ripping through space with a tail of fire and ice. A third image was of a tall beast ripping the tops of trees with sharp teeth. Gertie knew they were sharp because she heard the snap of tearing leaves.

Eventually the whipping pages slowed, and the old book settled on a paragraph of illuminated gold writing. There was also an illustration of a knobbly person in a green costume with long, pointed shoes.

"That doesn't look like a Keeper," Gertie said.

They all stared at the strange, sickly figure on the page who was sniffling and rubbing its joints as though they ached.

"Looks like the flu," said Kolt. "Better stock up on ginger and echinacea before we leave."

But then in another picture was a glass vial full of green powder. To everyone's disappointment, the glowing key downstairs was *not* the object to be returned. It was something from bedroom 469, medicine of some kind. It was *this* that the B.D.B.U. was telling them to take back, to someone called Dr. Girolamo Fracastoro, who lived in Italy in the late 1400s.

"A vial of green junk!" Gertie said. "It can't be!"

The old book let out a deep burp and snapped shut, making Robot Rabbit Boy's ears fly back.

"Well. Maybe next time," Kolt said.

"But the key was glowing!"

"That's true . . . maybe the B.D.B.U. changed its mind at the last minute?"

"There must be a mistake." Gertie was livid. "I'm not sure we can trust it anymore!"

"Come, come, let's not be rash. It's only one small mission to Venice; we'll be home before you know it."

Just as they were about to leave the room, the B.D.B.U. sprung to life again. The three Keepers turned around excitedly. The book flipped and flapped, as the thousands of pages turned.

Kolt seemed pleased. "It must be a double return! When we take two items back to the world, one after the other— like with the mathematician's stick and the watch!"

Gertie just stared at the B.D.B.U., waiting for the flipping to slow and then stop in the place with all the details of where else they would be going.

With a faint, repetitive drumming of four beats coming from the pages, Gertie leaned into the book and read the name *Sequoyah*.

"Who is that?"

"Hmmm, it does ring a bell—but look! North America in the early 1800s . . ."

"Is that good?"

"It's dangerous, Gertie."

Once again, the item was *not* the Keepers' key, as Gertie had hoped. It was a piece of thick paper with symbols written on it. Kolt couldn't tell why it was important, but was happy the item was conveniently located in the kitchen, hidden in one of Kolt's books on the healing power of plants.

All the way down to the basement from the tower,

Gertie was quietly seething about having to return a pair of items—neither of which was the key. Robot Rabbit Boy seemed annoyed too, and kept saying "strawberry mush dollop room," over and over again.

"I know you're upset," Kolt said, as they descended the basement stairs. "You have a right to be. If it makes you feel any better I agree with you—that old book has been driving me loony all these years, but it's still in charge. It's still the brains behind the Keeper operation."

When they were deep under the cottage, a Cave Sprite appeared—probably Thursday, as it was quick and a bit pushy.

Each Cave Sprite had once been the soul of a brave warrior, but the little glowing balls of light were now guides of the Skuldarkian underworld.

"I just don't get it," Gertie went on, as the Cave Sprite led them down to level four. "We *have* a Keepers' key with no Keeper, AND it was glowing!"

"Gertie, stop, please, there's nothing we can do. It wasn't glowing when we passed it again on the way down here, the B.D.B.U. knows things we don't, have faith. . . ."

"Yeah, yeah."

"Mush dollop."

BEDROOM 469 HAD A peculiar smell that had wafted out into the corridor before they even got a Keepers' key in the lock. It was like leather, eggs, and soil. Once they were inside, Gertie realized immediately that bedroom 469 wasn't like the other rooms with things just piled up, crammed into corners, and stacked dangerously on top of one another. This was a library of sorts, but instead of shelves, there were glass-fronted cases running along all four walls, and instead of books, there were specimens. The Cave Sprite lit the room by hovering in the center.

"Sorry about the smell!" Kolt said with a whistle. "But this room is all plant-based medicine in the form of lost herbs, powders, gasses, leaves . . ."

"And slime," Gertie said, watching a green blob move slowly around inside a glass bell jar.

"Yes, slime too, along with barks, vapors, and fungi . . ."

"Like those?" Gertie said, pointing at some glowing toadstools behind glass doors with a skull and crossbones painted on them. She recognized the symbol from her pirate book.

"Deadly poisonous!" Kolt said. "But only to men with beards for some reason—oh, there's really so much in here, Gertie, from powdered wolfsbane to crushed beetle wings, which are blended with unstable magnesium and dried kidney beans to make a formula that gives a person the ability to fly for about two minutes—or however long he or she can hold the burp for."

"Eggcup?" Robot Rabbit Boy said, reaching a paw toward the jar with the brown clumps inside. "Mush?"

"No!" Kolt said firmly, looking at Gertie. "If he can't get a plate of double-Dutch-chunk cookies across the kitchen without getting lost, then imagine what would happen if he learned to burp-fly."

Gertie sympathetically patted Robot Rabbit Boy's head. "I'll take you up in the Spitfire once we're back from this mission," she promised, "and we can pretend we're in that space film with the gold and white robots you like so much."

Robot Rabbit Boy blinked, then snorted rudely at Kolt.

In the center of the room were tall racks of different-sized test tubes and glass jars of pickled things. Some objects were in liquid that bubbled, giving off strange gasses. Kolt said these reactions often forced lids off, which accounted for the odor they were having to deal with.

Gertie sniffed. "It's like a wet forest meets . . . very old shoes, mixed with rotten eggs."

"Sorry to dampen your poetic nose," Kolt said, pointing. "But this particular aroma is from that giant fungus lurking in the corner. It broke out of its jar last year and is now moving around. If you see it, wave."

"Wave!"

Gertie looked down and noticed several sticky trails on the floor. Then she peeked around the corner. A gray mushroom with a red top slurped across the tiles. It was taller and fatter than Robot Rabbit Boy—who must have decided that he didn't like it, and went to wait by the bedroom door.

Gertie stepped cautiously toward the creature. "Hello," she said nervously. The entire mushroom turned and bent its red top toward the sound of her voice like an enormous ear.

"Aargh!"

Kolt laughed. "Oh, it likes you!"

"You speak Mushroom too?"

"No, but when it's afraid, it fires hundreds of tiny spikes."

"Thanks for telling me now!"

Then the Cave Sprite began blinking. Gertie and Kolt followed it to a cabinet of glass vials.

"This must be it," Kolt said, opening the door and taking out the glowing glass bottle of green powder.

Then Kolt led Gertie to another part of the room. He took two small bags and two little spoons out of his pocket.

"We're short on growing spice," Kolt explained. "If you'll excuse the pun."

Gertie watched him take the top off a glass jar and scoop some powder with a teaspoon into one of the bags. Then she looked around. "What's the other bag for?"

"The complete opposite herb—shrinking spice," Kolt told her, reaching into another glass jar. This powder looked exactly the same as the other one. Kolt brought up a heaped teaspoon carefully.

"Don't you have to measure it?"

"Not really," Kolt said. "One is for growing, and one is for shrinking, like in that book *Alice in Wonderland*. You only need a pinch to feel the effects. That author must have gotten hold of some."

Gertie stared at the two jars. "But they look the same. How do you know the difference?"

"I keep them in different pockets," Kolt said. "A big pocket for growing spice, and a little one for shrinking spice. Ready to go?"

"Shouldn't we do something about the creepy mushroom roaming around?"

"Live and let live, is what I say."

Then Gertie noticed the giant red top had turned to listen. She was worried it knew what she had said.

"It's such a *nice* thing," Gertie added.

"Maybe so." Kolt nodded—then in a loud voice said, "But if I come down and find any glass broken, or specimens on the floor—then it's back in the jar forever!"

Gertie watched as the rubbery mushroom blades trembled, and the living mold retreated to a far corner of the bedroom, where it tried to make it itself look smaller than it actually was.

"That should do it," Kolt said. "I wouldn't want to live in a glass jar, would you?"

"No," said Gertie, thinking about all the missing Keepers who were probably living in much worse conditions.

NEXT STOP WAS THE Sock Drawer, one of the biggest rooms in the cottage, and accessed directly from the kitchen.

At the center of the room was an enormous revolving globe, and beyond, rack upon rack of clothes from every period in history.

Gertie had learned that dressing for the time meant blending in, which made it easier to return an object. Early on, Kolt had told her that being fashionable for them was actually a matter of life or death. For the trip to Venice, they would need clothes from the Italian Renaissance.

For a while they stood before the enormous revolving Earth, mesmerized by the deep blue of the sea, and the way light crept along the continents. It was a beautiful sight, and the Keepers watched it spin from west to east, their faces like three bright moons.

Kolt said it was a complete mystery how the enormous globe had come to be in its current position in the Sock Drawer. It was clearly too big to fit through any of the doors.

"So remind me what happens with a double return?" Gertie asked. "Do we take another outfit?"

"If possible, yes," said Kolt. "Especially when it's somewhere dangerous like North America in the 1800s."

Kolt gave Gertie a large cotton bag to put the change of clothes in.

"Remember it's vital," he reminded her, "that we don't draw attention to ourselves."

After finding out which rack held the clothes for their adventures, they each went off and picked out things to wear. Once they'd decided on garments for North America, they searched a different rack for something that would blend in with the locals in Renaissance Italy. In Kolt's personal opinion it had to be practical—but with charm— which for him usually meant a sequin or two. Gertie, on the other hand, didn't know what she liked until she saw it, and could actually feel the fabric in her hands.

"I think we should take the new key with us!" she cried from her dressing room. "I mean, it *was* vibrating!"

Kolt shouted a reply from his own dressing room.

"But if we run into any Losers, that's a third key we have to worry about! Think it's worth it? It wasn't glowing when we came back from the tower, was it, Gertie?"

"I suppose," Gertie shouted back, dangling a corset in her hand, wondering why anybody would wear such a thing. "But the Losers can already travel through time because of Vispoth—so what use would a third key be?"

Kolt gave a muffled response, which meant he was putting something on.

Robot Rabbit Boy didn't have a changing room, as there wasn't much that fit his unusual rabbit body. He made himself useful though, by scooting back to the racks if a different size was needed—like a real-life shop assistant.

"What is the late fifteenth century like in Italy?" Gertie said, appearing before Kolt in a long black velvet dress with a red pleated linen overskirt and a black hooded veil.

"Oh, Gertie, you look more like a spider-woman assassin than a Renaissance maiden."

"There's such a thing as a spider-woman assassin?"

"Yes! And pray you never meet her . . . Now, are you sure you can walk in all that heavy fabric?"

"Well, I couldn't run a marathon," Gertie said, trying to look comfortable, "but check this out, detachable bouffant sleeves with embroidered slashing, just in case I get hot!"

"I'm afraid you'll have to leave the black veil hood thing behind."

"But that's my favorite bit!"

"Well, unless you're a widow, it's not going to work."

"I could be *the* black widow assassin!" Gertie said, "Who destroys her enemies with—"

Kolt cleared his throat. "What shoes do you have on?"

"Er, well, the giant platform clogs with pearls and lace were too much, which reminds me—that corset thing looked like a personal torture chamber, so I had Robot Rabbit Boy put it back on the racks with the clogs."

"Gertie, we have to fit in, we must—"

"I couldn't even stand in those shoes! They made me look like a cake decoration."

Gertie lifted the hem of her long red overskirt to reveal the green light-up sneakers Kolt had given her when she first arrived on the island.

"But, Gertie, those sneakers are twenty-first century!"

"But they're *so* comfortable."

"The whole purpose of the Italian pianelle platform sandal is to raise the hem of your skirt above the muck of the streets."

"I'll tiptoe," Gertie said. "And don't even get me started on the corset—humans wear their skeletons on the inside, thank you very much."

"Fine," Kolt said. "But if we stand out, it's your fault."

Kolt had opted for conservative robes in light green with olive tights to match. He had also picked out thin cloth shoes—which reminded Gertie of the ones she was wearing when she washed up on Skuldark.

Then, sheepishly, from behind a stand of wigs and false beards, Robot Rabbit Boy stepped out wearing a gigantic gold coin, which hung around his neck on a chain.

Kolt rubbed his eyes. "What the . . ."

It was the first time Robot Rabbit Boy had ever dressed up for a mission. He also had a silver dagger hanging from a leather sling, a purse, and best of all—a fake mustache.

"I don't believe this!" Kolt said. "He looks like the fifth musketeer!"

"Weren't there only three musketeers?"

"I can't remember, but none of them were rabbits!"

"Eggcup. Lavender. Smush," Robot Rabbit said matter-of-factly, admiring himself in the mirror. "Strawberry dollops."

"Fine," Kolt said. "I give up. Wear what you want, just don't get us killed with your strange facial hair."

Gertie gave Robot Rabbit Boy a secret thumbs-up, and his eyes flashed neon blue.

When they entered the kitchen to pack a few snacks for the journey, one of the old volumes in the bookcase was glowing. The three Keepers rushed over and took down a massive book on the healing power of plants.

"It's so heavy . . ." Gertie said, plonking it on the table. When she opened the pages, they found the important piece of paper they needed to return to the person called Sequoyah. It was thick, but had yellowed with age. Printed on the front in black ink were strange markings—some kind of written language that Gertie had never seen. She counted the symbols. They numbered 85.

Walking to the Time Cat, Gertie asked why fifteenth-century Italy was also called the "Renaissance."

"It means 'rebirth' in French," Kolt explained. "It was a time of great discovery and optimism, a rebirth of ideas and culture from the Roman and Greek periods."

"Oh no! Why would anybody want to bring back the cruel Roman ways?"

"It was more their arts and knowledge, Gertie, a time of rediscovering tools like maps that had been lost after the fall of the Roman Empire. In fact—many people during the Renaissance believed the Romans had been destroyed by God for their wickedness."

Gertie was relieved. If there was one period that sounded horrible to her—more frightening even than the age of dinosaurs—it was the Roman Empire, an epoch when people seemed to delight in being cruel.

"What was the name of the doctor the B.D.B.U. said we're returning the vial of powder to?"

"Doctor Girolamo Fracastoro." Kolt thought for a moment. "I'd have to check my books, but I believe he was the first person to come up with a germ theory. He wrote a long poem about it."

"A poem about germs?"

"Yes . . . the idea that diseases are caused by tiny creatures that get inside our bodies and multiply, I suppose. But don't get me started on parasites. . . . Anyway, people in his time thought the old chap was mad—but it turns out he was right all along!"

"I'm surprised they even had doctors back then."

"Oh, they did, but most *were* bonkers by our standards, basing their remedies on superstition, folk stories, or dots they could see moving around in space. But the Venetian food isn't bad. During the Renaissance, everything from cooking, to painting, to architecture, to music, and even dressing was taken to high levels."

"That sounds good."

"Don't get too excited, it was also a period when opposites thrived, and so we will have to be careful, because despite people's openness to new and beautiful things— they had a shocking appetite for savagery."

"Like their ancestors in Rome," Gertie pointed out.

IT HAD STOPPED RAINING when they reached the Time Cat, but it was still clouded over. Climbing inside, Kolt described the various dangers of Renaissance:

1. Gangs of toothless robbers

2. Gangs of robbers with a few teeth

3. Gangs of robbers with excellent dental hygiene

4. Robbers with or without a gang (or teeth)

5. Condottieri (professional killers)

7. Bravoes (hired thugs)

8. Mosquitos (tiny vampires)

9. The Black Death, a horrible disease
   spread by the bites of fleas

10. Getting burned alive in public—which
    hurts, but is also embarrassing as every-
    one sees your underwear on fire

Once Gertie had typed in the date for their new destination, they could hear the 101 automatic watches spinning
under the hood, but the Time Cat didn't want to go. Gertie
checked the fuel levels, but they had more than a quarter
tank of Skuldarkian seawater.

"I don't like this at all," Kolt said. "I have a funny feeling
the 1400s are not going to be one of my favorite historical
journeys—and it's a double return too."

"Don't be so superstitious! This mission might be the
one that leads us to finding those lost Keepers!"

Kolt noticed the end of the newly discovered Keepers'
key sticking out of Gertie's richly adorned black robe.

"If you have to bring it, Gertie, just keep it out of
sight," he warned her. "Don't fall prey to Venetian pick-
pockets. You're a real target in that velvet finery—I'll
be surprised if we don't get kidnapped and held for
ransom—especially with DJ Rabbit Boy," Kolt said, pointing at the Series 7 sitting quietly on the backseat playing
with his mustache.

"We'll be all right," Gertie reassured him, "and hopefully we'll make some progress in the hunt for missing
Keepers."

"You never know," Kolt said. "Let's just hope these back-to-back missions are a cinch."

"Mashed potato, fly."

"Hey, that's a new word for him!"

"What, *fly*?"

"He must us have heard us talking about Attercoppes!"

"Or . . ." suggested Kolt, "he's been spending too much time clamped to the Spitfire."

"Room, fly," Robot Rabbit Boy said again, "mush, fly."

"Well, there'll be plenty of flies where we're going," Kolt remarked, "because people of the fifteenth century were not known for their bathing habits—though they excelled at torture, witchcraft, and going to the toilet outside—while it's fair to say they completely failed at food hygiene."

"You're worrying too much as always. We can't let fear get in the way of our duties," Gertie said.

Kolt put his Keepers' key in the small wooden box that was the actual time machine, and the Time Cat began its usual fizzing. Then after a loud pop, everything went blurry. There was a white flash, a purple sizzle of gravitons, and they found themselves in the middle of a field.

But it was not an empty field. There were people all around who saw the Time Cat appear and were coming over to investigate.

14

Bird Boy

THE DAY AFTER CAVA Calla Thrax was in his new body, the hunt began. Posters were put up that read:

MAX FRANKS

WANTED ALIVE

(BARELY ALIVE OKAY)

HUGE

REWARD

They were nailed to trees, posts, signs, even the church door. It didn't say what his crime was, or even that Max Franks was a nine-year-old boy. But the reward was large

enough to draw every cruel, grizzly, rotten-toothed merce-
nary for fifty miles to the small town of Morrisville.

After hammering up some posters, Shard Pinch's
crew—along with Roland Tubb and Mandy Zilch—went out
themselves in search of the boy Vispoth had ordered them
to capture. Of course, just killing him would have been easy,
but it was not the preferred method of removal. Vispoth
had calculated with high probability that if any Keeper *was*
murdered, two or more Keepers would be selected by the
B.D.B.U. to take his or her place. The more Keepers they
killed, the more Keepers there would eventually be.

Max was on his way to town when he saw the posters.
He couldn't understand why the evil sheriff would have
offered *any* reward for his capture, seeing as how he was
on his way to Pinch's office that very morning to shine his
black boots. It was something he'd done for over a year. Why
couldn't Pinch have caught him then? It was a mystery Max
couldn't figure out.

But with a price on his head, Max turned around and
dashed home. He snuck in the back window, then crawled
under his bed where it was dark and cool. The perfect place
to come up with a getaway plan.

Thinking about the posters, Max decided there was no
alternative but to run away. His parents loved him, he knew
that—but there was nothing they could do against a mean
gang of outlaws with Max as their target. It would have
taken a vicious army of trained killers to defeat the motley
crew of people out searching for him. Max imagined himself

being taken. The faces of his mother and father as their son was captured.

He had to flee Morrisville.

Max felt for the coffin-shaped box where he kept precious things. Behind the box was a pair of folding wings he had been building for the last six months. They were just about ready to test, and were the best thing Max had ever constructed.

This is how they came to be made. Pinch and his men liked to shoot animals for fun. Whenever Max found one of their victims, whether it was a raccoon or a squirrel, or even an eagle, he would say a little prayer to the powers of nature. Then he would find a place to bury the remains.

After seeing so many dead animals, Max became interested in how bodies actually worked. Sometimes he could see inside the wounds to sinewy flesh and white bone. He was most curious about how wings enabled flight.

At first he simply sketched what he saw. The shapes and sizes of bones—which were hollow. The kinds of feathers on different birds. Soon, he had hundreds of drawings of bones and feathers.

Then one day, he was exploring a part of the forest he'd never seen before when he looked up in a tree and saw the complete skeleton of a buzzard. It must have died from old age while sitting on a branch, Max thought. If he could weigh and study each bone, it would help him figure out the mechanics of flight.

Not owning a set of scales, Max had designed a balance

system using rocks and old spoons. After weighing each piece of bone and estimating the weight of feathers, muscle, flesh, the animal's beak, and even food in its stomach, Max filled another notebook with mathematical calculations, trying to formulate an equation for lift force. Then he started work on his own pair of wooden wings that folded in and out. He constructed them with thin tree bark that was very light but strong. Instead of feathers, he used fabric, which he cut from the cloth his parents wrapped dead bodies in.

When they were finished, Max kept the wings under his bed, folded up like two fans. He had never *really* tested them, as his calculations from using Newton's Laws of Motion were not promising.

Sir Isaac Newton was one of Max's heroes. A long time before Max was born, he had come to recognize three laws about the physical forces around us—which were sometimes known as physics.

Max knew Newton's three laws by heart, and wanted to use them now to help him escape.

Newton's first law was about something called *inertia*. Basically, as Max understood it, objects like to continue doing what they were doing—whether it's being still, or moving in a straight line. An object that is still will keep being still until other forces act on it. The same goes for an object that is moving—it will keep moving in the same direction until a force (such as gravity) acts on it.

Newton's second law said that the acceleration of an

object depends on the object's weight and the force applied to change its current state—or inertia. A pebble has small inertia, and so requires a small force to move it, while a boulder has a large amount of inertia, and so would need a larger force to change its original state of being still.

Newton's third law stated that every action causes an equal and opposite reaction. So to fly, Max knew he had to generate enough force with his wings to push the air down, so that the air pushing back would be greater than his weight, thus giving him lift. But exactly how much force did he need to push the air down with?

The calculations in his notebook made flight seem impossible. He would need seven-foot wings at least. He also seemed impossibly heavy. From observation, he knew that birds had hollow bones and air sacs. According to his father, human bones were full of marrow, not air. Max also knew that his strength-to-weight ratio was very low—if he remained his current weight, he'd need massive muscles to power the wings—and that would add even more weight to his frame.

Then if by some miracle he *could* get in the air, Max knew gravity would be trying to pull him back to earth every moment.

But now with a price on his head, running away was probably not as effective as *flying* away.

Max put the artificial wings into his knapsack, then opened his coffin-shaped keepsake box to grab the strange key that had appeared in his pocket one day. Except that the key was not there. Max felt around under the bed again, but couldn't find it.

Suddenly he heard pounding on the front door. There was no time to look for it now. As his mother's footsteps echoed in the hall, he scrambled out of his window.

Max hiked through dense woods for most of the morning. Sneaking away had given him a head start on Pinch's gang and probably saved his parents' lives. He stood in the shade of a cedar tree and thought about where he would go, and what his life would be like as a boy of nine living alone in the world. He felt sure he'd see his mother and father again, but not until he was much older—a man perhaps.

He remembered the wings in his bag. With aching legs and sore feet, he felt it was time to test them out.

He had no idea where he would go if they worked, but imagined himself soaring high up in the sky like some kind of bird boy. Maybe he'd make it as far as New York City? Or across the sea to merry old England? He would be like Icarus—but obviously without the going-too-close-to-the-sun-and-resulting-death-plunge part. Even though Newton's laws told him flight was completely impossible, he knew he had to try it.

Max spat on his hands and pulled himself up into the tree. It was a hot day, and the air was sweet with the scent of forest. He wondered why trees didn't start growing branches until they were a certain height, and figured that it must have been to stop animals from feasting on the young leaves. After climbing for several minutes, Max was on a thick limb. Although he wasn't very high, it felt danger-ous. His plan was to edge out to the end of the tree branch, and sort of drop into what he hoped would be a miracle of flight—like the bumblebee. All around were trees and thick bushes, which he hoped might cushion his fall if it went wrong.

Max carefully unfolded the delicate wings from his knapsack. He strapped them onto his arms using leather pieces he'd made in his father's coffin workshop. He tied the knapsack around his chest, leaning forward to lie on the wide branch. It was warm from the sun and there was a light breeze. But then uncertainty and fear gripped him, churning his insides. He felt suddenly foolish up there in a tree wearing fake wings. Max leaned against the tree trunk and pulled out his book of notes. He would think through Newton's laws again and go over the numbers. Perhaps there was some factor he had overlooked that would make flight possible? Some miscalculation that would mean the difference between soaring majestically over the woods, and plunging to the ground with a splat.

15

Walking Hunks of Flesh

GERTIE AND KOLT HAD landed in the middle of an open field, with trees at one end and a dirt track on the other.

"Is this Venice?" Gertie asked. "It looks more like a swamp."

Kolt was annoyed. "The B.D.B.U. has done it again. It's definitely not Venice, but by the looks of those cottages, we *are* at least in Renaissance Italy."

"Lavender?"

"I'm really losing patience with the B.D.B.U.," Kolt admitted. "We were supposed to be over *there* some-where, on the edge of the city, not miles away in a swamp!" He pointed toward a dark, gray sky in the distance.

"Why on earth would the B.D.B.U. plonk us down so far away?"

"At least we have the Time Cat, and the air is fresher here...."

"Fresh air?" Kolt said, suddenly noticing movement in the distance. "Oh no, look!" A ragged human figure was approaching. After a few seconds, dozens of other bodies began to emerge from all directions, limping slowly toward the Time Cat, with blank, hollow looks on their faces.

Kolt was pale with fright. "Gertie, I don't suppose you know what a zombie is, do you?"

"Um, um, let me see . . ." she said, "some kind of spicy chewing gum?"

"Er, no—trust me, you wouldn't want a zombie in your mouth."

"Mashed potato?" said Robot Rabbit Boy.

Kolt turned to glare at the Series 7.

Gertie could feel Kolt's fear now, and panic began spreading through her body at the sight of so many strange people coming toward them.

"Why are they walking so slowly like that?"

"Because they're zombies!" Kolt yelled. "Walking hunks of dead human flesh!"

"Zombies?" Gertie said frantically. "What do they want with us?"

"Let's just say they're not vegetarian."

Kolt slammed the Time Cat into first gear. But when they tried to drive away, the wheels spun in the wet grass. Clumps of dirt flew up from the tires and mud splattered the windows.

"We can't get traction!" Kolt shrieked. "This ground is like butter."

"Butter!" Robot Rabbit Boy exclaimed. "A dollop of butter?"

Suddenly there was a type of disorderly music made by tiny bells and wooden clappers—instruments being carried by the people now surrounding the Time Cat.

"Er, that's weird," Gertie said, "they're putting on some kind of zombie concert."

Then something occurred to Kolt, as his expression of fear changed to one of delight. "This is no zombie concert! Those are bells used by people with leprosy! We're saved!"

"Phew," Gertie said. "So not zombies?"

"I don't suppose you know what leprosy is?" Kolt asked in a voice that Gertie found slightly annoying.

"Not exactly," she said, "but I suppose you're going to tell me it's something horrible, using a very long word that I don't understand?"

Kolt frowned. "I wouldn't dream of doing that! I hate it when I'm reading a book and the author uses a super-long word to make herself look clever."

They were now completely surrounded by a hobbling mass of bodies. Men, women, and small children, all suffering from a disease called leprosy and thankfully not another condition known as pneumonoultramicroscopicsilicovolcanoconiosis.

Gertie cleared her throat. "So what is it then?"

"People with leprosy have been infected with bacteria

that causes skin growths, which can disfigure the person—even stop them from feeling pain, which means they may not know if a limb is broken or infected."

"That's a really horrible disease," Gertie said sympathetically, noticing that some of the victims of leprosy were missing hands or legs or feet. "Can we help them?"

"Sadly no, the cure hasn't been invented yet."

"We should have brought it! I bet it's down in bedroom 469 with that walking mushroom."

"Tempting I know, but we have to let progress unfold naturally, Gertie."

"Well, we could at least have brought them wheelchairs or something—some of those children might be our missing Keepers!"

Robot Rabbit Boy (who'd been in the backseat near the emergency juice boxes) hopped onto Gertie's lap.

Some victims of the disease couldn't walk and dragged their bodies along the ground. Some had lost fingers or whole arms. Nearly all had some kind of facial deformity.

"Usually the bells and clappers are used to get someone's attention after a victim's voice has fallen prey to the disease, but in this case, they are warning us to stay away," Kolt explained. "They're trying to let us know we're in danger of catching their disease, despite their terrible pain."

"I feel very sorry for them," Gertie admitted. "They might look weird on the outside, but inside they have the same thoughts and feelings as us, right?"

Kolt nodded seriously.

"History really is a nightmare. They're doomed and there's nothing they can do but suffer."

"Which is why it's so important we defeat the Losers. Without science and education, there would never have been a cure."

Just then, the Time Cat's wheels found some traction in the dirt and they were sliding sideways.

"Finally moving!" Kolt said, turning the wheel to get them going straight.

"Go slowly," Gertie said. "In case anyone falls in front of us."

"Good idea."

"Fly," said Robot Rabbit Boy, "mush."

One person they passed was ringing his bell so vigorously that the metal bit came flying out and hit the windshield. Behind him stood a child who was missing both her hands.

"When was the cure for leprosy invented?"

"Er, um, let's see, 1980, I think . . ."

"WHAT?!?! That's almost five hundred years from now!"

Gertie was determined to do something, and rolled down her window.

"Well, if we can't get them the cure . . ." she said, pulling all the money they had brought with them from the pockets of her gown (and from Kolt's leather satchel), "then at least we can make them rich!"

With the window down, Gertie began flinging out gold coins, silver pieces, even emeralds and rubies.

"Butter!" Robot Rabbit Boy said, taking off the gold coin from around his neck and chucking it out into the field.

"What are you both doing? We need that! How will we buy food?"

"We can live on the emergency cakes and moonberry juice!"

As they drove across the field in the direction of the road, Gertie looked back and watched the victims waving madly as best they could.

"What are they doing?"

"They're thanking you," Kolt said. "You've made them wealthy beyond their wildest dreams."

"I'm glad," Gertie said, "but I wish we could give them the cure now."

"Well, we can't, but thanks to you, they'll be able to live in decent houses, and eat soft food that doesn't hurt their gums, and take baths and have the nice things we don't even think about—like comfortable straw beds."

Gertie checked her pocket for the glass vial of medicine they had come to return. In her heart she felt, more than ever before, the reason she had been chosen to be a Keeper of Lost Things.

"I think I understand now why knowledge is so vital, and why our duty is more important than the lives we had before, the ones we lost."

"Yes, it's paramount"—Kolt smiled, driving up onto the dirt track—"because knowledge fills a space in humans that would otherwise fill up with fear."

"The Losers want people to be afraid, don't they?"

"Eggcups fly."

"Yes, but what they don't realize, Gertie, is that when people live in fear, they're easy to convince that attacking others is the only way to feel safe."

Gertie thought of her brother, and wondered what he was doing at that exact moment, wherever in time he was.

"And so if humans were to lose knowledge," Kolt said, steering the Time Cat around an enormous brown puddle, "the result would not be mindless harmony as the Losers think, but endless war, disease, and suffering."

Gertie thought for a moment. "So ignorance is not bliss?"

"No," Kolt said seriously. "Ignorance is danger."

16

A Dream Home for Fleas

Soon the marshy field was behind them. The sounds from the tiny bells and clappers was replaced by the buzzing of insects and the smell of damp wood. Gertie leaned out her window to guide Kolt onto the road.

"Watch out," she said. "There's a giant hole—move to the right."

Kolt steered around the hole, but instead of pulling onto the narrow dirt highway he parked the Time Cat under some mulberry trees.

"There's no way we can drive an E-Type Jaguar into Renaissance Venice."

Gertie looked at the road, a narrow track of mud with deep puddles and the occasional pyramid of horse droppings.

"Dollops."

"But Venice seems like a long way."

"Sorry, Gertie, it's too risky to drive any farther."

"But we can't come all the way back here for the Time Cat after?"

"We have to, it's a double return, remember? We have eleven hours in each place."

"Oh, but it's too far, I was hoping we could use the extra time to look for Keepers?"

Kolt cloaked the Time Cat with the Narcissus button.

When they started walking, Robot Rabbit Boy ran ahead with one hand on his fake mustache and the other on his leather belt.

"Why is he in such a hurry?" Kolt asked.

"If there's one thing I've learned since he came to live with us, it's that what goes on in a rabbit's head is one of the great mysteries of the universe."

Kolt was about to say something when his foot disappeared in a puddle.

"Wet feet again! What's the deal?"

The road was indeed much sloppier than it looked, with flies hovering over each slimy puddle. When they reached an enormous one, Robot Rabbit Boy used his dagger to measure the depth.

"Lavender."

"Ugh, this stuff is a nightmare!" Kolt said.

"I told you we should have driven!"

"It would have been too dangerous."

"Well, we could have gone a little farther . . . we haven't even seen anyone!"

"Renaissance Italians loved anything beautiful and well designed. The Time Cat would be taken from us for sure, then pulled apart in a frenzy of grabbing, so they could learn how to make it before anyone else in the surrounding towns."

"If the Italians loved design so much, why is this road such a mess?" Gertie said, still annoyed at the time it was taking to walk.

"Because there was no central government in Italy."

"Eggcup."

"I mean no one was in charge," Kolt said. "The cities of Renaissance Italy were ruled by rich families with private armies who were constantly fighting for power."

"Weird," Gertie said. "So if you weren't in one of these rich families?"

"Then you were at their mercy," Kolt explained. "The Renaissance might have been a time of discovery and invention, but it was also a period of constant bickering, murder, poisoning, hanging, public burning, and other brutal forms of persuasion and torture."

Kolt was about to say a bit more about the very creative approach taken to torture, when they noticed someone coming toward them.

"A local!" Gertie said. "Thank goodness, we can ask directions."

But Kolt seemed anxious. "Just act normal," he said. "Like we're from a powerful Venetian family, living out simple, short, smelly lives in Renaissance Italy." Then he looked down at Robot Rabbit Boy, who was using his dagger as a pointed walking stick. "For goodness' sake put that thing away and straighten your mustache!"

"Strawberry fly butter?"

The man had a round, sweaty face, and rough, straggly hair that looked as though it had never been washed—except by rain.

He stopped a yard or so away and pointed at Robot Rabbit Boy.

"Carnival monkey!" he said, gawking.

"Excuse me, local . . . person," Kolt said, "but is this the highway to Venice? And do you know what a doctor is?"

The man scratched his head, though not because he was thinking—but on account of lice, which at that moment had all begun a mass scramble at the sight of Robot Rabbit Boy's fake mustache, which greatly resembled the dream home they had recently been discussing.

The man nodded. "This is the road to Venice, sir, and for telling you I want your circus monkey."

"Lavender fly?" Robot Rabbit Boy said.

The man jumped back so fast at hearing the rabbit speak, that he slipped and fell into a puddle. "It can talk!" he cried, pointing with dripping sleeves.

"Oh dear," Kolt said. "This isn't going well."

The man then pulled a rusty knife from his cloak.

"Give me that talking monkey or I'll slash thee!"

"Thee?" Gertie said, looking around. "Who's *thee*?"

"He means us!" Kolt told her. "He's some kind of Renaissance loony."

Gertie was amazed by how easily the stranger was prepared to use violence against them. She had to think quickly.

"He's not a monkey!" she blurted out. "He's my brother, a rabbit boy, and he's dangerous."

The arm with the knife dropped slightly.

"Rabbit boy? Dangerous?"

"Yes—he's part-boy, part-rabbit."

Then Kolt interrupted, "And part-robot."

"PART RHUBARB!" Gertie shouted, glaring at Kolt. "I mean rhubarb is what he eats, nothing else."

"Lavender," said Robot Rabbit Boy.

"And lavender, which . . . is why he turned into a rabbit," Gertie said.

"Butter," Robot Rabbit Boy added.

"Yes, rhubarb and lavender dipped in butter," said Gertie.

Robot Rabbit Boy touched his fake mustache. "A dollop of mashed potato."

The Italian peasant was understandably confused. "He certainly eats a lot, and he's your brother, you say? But he doesn't have a mark on his face like you?"

"That's actually a birthmark," Gertie explained. "I was born with it. My brother has a mustache instead."

"Well, I can't steal him," said the man, getting up out of the puddle. "Seeing as he's family."

"That's right," said Gertie. "It would be rabbit-napping."

"So just tell me your price?"

"Price?"

Kolt stepped toward Gertie. "He's serious. Buying and selling people was sadly normal before the end of the twenty-first century."

"Come on," said the man. "I haven't got all day. If you want me to let you live, I need a price."

Just as Gertie was about to get *really* angry—and agree with Kolt that the Renaissance was a brutal time where bullies ruled—they heard a clobbering and splashing in the distance as a chestnut horse in armor came galloping toward them.

"What now!" Kolt said. "We've got enough on our plates without King Arthur showing up!"

But it wasn't King Arthur. As the horse and rider got closer, they saw it was a woman, sitting high and straight in the saddle, with a shiny metal breastplate strapped to the upper part of her body. On her body armor was a painted rabbit head.

Gertie and Kolt could hardly believe their eyes.

"I don't believe it," Kolt said. "Robot Rabbit Boy's fairy godmother."

The woman's long hair had been tied up in braids, which were rolled neatly to the sides of her head in buns. She wore a shimmering sword at her hip, which bounced as she cantered toward the strange group in the middle of the road.

The peasant's eyesight must have been poor, because he kept his knife held high until the rider was close enough for him to see her. The woman steered her horse right up to the man. Then she booted him in the chest so that he went flying back, dropping his knife and losing one of his ragged shoes.

"Get off this road, you terrible man!" the woman growled. "If I ever see you harassing people again I'll quarter you myself!"

"What does she mean by *quarter*?" Gertie whispered to Kolt.

"You don't want to know—seriously you don't."

"Actually I do."

"Okay, fine—pieces of rope are tied to a person's wrists and ankles, then the other ends of the four pieces are tied to four different horses. When the horses bolt, the victim's body is torn into four quarters, hence, quartering."

"Gross! Who would do such a thing?"

Kolt pointed to the woman, who was still shouting at the thief. "Er, rabbit girl for one, so keep you wits about you."

Then something occurred to Gertie. In Mrs. Pumble's book—the one she had written about miraculously finding her way home—she talked about going back to her original life, discovering her true identity, but then giving it up and returning to the Island of Lost Things to take her place as a Keeper. Gertie was only a few chapters in, but if Mrs. Pumble's home was a place like this, where human lives were short, painful, full of fear and violence—then it made sense she had wanted to return to Skuldark.

"And who might you lot be?" barked the woman on the horse at the three Keepers. "You don't look like thieves."

Kolt smiled weakly. "Um, we're simple travelers trying to get to Venice with dry feet and failing."

"I like her braid buns," Gertie whispered. "Her hair is so blonde, it's cool."

"It was the fashion. People put on wide-brimmed hats with no center, then sat on roofs for hours on end, as the sun dyed their hair yellow."

"You can dye your hair in the sun?"

"Oh, sure."

The woman cleared her throat loudly, as if to stop their muttering.

"Who are you, exactly? Not spies, I hope. . . ."

If not for the symbol painted on the woman's armor, ,Gertie would have been more afraid of her wrath. But how could anyone who loved rabbits be mean? And she *had* saved them from the weird peasant, who had now disappeared along with his rusty knife and army of head lice.

Before Kolt could tell this girl warrior how they certainly were not spies, Robot Rabbit Boy marched toward the horse, smoothing out the ends of his fake mustache.

"Butter!" he said pointing at the rabbit emblem on her armor. "Butter fly mushroom?"

There are only two words that can describe the look that seized the woman's face at that moment: *cuteness overloadus.*

17

An Invitation They Can't Refuse

"WE'RE LOOKING FOR VENICE," Gertie said in a deep voice, "and it's pretty urgent."

The woman studied the young Keeper from the top of her horse. Gertie knew she was looking at the birthmark that covered one side of her face.

"What fine clothes for a child . . ." she said. "Detachable sleeves with designer slashing? Very nice."

Gertie looked down at the clothes she had picked out.

"And what an unusual, well-trained animal soldier you travel with. Though I've never seen a rabbit with a mustache before. You must be important people from kingdoms far off."

"Very, very far off," Kolt said. "And yes, our rabbit is well trained—just don't ask him to get you a plate of chocolate chip cookies."

The woman looked around. "Where is your escort?"

"Our escort?" Gertie said, wondering what such a thing was.

"We lost it," Kolt interrupted, "it was terribly bad luck."

"You lost it!" said the woman. "How unfortunate."

Gertie looked at the ground. "It must have fallen out of my pocket."

The woman smiled and patted her horse. "No, really, c'mon," she said, "where are the private soldiers all wealthy merchants travel with?"

Kolt took a step forward. "The truth is, our escort was involved in a tragic accident involving..."

"A dollop of mashed potato."

"It was very bad . . ." Gertie said, trying to salvage the conversation, "their horses slipped on . . ."

"Strawberry mush."

The woman on the horse was now just looking at them with a blank expression.

"I know what you are," she said. "You can't fool me with your humble traveler story—I know the truth about you, there's no point denying it."

"Well, you're wrong," Kolt told her nervously. "We're not an ancient order of time-traveling heroes, battling an evil sect of neophobic losers for control of human destiny using a time machine in the glove box of a British racing car."

"You're clowns! From the commedia dell'arte," the woman said.

"Look, the absolute truth," interrupted Gertie, "is that

we need to see a very important doctor in Venice, and would be very grateful if you would help us find him or her."

"Very well, I will escort you into the city of Venice where my family is on the Counsel, close with the Doge himself—he'll get the truth out of you . . . or more merriment perhaps?"

"What's she talking about?" Gertie asked Kolt. "Merriment?"

"She thinks we're Italian clowns from an early tradition of comedy, so just try and be funny until we get to Venice."

THE CITY WAS SEVERAL muddy miles away, and the track widened as they walked behind the woman's horse.

"If the Renaissance wasn't such a dangerous time," Gertie said, enjoying the chatter of birdsong from the woods, "then Italy in the 1400s would have been a fun place to hunt for lost Keepers."

Kolt pointed out that the Renaissance in Italy was actually one of the safer times in human history.

"But it's so dangerous with robbers on the road!"

"It was better than what came before," he told her.

"What about all the diseases? Like leprosy."

"You simply couldn't avoid them," Kolt said. "But the real problem was that no one questioned anything. People just did as they were told. The lord who owned the land also owned the people who lived and worked on it."

"People weren't free to go anywhere they wanted?"

"Absolutely not."

"But at least they could *think* whatever they liked, right?" Gertie said, trying to be optimistic.

"I'm afraid they couldn't do that either," Kolt said sympathetically. "Your body belonged to the landlord, and your soul belonged to the priest who served another kind of lord. People thought that if they disobeyed the rules, they would burn at the stake, or burn in hell, or both, but everything will change dramatically about two hundred years from now, with a new fashion called science and people called humanists who want everyone to be educated and free."

"They sound like Keepers!"

Kolt nodded. "Yes, I've always wondered if they knew about us; one chap in particular called Rousseau, he had all the hallmarks of a Keeper who found a way back...."

"Once we've completed the mission, Kolt, let's sniff around a few dungeons and see what we turn up? We'll know if there's anyone down there, because the key in my pocket will probably do something."

A look of concern crept over Kolt's face as they neared the entrance to Venice. "You want to explore the dungeons?"

"Oh, stop worrying!"

When Gertie noticed long-haired children her age playing in the street, she waved and smiled. They beckoned for her to come and join their game, but the woman on the horse was walking too quickly, and Gertie knew she had to keep up.

As they passed an open barn, where people were

blowing glass, Gertie heard rushing water. Then they turned a corner where the main street was a brown canal. Kolt explained that Venice was a river city where the main roads literally gushed with brown water, and bobbed with the traffic of small, thin boats called gondolas.

The streets stank of rotting food, dirty water, pee, and animal droppings. Robot Rabbit Boy was able to step over most steaming piles of animal waste, but some of the streets were very narrow, forcing them to squeeze past local Venetians, who smelled of incense, perfume, burnt wood, and sweat. One woman hurried by with a goose pulled to her chest, while a boy in red tights steered his greyhound on a leash through the crowd. Gertie felt a tingle of excitement at the idea of nodding and saying hello to the boy and his dog, but before she could get close enough to talk, their path was blocked by a line of donkeys with hay loaded onto their backs.

All the windows at street level had iron bars over them, and in the walls, Gertie saw carved lion faces with thin slots for mouths. She asked Kolt what they were for, but he didn't know. When Gertie touched one, and Robot Rabbit Boy put his whole paw into one, the people all around her stopped what they were doing and stared in horror.

The woman on the horse turned to see what had happened.

"Don't they have those where you come from?"

"No." Gertie said, touching the carved lion face. "What are they?"

"People write the names of those who break the rules of the city, then drop the paper in there. If a person is found guilty—"

"They're quartered?" Gertie asked with a gulp.

"No! Nothing usually so brutal as that," the woman said. "They're just strangled in a dungeon."

Gertie backed away from the deadly lion's mouth, but it was clear Robot Rabbit Boy's paw was stuck.

"Butter," he said, his fake mustache twitching. Everyone in the street burst out laughing. "A dollop of mashed potato," he cried, his eyes glowing neon white, as he pulled and pulled on his trapped paw.

Kolt sighed and shook his head. "This is not what I meant by blending in!"

Eventually Robot Rabbit Boy wriggled free and they continued their journey.

"Did you hear what she said, Kolt? Dungeons!"

"I suppose you want me to get directions for you?"

"Or we could just write our own names on some paper and drop them in the lion's-mouth box."

"Get ourselves arrested, you mean?"

"You brought the time machine from the glove box of the Time Cat, didn't you? We can just put the key in and fizzle home if things get too hairy. It would be worth it to look for lost Keepers."

"Hmm, I'll think about it, but if we can get to the dungeon after we've completed our task, let's try and visit as guests of Venice and not prisoners, eh?"

In the center of town, the brown buildings got taller and grander.

When they walked through a large town square, it echoed with the deep, haunting tones of church bells. Gertie found it strange that in the countryside there were people in worn-out cloaks, with missing limbs from leprosy, while the city had tall stone buildings, and enormous, beautifully detailed churches. It amazed her that such magnificent structures could have been made without the technology that would come later.

The smell near the Grand Canal was less *rotting food* and more *decaying fish*—with the occasional blast of wind that felt good on their cheeks and in their noses.

There were wooden stalls with many different things for sale, from paintings of the city, to tall cups of colored glass, to sleeves of lace that could be stitched onto clothes or pillowcases.

"Are you impressed with our city?" the woman asked. She had slowed her horse and was now walking alongside the three Keepers.

"Our Venetian craftsmen and craftswomen practice their art only here, in our fair city."

"Yes, there are many nice things," Gertie said politely, but there was nothing she wanted to buy personally, and Kolt only liked doughnuts.

"The people who make all these fine things must really like it here in Venice," he told the woman, "despite the aroma."

"Oh, the artisans who work here have no choice; if they practice their craft anywhere else, we send private soldiers to kill them."

"I see," Kolt said, making a face at Gertie. "That's one way to limit competition."

As they neared the woman's home, a brick building with balconies overlooking the canal, she stared down at Gertie.

"I have a young brother, about your age. He's extremely strange, but perhaps you'll like one another. He's twelve and not married."

Gertie shot Kolt a panicked look.

"Calm down," he whispered, "don't panic, no one's getting married."

"I'd rather get snatched!" Gertie hissed quietly. "Ten times in a row!"

Robot Rabbit Boy's eyes turned raspberry. "Dollops. Mush. Fly."

"Relax. Both of you, calm down. We're going to return the medicine and then get out of here."

"Good!" Gertie huffed. "The sooner the better."

It was starting to get dark, and they could smell the smoke from people's evening fires.

"And here we are," the woman announced, as they reached the grand villa with iron gates and guards who were also wearing pieces of armor with rabbits painted on them.

"First thing we should do," Kolt said, "is try and get some leads as to where the doctor this powder belongs to lives."

Gertie agreed.

The guards saluted the woman on the horse and pulled open the heavy wrought-iron gates. "Are you travelers hungry?"

"Funny you'd ask," laughed Kolt, "because I'm actually starving."

"Food?" Gertie said, nudging him. "I thought we were in a hurry!"

"Well, you gave all our money away! We'll just nibble a few things, then go, I promise. . . ."

18

Birdy

SOMEWHERE IN THE MOUNTAINS over the town, a Cherokee village was preparing for the Ceremony of Green Corn.

It was a time to start again. Old things would be tossed out. All crimes except murder forgiven. It would be a celebration with turtle rattles, drums, dancing, eating, and singing.

A visitor to the village named Sequoyah was in the woods with some children. They had found a cool, shady tree to sit under and listen to the story of Uktena. Sequoyah was wearing a blue tunic with a red turban tied around his head. He had a soft voice, and kept pointing to the sky as he described how the horned serpent clawed marks in the cliff with giant talons. In the forests grew wild plants and herbs that possessed magical powers to cure the sick. Then Sequoyah began telling the story of how the valley had been carved out by Great Buzzard.

But as the children started to imagine this majestic bird, they heard tree limbs snapping over their heads. They all jumped up and scattered.

"It's Uktena!" yelled someone in the group.

"No, it's Great Buzzard!"

But it was neither. Instead, a nine-year-old boy, with a pair of homemade wings on his back, came crashing through the branches to land in a heap at the base of the tree.

After a moment of astonishment, Sequoyah bent down to see if the boy was dead.

"Urrgh," he moaned. A few of the children giggled.

Then Max slowly lifted his head, and turned to Sequoyah. "Sorry," he rasped, "and hello . . ."

Sequoyah removed a pouch of herbal medicines and checked to see if Max was injured.

"It really was an accident. I couldn't help it," the boy confessed.

"Are you in pain?"

"Not really," Max said, lifting his arm to reveal a small wound. "Truly it was an accident. I didn't mean to fall on your heads."

"It was no accident," said Sequoyah, rubbing cool green sludge onto a bleeding elbow. "The Great Spirit has sent you."

"It has?" Max said, trying to sound polite. He had never really believed in anything except Newton's Laws of Motion and the laws of nature he had experienced firsthand."

"I am Sequoyah," the man said. "And these children were here learning about plants."

"How come you speak English?"

"My father was a Virginian fur trader, and my mother was the daughter of a Cherokee chief. And I have done many things in my life," Sequoyah told him. "I was once a soldier, and a silversmith. But then I discovered what language can do, and now I teach, after working many years on a syllabary for my people."

He took a stick and wrote something in the soil.

$$4 \cdot V^{\circ} \mathcal{C} \mathcal{D}$$

"That's my name in Cherokee," Sequoyah said.

The children had crept forward to look at Max. Then one of them whispered something and they all hooted with laugher.

Sequoyah chuckled along with them. "They call you Bird Boy."

"Bird Boy?"

"Yes." He smiled. "As you came from the sky, you are Bird Boy, or Birdy for short."

Max blushed. "The truth is I tumbled out of a tree because I fell asleep reading my notebooks. Before that, I'd been walking for most of the day."

Sequoyah laughed and helped Max brush off leaves and dirt. Then Max followed the children along a path through dense woods toward the Cherokee village that Sequoyah was visiting with his daughter.

"How did you learn to build bird wings?" Sequoyah

asked when they stopped to quench their thirst from a stream.

"From studying the bones themselves, and from reading. Do you have any books?"

"My dream," Sequoyah told him, "is to have books in the Cherokee language, which is why I have been working on a system of symbols, where each symbol stands for a sound, or a syllable. With it, my people can keep our history safe, make sure the wisdom of our ancestors is passed down to each generation. Everyone thought I was mad when I first had the idea, so I built a small cabin close to my wife and family where I could be alone to work. At first I made a symbol for each word, scratching into slats of wood. But there were so many words. Even my friends and family thought I was being foolish."

"Did that make you want to give up?" Max asked.

"No, it made me more determined. About then I realized, there are too many words in my language for each to have a different symbol, but each word shares sounds, so the symbols would stand for syllables that could be put together to make words."

Sequoyah stopped walking. In the distance a family of deer were very still, looking at them. After a moment they just walked on. "I arrived only yesterday with my daughter, to teach my people a written version of our language, but I must have lost the page on my journey—despite being very careful."

"Lost it!" cried Max.

"Yes, so I'm telling the children traditional stories and

teaching them about plants until I can find it—or at least write down all I remember."

Max was sad to hear this, and remembered all the notebooks he'd left behind at home. "Maybe I could help you look?" he said. "I'm pretty good at finding things."

"Thank you," Sequoyah said. "Maybe I will accept your kind offer." Max noticed then that Sequoyah walked with a limp. He was going to ask if the kind Cherokee was okay, but a moment later they arrived at the village.

"Welcome," Sequoyah said. "Here you will meet my daughter, Ayokeh."

Max was staring now at all the homes built from wood and clay. Children his age stood pounding cornmeal that would be baked into cakes. Sequoyah explained that preparations were under way for the Green Corn Ceremony, in the month of the green corn moon. Sequoyah adjusted his turban and described how every family was given a piece of land by a chief. But as Cherokee people believed in *gadugi*— working together for the greater good of the community—no one family worked on just their own fields. The planters of the tribe worked on all the fields together.

Sick people, widows, and old people had their fields planted for them.

As Max had secretly feared, the sight of a stranger entering the village pulled curious stares from every direction.

"Worry not, Birdy," Sequoyah said. "They're just surprised to see you here. These people don't interact with the settlers as much as other Cherokee people."

Then a girl came running to greet them.

"This is my daughter, Ayokeh," Sequoyah said. She was about Max's age, and wore deerskin clothes with moccasin shoes. Her hair was long and black as a crow's feathers.

Ayokeh couldn't hide her surprise. "How did *he* get here?"

"He flew." Sequoyah smiled, pointing up into the trees.

Ayokeh looked at her father with a confused scowl.

"Come, daughter, walk with Birdy and me through the village."

A moment later they arrived at the house where Sequoyah was staying. It was a rectangular hut made from hickory wood with clay walls.

"What's your house like, Birdy?"

"Full of dead people," Max said with a smirk.

"A spirit lodge?"

"Er, kinda."

Then Sequoyah interrupted. "Birdy, if you are hungry you can feast with us, on corn and deer meat—as an honored guest of Sequoyah of the Red Paint Clan."

"Anything's better than beans," Max said.

"Where are you from, Birdy?" asked Ayokeh.

"I'd rather not say because it might get you in trouble if you know too much about me."

"Are you some kind of outlaw?" asked Sequoyah. "I've known many in my time."

"I am actually," Max admitted. "And though I haven't broken any laws, there's a price on my head."

Ayokeh looked at Max's head closely, as though trying to

see what he was worth to the people who wanted him. "You don't seem that dangerous." She shrugged.

"Er, thanks," Max said, looking around. "I'm not sure I can stay and eat, even though I want to. If someone captures me then they can turn me in to the sheriff for money, so I'm being hunted."

"How did you offend your people?" Sequoyah asked.

"They're not really my people," Max said, "and I didn't do anything. I left home so I wouldn't put my family in danger, and I don't want to put you in danger either, so I'd best be on my way."

Sequoyah thought for a moment. "It is clear to me that if we let harm come to you, then harm will also come to us. Let me talk with the White Chief and the Red Chief in the council house on the mound."

"In the meantime we'll go to the river," Ayokeh said, "and lay swan feathers for Big Brother Moon to see. This helps the corn!"

As they were leaving the village, a few Cherokee warriors glared at Max with such fierceness Ayokeh had to say something quickly in her language. When the warriors had gone, Ayokeh tried to reassure her new friend.

"Don't worry, Birdy, my father will convince everyone that your arrival has meaning for us. They respect him because he has given his people the gift of a written memory through his syllabary."

"Thanks," Max said. "I don't want to be any trouble. I don't like fighting and avoid it wherever I can."

Ayokeh was amused. "You sound like the spirit of Little Deer."

Max tried to imagine Little Deer, and wondered how humans can love animals while also eating their flesh. When they reached the gushing river, Max and Ayokeh stood at the edge, staring down at the cold, clear water.

"Let's try and find some feathers!"

But Max wanted to know more about Little Deer.

"Our stories are sung and danced to, Birdy, but I suppose I could try and explain what happens."

"I've only heard music through the windows of Tara's Tavern," Max said, "where people dance and get drunk."

"Our songs are gifts from the Great Spirit; they put us in harmony with ourselves and with nature. We have songs for journeys, homecoming, memory, love, war songs—even songs my father and I sing when we are away from each other."

"Will you teach me that one?"

"It's private," Ayokeh said, "only for my father and me—but maybe we could have a song to mark the occasion of our meeting?"

"Yes!" said Max.

"But remember, Birdy—it's not the song that's important, but the feeling it gives you—that's the true gift."

"Let's make up a song...."

Ayokeh pushed him playfully. "Don't you want to hear the story of Little Deer first?"

Max nodded.

Ayokeh made herself comfortable on the trunk of a

fallen tree. "Long ago, the animal people and the human people could talk to each other. They lived in peace, and the humans only killed animals when they were hungry or for clothes to keep warm. But then, a new weapon came along that gave the animals less chance to run away or fight for their lives."

"A gun?"

"No, Birdy," laughed Ayokeh. "This is a very old story, before strangers came—the weapon was bow and arrow."

"Couldn't the animals just run away?"

Ayokeh shook her head. "The arrow was swift, and soon humans killed animals even when they did not need food or clothes. The animals got worried they would die out, and so called a meeting of the council of elders. There was buffalo, bear, beaver, rabbit, eagle, mountain lion, even field mouse. Every animal got the chance to have a say."

"So it wasn't just the toughest, greediest animal telling everyone what to do?" Max said, thinking of Shard Pinch and how he had taken over the town of Morrisville.

"No, that is not the Cherokee way; remember *gadugi*. Working together for the good of everyone around you."

"So what did the animals do?"

"First they decided to try and learn how to use the bow and arrow themselves. But Bear's claws got in the way, and Mouse's tiny arrows couldn't even pierce a blueberry. So, the animals felt lost and helpless, until Little Deer said that hunters had *always* killed animals for food and clothes. That was how it had always been, and it was natural. So the real problem was that now humans were doing it the *wrong* way. Little Deer explained that if humans wanted to kill animals, they should do it in the *right* way. Then all would be well. The animals asked Little Deer to describe the right way, and Little Deer said there should be a ceremony where the hunters first ask permission to kill the animals. Then, if they are granted this right by the Great Spirit and kill an animal on the hunt, they must show humility and ask forgiveness from the animal's soul."

"That's nice," Max said, his mind going back to the cruel way people in the town often slaughtered animals, with no thought for the feelings of the poor creatures. "Did Little Deer's plan work?"

"Little Deer went to all the hunters that night and whispered in their ears the *right* way to kill, and that if they failed to follow these laws, Little Deer would use magic to cripple their limbs so they could not hunt. And that is why we ask forgiveness from any creature's soul before we enjoy its meat, or wear its skin, and we only take what we need."

Max liked the story, but still felt sorry for the animals who had to die. "I guess I'd sooner stick with beans," he admitted, "and let the animals live out their lives in the woods."

Ayokeh smiled. "I think that too sometimes. We'll tell my father and see what he says. One of his favorite meals is bread and honey."

"You have a good life among the Cherokee," Max said, thinking about his parents, wondering if they were in danger. But he needn't have worried, for the worst, most violent outlaws and mercenaries who were hunting him had already entered the forest, and were beginning to surround the Cherokee village that was preparing for the Green Corn Ceremony.

19

Something Rather Awkward Happens . . .

STABLE BOYS IN RED tights and pointy cloth shoes guided the woman down from her tired horse. She was short, with strong shoulders, a round face, and pale green eyes. The attendants helped remove her rabbit-painted breastplate armor.

"Let me introduce myself as Isabetta," the woman said. "Now, please, let's go inside."

She led the three Keepers from the brick courtyard through spiked wooden doors into the Venetian palace that was her home.

The air carried the aroma of wood smoke and cooking food. Isabetta's servants wondered who these strangers were. Their staring made Gertie nervous, but she told herself it was ridiculous to be frightened of people dressed like characters from a deck of cards.

They were led by their host across a red tile floor to some comfortable chairs near a warm fire.

"They've got the right idea," Kolt said. "This is just like home!"

Gertie nodded, but hoped they would get moving soon. She wanted to eat quickly so they could start looking for the doctor.

The woman's blonde braids were studded with pearls, and all her hair had been shaved from the front part of her head, so that her forehead looked huge.

"It was a fashion," Kolt whispered. "The more forehead the more beautiful, apparently."

Suddenly they heard shouting. A boy's voice echoed through the hall from one of the palace's many chambers.

"That'll be my brother," Isabetta said. "He's always messing around in his room with herbs and potions. I don't think he's right in the head, to be honest."

"Probably why he's not married," Kolt said with a chuckle.

Isabetta laughed too, but Gertie shot him a disgusted look. "Why would you even bring that up?" she muttered through gritted teeth.

"Just trying to lighten the mood before supper..."

"Well, do it some other way ... and I thought you said we were in a hurry? Maybe I should show her the powder?" Gertie asked. "She might recognize who it belongs to."

"It's worth a try," Kolt agreed. "But let's meet her family first."

"You mean, let's eat first," Gertie said wryly.

"Travelers, honored guests," Isabetta announced, "I know you have someone very important to see here in Venice, but as visiting nobles and players of the commedia dell'arte, you will first take a meal with us, so that I can properly introduce you to my father, Doctor Fracastoro, and my mother, Camilla. They are personal friends of the most powerful person in Venice—the Doge—and will help you find this doctor you seek."

"That must be him!" Kolt said, nudging Gertie. "I don't believe it, what luck!"

"Who?" Gertie said.

"Doctor Fracastoro!"

Gertie felt a surge of appreciation for the B.D.B.U. It was clear now why they had been sent to a field outside the city. The run-in with the outlaw and Isabetta must have been the old book's intention after all.

"So your father is a doctor, Isabetta? How marvelous."

"He's more an astrologer."

"Oh, that's right," Kolt said. "In Renaissance Italy, doctors were also astrologists."

"But astrologists study things in space," Gertie said. "How would that work?"

"Actually, astronomers study things in space," Kolt tried to explain. "Astrologers are interested in how things in space affect people's lives on Earth."

"Do they?" Gertie asked.

"Do they what?"

"Do things happening in space affect us?"

Kolt lifted his arms and raised his voice, as though he were on a stage. "There are more things in heaven and earth, Horatio, than are dreamt of in your philosophy!"

Gertie shook her head with irritation. "What does that mean?"

"It's a quote from a play written by a chap I met on a return, Bill Shakespeare, interesting man, great writer, but a really amazing cook...."

"But what about space?"

"I hardly go up there, it's very dangerous ... hard to breathe, impossible actually ... but during the Renaissance, people thought every part of the body was governed by a different planet."

"You're rambling," Gertie said. "You've been doing it a lot lately."

"Yes, most people get angry when they need a meal, but I just talk endlessly."

"So then, Isabetta's father is the doctor we need to return the vial to?"

"It would appear so."

Gertie was about to ask if they could just leave it on the table and go find a dungeon, when a boy with long flowing locks of hair strode nervously into the hall followed by an elegant man in blue velvet robes and a red stocking hat.

Walking next to the man and his son was an older version of Isabetta, who Gertie assumed was her mother, Camilla.

Isabetta introduced the three Keepers as traveling noble comedians whom she had rescued from a ruthless bandit.

"I wish you wouldn't engage in such Spartan shows of force, Isabetta," her father grumbled. "Your mother and I are getting too old to worry about you roaming the countryside unescorted on an armor-plated horse."

The girl bowed her head. "Sorry, Father."

Gertie cleared her throat. "If it hadn't been for your daughter, sir, I don't know what would have happened to us."

"Fly butter."

The old man raised one of his eyebrows. "Fly butter? What's that?"

Isabetta stifled a laugh with her hand.

"Mashed flies?" said Robot Rabbit Boy innocently.

"Flies?" said the old Venetian doctor. "Where?"

"We're actually from Verona," Camilla interrupted, "but trade has brought us to Venice for a little while. Tell us about *your* country? Your accents *are* Italian, but I can't quite place the region. . . ."

Kolt laughed. "Let me explain. It's very interesting. We're speaking an ancient, and you might even say, chameleonic tongue called Skulda—"

"Skuldarkoni," Gertie interrupted, wishing that Kolt would just eat something, and stop giving speeches. He really was dangerous on an empty stomach.

"Skuldarkoni?" the doctor said. "I've never heard of it."

"It's a tiny island," Gertie told him. "Tiny and very boring, no magic, no talking mice or weirdness whatsoever."

They were led into yet another room with a high paneled ceiling, painted with different scenes from nature. Gertie followed the pictures with her eyes. There was a green field dotted with lambs, and a blue sea with a scaly sea monster that reminded her of Johnny the Guard Worm. Several other ceiling panels had been decorated with tall, wooden ships—the sort Gertie had been reading about in her pirate book.

In the center of the room was a wooden table laid out with food. They all sat down. Gertie made sure she was sitting at the exact opposite end of the table from the long-haired brother. But then Isabetta said the two youngest should sit together. Gertie went red with embarrassment, and pulled on Kolt's green robe.

"Shouldn't we just give him the powder then get out of here?" she said. The vial had begun to glow and warm up, which she knew meant they were close to the intended target.

"That will make them think we stole it," Kolt said, eyeballing the dishes of food, "as why on earth would we have it if we couldn't even say where we found it?"

Gertie felt her hands going numb and tingly. The long-haired boy was now sitting *right* next to her. Kolt was on her other side, and she leaned toward him.

"The idea that people can get married here at twelve is completely freaking me out!"

But Kolt was too busy grinning at their hosts. "Your palazzo is magnificent, and once again I have to thank your daughter. She saved us from highway robbery!"

"I shall have my condottieri patrol the area," Dr. Fracastoro said, "and bring these brigands to justice without mercy."

"Oh, you don't have to do that!" Gertie said loudly.

Isabetta's father raised both his eyebrows. "That's forgiving of you, young lady. One day I'm sure you'll run a magnificent household."

But his wife winked at Gertie. "One day," Signora Camilla said, "women will be able to do more than run households, read poetry, embroider, play the lute—"

"That's right," Gertie said, remembering her first solo Keeper mission. "One day, a woman might even swim from France to England!"

Everyone at the table stopped what they were doing and stared. Even the servants couldn't believe what Gertie had suggested might happen. Gertie realized that anyone swimming from France to England was as unimaginable to them in the fifteenth century as a person going into space (which was only about four hundred years away from actually happening).

"Be careful!" Kolt whispered to her. "This sort of information might blow their minds!"

"Would that be such a bad thing?" Gertie said, chewing on a bread stick. "Might speed things up a bit."

At one end of the hall was an open fire, and beside it, mouth-like openings with flat wooden paddles hung next to them.

"Look at those authentic bread ovens," Kolt said.

"Be great for pizza."

"I don't know if it's been invented yet!"

Above the fire, an iron wheel was turning in the heat's path. The wheel had spokes, upon which were chickens, ducks, pheasants, thrushes, and pigeons, all roasting slowly.

"Heavens alive!" Kolt cried on seeing it. "What a fowl massacre!"

"Aren't you going to tell them you're vegetarian?"

"They wouldn't understand—in this time only the poor ate vegetables."

Also on the table were boiled carrots, grapes, turnips, fish fried in oil with rosemary leaves, larks stuffed with sage and bread—and what would turn out to be everyone's favorite, gooey chestnut pudding sweetened with wild honey.

The walls were hung with fabric tapestries like the one Gertie had seen in the Gate Keepers' Lodge.

One of the servants, a girl just a little older than Gertie, brought over a bowl of rose water for the guests to wash their hands. When it was Robot Rabbit Boy's turn, instead of washing his paws, he pulled out several of the rose petals and ate them.

The girl holding the bowl laughed.

"Eggcups," Robot Rabbit Boy said, his eyes flashing neon yellow. The girl screamed and dropped the bowl, but Robot Rabbit Boy caught it. Series 7 reflexes were lightning fast.

The boy next to Gertie suddenly sat up. "Who is that furry person with the mustache?"

"Er, Robot Rabbit Boy?"

"I long to pet him."

"Oh, okay, maybe later."

"Do you go to clown school? Most girls in Venice don't go to school at all, but my mother made Isabetta take lessons. I have six older brothers, but they are off doing things, university and such."

"We're not actually clowns, and there is no such thing as school where *I* live. It's a rocky island with snowcapped mountains and underground tunnels."

"So what do you all day if you're not in school?"

"I work," Gertie said, and nodded in Kolt's direction, "with him."

Warm food was now being served onto their plates by young servants.

"I'm Girolamo," the boy said. "Giro for short."

Gertie stared at the boy sitting opposite her. He didn't look like a doctor, but his first name matched the name of the person whose vial they had come to return.

"Um, so . . ." she said, "your father is an astrologist?"

"I'm afraid so."

"What? You don't believe in planets controlling our body parts?"

"No I don't," Giro said passionately, but making sure his father wasn't listening. "You might think I'm dumb, but I think diseases are caused by tiny creatures, like little animals too small to see, that get passed from one person to the next in fluids, or through coughing and sneezing."

Germs! Gertie thought. She *was* sitting next to the medical genius, to whom the green powder belonged!

"That's why I want to build hospitals," Giro said, "so that people can be kept away from others and get better without the little creatures spreading."

Gertie pictured the people she had seen with leprosy, and suggested that Giro find a way to help them too.

"If I can't find a medicine to cure leprosy, then I want to find out how it spreads, and then control it. My dream is to stop the spread of disease by spreading knowledge instead."

Gertie smiled.

"My sister thinks it's stupid, but then all she can think about is riding around the countryside like a soldier, and trying to get our parents to find her a marriage partner. That's our custom. Parents choose the person you get married to."

"Oh, huh, well, that's a pretty boring subject if you ask me."

"I agree," Giro said. "I'd rather spend time with my mushroom collection than a *girl*!"

Gertie breathed an enormous sigh of relief.

"Perfect! That's exactly how I feel," she said, extending her hand to shake. "I'm Gertie."

Giro looked at it awkwardly. "Um, when was the last time you, er, washed your hands?"

"In the rose water that was brought around."

"Oh, that's fine then—can't be too careful with little creatures lurking everywhere."

Giro's parents were now ogling and petting Robot Rabbit Boy, who by his glowing neon pink eyes was enjoying the attention.

"Lavender!" Robot Rabbit Boy said, showing off. "Room butter strawberry fly dollop lavender cup eggcup fly mush potato mashed."

Gertie leaned toward Kolt, who had finished his vegetable course, and was now gobbling up chestnut pudding.

"It's him," she whispered.

"Who is?"

"The *boy* is Girolamo Fracostoro—not the father."

"Okay, great! Ask if he can get us the recipe for this, would you? It's unbelievable."

Robot Rabbit Boy was also getting fed giant globs of chestnut pudding from golden spoons. Everyone but Gertie seemed to have forgotten about the mission, and the importance of trying to reunite a Keeper with their key.

She was about to take the glass vial of powder out of her velvet Renaissance dress and hand it to Giro when he started to apologize.

"Sorry if you heard me shouting earlier, Gertie. I've been in a state of panic and fury for days now."

"Why?"

"I know I'm only twelve, but I have a patient already."

"A sick person?"

"A very ill woman on the other side of the city."

"Who?"

"My nanny's mother," Giro said. "And she has a disease, a terrible one."

"Will she die?"

"I'm afraid she might, which is why she's gone back to her husband, and is no longer living here with us," Giro said, his eyes filling with tears. "I spent weeks preparing a medicine for her, but lost it. And now I can't recreate the formula. I've looked everywhere, but . . ."

Gertie whipped out the vial of powder from her velvet dress.

Giro's eyes widened with disbelief.

"It was on my seat when I went to sit down."

"Gertie!" Giro said, staring at the vial of green medicine in astonishment. "That is an old woman's life you hold in your hands. I have to get this medicine to my patient! Do you want to sneak away from this dull supper and go on a wild adventure to save an old woman's life?"

It was probably the worst idea in the history of bad ideas—an insane, deadly suicide mission with a twelve-year-old medical genius who was also a clean freak. But they weren't going to find any trapped Keepers at the bottom of a dish of chestnut pudding.

"I'm in!" Gertie said. "Let's go."

20

An Adventure at Sea

THE ADULTS WERE SO busy talking about the different customs of Venice, and marveling at Robot Rabbit Boy's glowing eyes, that Giro and Gertie slipped away from the table unnoticed.

It felt weird going on an adventure without Robot Rabbit Boy and Kolt, but there was no way of getting their attention without being found out.

Giro led Gertie out of the main hall, through a low stone opening, down some damp stone stairs, until they were outside at the edge of the rushing Grand Canal. Distant church bells were tolling, as though urging Giro and Gertie forward, on their mission of life and death.

"This is my boat," Giro said, pointing at the long vessel bobbing up and down on the river current. "It's completely custom, and took four carpenters and five normal-sized gondolas to build it."

They jumped off the stone jetty onto Giro's special watercraft, which had a high black hood of canvas stretched over it and two tall wooden arms at each end. A shirtless man with scars all over his body and an eye patch was at the back of the boat: Giro's private gondolier.

Once inside under the heavy canvas, Gertie was amazed. It was a science lab with vials and pots of bubbling smoke.

Between them in the middle of the boat was a bench and narrow table upon which stood dishes, bottles, glass pipes, and vials, all with different colored liquids running through them. One pipe went very high up, then curled around countless times as the liquid went from clear to purple, then to a strange smoke that was slowly filling a giant bottle suspended by ropes. It was like a smaller, floating version of the lab where Marie Curie was isolating elements. Gertie wasn't sure if elements had been discovered yet, and decided not to say anything about the other great scientist she had met only days ago.

On a smaller table near the back of the boat were various vials exactly like the one Gertie had brought from bedroom 469. The front of the vessel was literally a jungle of plants.

Giro untied the ropes so the shirtless gondolier could push them off into the fast current.

"Welcome to my laboratory," Giro said.

"You built it on a boat?"

"It was the only place, as some of the plants I need for experiments are deadly, and so I didn't even ask if I could grow them in my bedroom."

Gertie stepped away from a waxy tree with orange and red spikes growing from it.

"That's ghost pepper," Giro said. "If you touched it, then you would have to quarantine your hands for four hours until the burning wore off—some mad people actually eat them."

A different specimen had green berries with black dots all over them. Giro said these helped with muscle stiffness for very old people. In another corner was a mini pineapple plant.

The boat swung out into the fast-moving mass of water. The legs of the tables had been cut and joined back together inside sealed glass cylinders that were full of olive oil. When the boat rocked from side to side, the table legs moved, keeping the surface level.

"Another reason I keep my lab out here," Giro confessed, "is that if I had live animals in the house, they would wake everyone up—especially if they escaped."

"What animals?" Gertie said.

Giro pointed to the wooden compartments lining the sides of the boat. From inside, Gertie saw countless pairs of tiny eyes watching her. Some of the compartments had doors, and some had bars. Giro's modified gondola was not only a lab, but a floating zoo of small creatures.

"Do you test things out on them?" Gertie said.

"Goodness no!"

In the closest compartment was a frog.

"You can take him out," Giro said. "He's completely cured."

Gertie nervously reached her hand toward the opening, and the frog blinked twice then pushed off his back legs and crawled onto her hand.

"Hello, froggy," she said, wondering what the small amphibian thought of her.

In addition to the frog, there was a mouse, squirrel, vole, fox cub, and several birds rescued from his parents' kitchen. Giro also had a pig called Lester who lived in a straw basket. Giro said that Lester kept the boat clean by eating any food scraps and by chasing rats away without hurting them.

"That medicine you found," Giro said as they bobbed along the canal on their lifesaving mission, "was something I had been trying to make for a long time—but I couldn't get the cooking temperature right—too hot and it flamed, too cool and it wouldn't harden into a chalky block so I could grind it with my mortar and pestle."

"I'm impressed," Gertie said. "You really are a doctor. But wouldn't your parents be proud of you, Giro? If they knew?"

"They wouldn't understand," he said sadly. "Especially my father; he'd think all this was too dangerous somehow, or that it was just a child's game. Grown-ups always think they're right and never listen to children," Giro went on, "but if you look at history—the old ruin the world, while the young are always saving it."

Because the old are afraid of death, Gertie thought, remembering what Kolt had told her that first night they visited the rooms under the cottage—about how the human fear of death is what causes most suffering.

"So will we ruin the world when we get old?" Gertie asked.

"Hope not!"

"Me too," Gertie said, wondering exactly how she would age on Skuldark.

By now the boat was ripping along in the current at a frightening speed, with the gondolier still steering bravely through the tumultuous water.

When the boat began to rock back and forth violently, the animals cried out in their little voices.

"Don't worry, my friends!" shouted Giro, throwing his hands around as though he were conducting a pet orchestra of squeals and squeaks.

"I knew this trip would be dangerous—but if we survive, something incredible will have been achieved."

"*If* we survive!" Gertie said. "I thought you said we were going to rescue an old woman?"

"I didn't mention we'd also be in grave danger?"

"No! You said *an* adventure, and nothing about being on a deadly river in a floating zoo with poisonous plants and a pig called Lester."

"Oink," went something under the table.

Then the boat began to turn sharply in the fierce currents.

Giro went up the steps to brave the terrifying storm outside. Water was splashing up and over the sides of the boat. It was *so* rough they had to tie themselves to a varnished railing with leashes of rope.

"Why is it so bad!"

"The tide!" Giro said. "We should have timed our departure a bit better. We have to cross sandbars, and there's a growing wind swell making high rollers that we're going to have to get past before the long journey."

"What long journey!?" Gertie screamed over the furious sloshing. "I thought it was just a dangerous adventure to save an old woman! Now it's a long journey? How long?"

Her panic at sinking in the mud-brown water was now replaced by a worse fear. Although she had returned the vial of medicine to its rightful owner, she had only seven hours left in Venice to reunite with Kolt and Robot Rabbit Boy.

"We're going out into the Adriatic Sea," Giro said, "to a ship moored in deep water."

"A ship? I have to get to the dungeons before Kolt finishes dessert!"

"I didn't tell you the sick old woman is on a ship?"

"Er, no, and couldn't they have sailed into Venice? It *is* a river city."

"I'm afraid not, Gertie—you see, my beloved nanny is married to a pirate and no doctor in Venice will treat outlaws—it's forbidden by the Doge himself. She doesn't sail with him, preferring a more tranquil life with us on land. But at the prospect of death, they reunited."

"Pirates!" Gertie said, remembering her book and the insect movie. "Great!"

"You're happy about this? For helping pirates we could get put in prison or worse! That's why this is such an exciting mission, because we'll either drown, be caught by the authorities and have our heads chopped off, or be put in prison—*or,* and this is probably the most likely option, get kidnapped by the pirates who decide they need two ship doctors."

"But I'm not a doctor!"

"Neither am I!"

When Gertie looked back, Venice was just a cluster of flickering lights under a cloud of gray smoke.

Gertie took deep breaths of sea air and remembered when she had been alone on the cliffs that first morning on Skuldark.

She wished now she had told Kolt where she was going. If they did sink, she'd have to swim for it—try and stay alive long enough to get snatched, as Kolt had the time machine, which she would have needed to escape.

In the distance, peaks of open sea loomed like dark, watery mountains.

Without the rough-looking gondolier's expert handling, they would all have drowned for sure. But he knew how to take the waves, steering masterfully up the heaving chest of one, then down its slippery back.

"If we hit the swell at the wrong angle, we'll capsize," Giro shouted over the wind, which was now whipping up sea spray and stinging their cheeks.

After plowing over the crest of the most enormous wave, they glimpsed a yellow glow in the distance, somewhere between the sea and the sky. Then they lost sight of it, as another set of monster waves rolled toward them.

They were now completely soaked to the skin, and at least half the animals in the boat had thrown up in their cubbies.

The yellow glow, which had looked like a faraway candle only minutes before, was now a massive warship right off their starboard bow. It had been stolen six months ago from the country of Portugal by the most vicious, cutthroat band of sailors who had ever sailed the seven seas.

Pirates.

"Weird-looking gondola-boat-thing ahoy!" came a gruff voice from the deck of the pirate ship. Two more faces appeared, then ropes were thrown down through the mist. Once Giro's floating science experiment had been secured, a rope ladder unfurled over the side of the enormous stolen warship. Giro and Gertie pulled themselves up along the slick hull of the four-mast caravel—hoping that whoever was holding the top rope wasn't going to let go. The brave shirtless gondolier climbed down from his steering platform, and went inside to nurse Giro's seasick animals.

Gertie had read terrible things about pirates in her book, and half expected to be chased around on deck by one-legged sailors, with lice-filled scraggly beards and parrots on their shoulders.

When they were safely standing on the deck, Gertie took a deep breath at the sight of such scary-looking men and women, who represented so many different nations from Jamaica to China. Some of the sailors were very old, while one or two were younger than Gertie. She hoped they knew Giro had come to help.

Then a man with long black hair and two sparkling earrings growled at them.

"Giro, ye old barnacle! Where have you been? We were worried sick about you in such a boiling sea—and with Martha still so unwell."

Then the old pirate turned to Gertie, flashing a smile that revealed several gold teeth, and a few black ones.

"Is this your wife, Giro?"

For the first time ever in her whole life, Gertie felt seasick.

Everyone on the ship burst out laughing, except Gertie and Giro, whose faces turned the color of overripe strawberries.

"This no time for jokes, Captain," said Giro, holding up the vial of powder. "Thanks to Gertie, I have the medicine for Martha."

The gnarly crew of disfigured, tattooed, patch-wearing, dagger-wielding pirates separated, and Giro ran up some steps to a small cabin at the stern of the ship. After hesitating for a moment, Gertie followed.

In a small wooden bed in the captain's quarters, an elderly woman was curled up in great pain. When she saw Giro, she reached out feebly. "My boy, my boy . . ."

The unofficial child doctor went to work quickly.

The old woman sat up and took a few trembling sips of the medicine Giro had mixed with water.

"Will she be all right?" the captain asked, his earrings glinting in the candlelight.

"Most likely," Giro said. "But as soon as she can stand, you need to set sail before the Venetians discover you're hiding out here in the mist."

21

The Losers' Master Plan

ALL THEY NEEDED NOW was the boy. Through the dusty glass window of the sheriff's office, Thrax watched people hurrying home as darkness fell upon the town. Then someone knocked on the door.

"Enter," Thrax said. It was Roland Tubb.

As the giant Loser bounded in, Thrax held up a hand to stop him.

"You haven't even opened your mouth and you're already insulting me."

Tubb froze.

Thrax pointed at the dirt tracked in by Tubb's leather-soled brogue boots.

"Do you know how spotless that floor was before you barged in with an entire forest on your shoes?"

"What?"

"If things don't start getting clean around here I'm going to get very, very upset."

Tubb removed his shoes, trying to sweep up the dirt by swishing around in his socks.

"What are you doing?"

"I'm cleaning up my mess, sir."

Thrax smiled with both amusement and disgust. "You silly, silly man."

"But, sir, I . . ."

"Don't speak! Just tell me, is the boy captured yet? I can't wait to get out of this place and see a dentist. This body is the ultimate fixer-upper."

Tubb pointed to his mouth.

"What are you doing now!" Thrax snapped.

"You told me not to speak, sir."

"Stop being an idiot and tell me if you have the boy."

"Er, he should be in our custody by tonight, as we have him surrounded. What should we do with his parents?"

"Parents? He has parents?"

"He does, yes."

"How many?"

"Er, two."

"That seems like a lot."

"Most children have at least one, sir."

"They do? Did I?"

Tubb shrugged and looked down at his socks. "Yours would have been Romans, sir."

"Well, I've forgotten, so they must have been idiots."

Thrax checked his fingernails for micro-specks of dirt. "Listen, Tubb, I wouldn't worry about his *parents*—they've only had the boy nine years. How attached could they possibly be? You've worn underwear for longer than that, I'm sure. Now listen—once we get rid of the undertaker's son, this Max Franks fellow, Vispoth has uploaded the details of our master plan to *Doll Head*, which will put us within striking distance of the three remaining Keepers. If all goes well, that wretched cottage AND the Swiss-cheese cliff full of junk it sits on will be destroyed once and for all."

"What is the plan exactly, sir?"

"You don't need to know. Let's just say we're giving the Keepers a bit of a *hand*. Now find the boy!"

"Did we decide on a place for him yet?" Tubb asked.

"Vispoth came up with the Black Hole of Calcutta."

"Is that bad, sir?"

"It's a black hole, you idiot—yes, it's bad. And a wonderful irony, considering how the master plan involves exactly that."

"A boy in a hole?"

"Oh, stop blathering and get back out into the woods. Make sure this Keeper business is taken care of—and find out if pedicures have been invented yet, as inside these boots it's a chemistry experiment."

22

Surrounded with No Escape

AFTER TELLING MAX THE story of Little Deer, Ayokeh suddenly seemed afraid.

"We should go back," she said. "I smell something."

All Max could smell was sweet forest air and the cool gushing river.

"Come on," Ayokeh said, pulling on his arm. "We must return to warn our warriors."

Max trusted his new friend, and raced after her up the grassy path toward the Cherokee village.

"What do you smell exactly, Ayokeh?"

"Alcohol and rotten teeth."

Max froze with terror. He knew exactly what that meant.

"Come on, Birdy, we must tell my father. He'll know what to do."

"But all this is my fault!" Then he had an idea. "If I

disappear into these woods, then they'll leave you alone. They'll come after me."

"No," Ayokeh said wisely, "they will think we are hiding you."

WHEN THEY ARRIVED IN the village, Ayokeh and Max ran straight to the great council house where her father was meeting with the elders. They burst in as the Red Chief was speaking. Sequoyah rose awkwardly.

"Ayokeh?"

"There are bad men coming!" she said. "I picked up their scent."

"I will go call the warriors," one of the chiefs said.

Max couldn't believe there was going to be a war because of him.

"I'll give myself up!" he shouted.

Sequoyah put his hands firmly on the boy's shoulders. "We all agree the Great Spirit wants us to protect you."

"So I could get your village destroyed by gamblers and drunks?"

Sequoyah whispered something to his daughter.

"Yes, Father," she said, then grabbed Max's hand and led him back out into the village. Warriors had heard the chief's call, and were assembling. Women and children hurried toward the trees carrying six-foot-long blowpipes made from river cane.

Ayokeh took one of the blowpipes and gave it to Max.

"There is a dart inside," she told him. "Just blow."

Max examined the strange weapon, telling himself not to suck.

"But if anyone gets hurt," he said, "it will be my fault."

"No, it won't, don't be silly," Ayokeh said. "Now follow me to our hiding tree."

Ayokeh led Max to the edge of the village and they began to climb. Just in time too, for as soon as Max was settled in a wide branch with his enormous (but very thin) blowpipe at the ready, he saw a figure sneaking through the woods with a rifle.

Max glanced up at Ayokeh, who was on a higher branch, but she shook her head and the man passed beneath their tree toward the village unharmed.

Then Max saw something he couldn't believe. He rubbed his eyes, and blinked a few times, but she was still there—a girl just a few years older than himself stepping through the forest trailed by a pack of wolves. She was wearing a tartan day dress, and where her bonnet should have been were tiny flashing lights—like little candles that were too small to hold. Max had never witnessed anything like it. How was she able to control the wolves? It had to be connected to the lights on the side of her head, he thought.

As the bounty hunters reached the fringe of the Cherokee village, Max knew that at any moment, the brave warriors would burst from the houses with their weapons raised, then a terrible, violent battle would commence. Without thinking, he swallowed his fear in one gulp, and scrambled down the tree. Ayokeh called after him, but

Max ignored her voice and sprinted to the center of the Cherokee village before anything could happen.

"It's me, Max!" he cried, waving his arms around. "I'm surrendering, hello! Everyone! It's me, Max! Fresh from the woods! The kid in the wanted poster! Here I am! Hi! Better take me in!"

There was a great commotion from the men hiding, as well as movement in the trees.

"He's mine!" shouted one of the mercenaries who'd come fifty miles to claim the price on Max's head.

"Get out of it!" shouted another as the two men began fighting it out with fists. Suddenly the truth dawned on the dozens of outlaws in the Cherokee village. There was only one bounty to be collected. In a mad scramble, they came for the boy all at once. At that exact moment, Mandy Zilch let loose the wolves she had been controlling with a frequency modulator. As if there wasn't enough chaos already, thirty-three Cherokee warriors came barreling out of their houses with deer-bone knives held aloft.

The battle Max had tried to prevent was about to take place. And it was going to be a slaughter.

But then something unexpected happened. There was a blinding flash of light as the Cherokee village was hit by an electro-graviton pulse. Then another flash—this time green—out of which came something no one had ever seen, except in myths and legends.

23

Venetian Warships

A FEW MOMENTS AFTER drinking Giro's medicine, the elderly woman in the white nightgown blinked her eyes and sat up. Then to everyone's surprise, she got out of bed and did a little dance on the spot.

The captain was delighted and clapped Giro on the back. "You're a clever barnacle, ain't you, boy?"

But the celebrations didn't last long. A cannonball whizzed past the cabin, hitting the wooden case of the ship's bell and smashing it to pieces with a disorderly clang.

"Shot!" bellowed the captain. "Looks like the Venetians have found us! Shot! Shot!"

They cleared out of the captain's quarters as quickly as possible. Pirates were rushing around in the scramble for weapons, amidst the deathly whistling of cannonballs.

Giro led Gertie to the starboard side of the ship, where

she climbed down the rope to his special gondola. The rope was rough and stung her palms.

With an attack under way from the Venetian navy, Gertie's first thought was for Giro's floating zoo, still bobbing at the side of the pirate ship. If even the smallest cannonball hit, the furriest, cutest little creatures in Venice would be sent to a watery grave.

Then Giro shinnied down into his gondola, where his loyal gondolier was waiting for orders.

"Untie the ropes!" Giro shouted.

As if sensing the danger, all of Giro's little creatures were mewing, meowing, chirping, squeaking, bawling, screeching, and ribbiting, as iron balls of death whistled about their heads.

Gertie frantically tried to undo the knots that held the two boats together.

But just then, the bow of a beautifully crafted hull cut toward them through the mist, only missing the side of the gondola by a few feet. It was a boat of the Venetian navy.

Suddenly grappling hooks flew over their heads and caught in the rigging of the pirate ship—like hooks in a spider's web. Then from out of the mist burst two daring figures on ropes, swinging wildly. Giro rubbed his eyes in disbelief. "It can't be!"

"It is!" Gertie screamed, as Kolt and Robot Rabbit Boy landed with a thump on their bobbing gondola.

Robot Rabbit Boy bowed, his fake mustache twitching.

"We found you at last!" Kolt said.

"You're not angry?" asked Gertie.

"I don't get angry, you know that—I just worry myself into a state of oblivion."

"Sorry, Kolt, but I wanted to see Giro's medicine in action for myself—and it worked! But I don't think we should stick around any longer—do you have the time machine?"

Kolt had already pulled it out of his Renaissance cloak.

"What about the Time Cat?"

"It'll find its way back as it always does."

"Okay, but we don't have the clothes for North America. They're in the car!"

"How can you worry about what you're going to wear at a time like this? It was the same in ancient China! Listen, the main thing is I brought the page of important symbols we have to return."

"Fine, whatever!" Gertie said, as several cannonballs came whistling toward them. "Let's link up!"

They quickly grabbed on to each other's hands, unaware that Robot Rabbit Boy's other paw was still touching the side of the massive pirate ship, which could mean only one thing.

24

Unexpected Guests

As THE LAST EXPLOSION of green light tore through the Cherokee village, some outlaws believed it was divine punishment for the evil things they had done.

The Cherokee took it as a sign that Great Spirit had come to their aid. So then everyone was *really* surprised when out of the blinding flash came a three-hundred-year-old heavily modified Renaissance gondola, with outdated scientific equipment, small animals at various stages of throwing up, a bare-chested gondolier, a stunned-looking professor type, a young Italian holding an escaped frog, a rabbit with facial hair, and a soaking-wet girl in light-up shoes clinging to ropes at the side of the vessel. The small Venetian watercraft crash-landed on the grass outside Sequoyah's house, to a stunned silence.

Gertie stared at the strange-looking men in long-tailed

jackets, who were carrying rifles. On of the other side of the boat were Cherokee warriors, and behind the gondolier—a pack of bewildered wolves.

Then one of the older outlaws pointed a bony finger at Giro.

"Look, it's Jesus!"

Gertie didn't understand what was happening. "How can we have traveled over the graviton bridge with the gondola, and Giro, and all the animals?"

"The boat must have been attached to us in some way," Kolt said quickly, "and the B.D.B.U. thought we meant to bring it with us. It happens from time to time, as does landing in the middle of a battle."

"Keepers!" Mandy Zilch screamed, unable to contain her disgust.

"Losers!" Gertie cried. "This gets weirder and weirder."

"Mashed potato fly?"

"It could always be worse!" said Kolt, noticing a piece of rope hovering in midair as though the gondola was attached to something invisible.

Suddenly, in a blinding pink flash, a three-hundred-ton stolen Portuguese warship, with a crew of sixty-four blood-thirsty pirates, exploded through the time portal and came to rest (leaning but upright) atop several crushed clay-and-wood houses.

The outlaws, the Cherokee warriors, and even the pack of wolves were now completely bewildered by the sight of a pirate ship with a full pirate crew, who were just standing around on deck wondering why they were no longer floating.

The captain looked sheepishly over the side of his ship. "Who be you people in strange clothes with hand muskets!?"

"And where be the sea? It was here a minute ago," Gertie heard one of the other pirates say.

An outlaw stepped forward. "Er, we're evil mercenaries who've been hired by a cruel sheriff to capture a small boy for an outrageous amount of money, and these are the rightful people of this land, the Cherokee, who were about to try and stop us."

"Oh, I see, sort of a battle then?" said the captain.

Everyone on the ground looked at one another and nodded.

"Yes, exactly," said the outlaw.

"And might you know," the captain went on, "where the sea has gotten to?"

"Can't help you with that one . . ." said the outlaw. "I don't even swim."

"Me neither," said another voice.

"Nor me," said another.

Then one of the Cherokee got to his feet. "I'm Sequoyah!" he shouted to the pirate captain on the boat. "Welcome to our village."

"Sequoyah!" Kolt said. "I know you! Hello, hi, hello!"

The kind inventor raised his hand in greeting. "We know each other?"

"Not really, but I have something for you! Some kind of alphabet."

"Not a syllabary?"

Kolt looked at the paper in his hands. "Yes, it could be that actually. . . ."

"If it is, then praise Great Spirit! I thought I was going to have to start all over again. Thank you, stranger!"

"I'll bring it down after this battle business is decided—wouldn't want it to get damaged."

"Who are you, stranger?"

"Well, I'm a sort of a curator of objects, and these men are bloodthirsty pirates, who terrorize the Adriatic Sea on stolen ships."

The pirate captain nodded. "We were just about to be cannonballed by the Venetian naval fleet, after dropping anchor just outside Venice so that my wife, Martha, could get medical treatment from a small boy with a floating chemistry set."

Giro put his hand up to signal that he was the "small boy."

"It really is Jesus!" said a voice in the crowd. "Performing miracles with the help of that magic frog."

One of the outlaws took off his hat and scratched a bald head. "Pirates?" he said. "I think I read about you somewhere? Bandits on boats, right?"

The pirate captain smoothed his hair. "Oh, so you've heard of us then?"

"Yes, of course," said the outlaw. "You terrorized the

seas for hundreds of years, and as such were a great inspiration to me as a boy, hence my current profession."

"Me too." One of the other outlaws nodded. "I love how you made people walk the plank; that was just so original."

The captain chuckled. "Well, we *honestly* try our best."

The outlaws laughed at that.

"Who is the rabbit soldier with the mustache?" shouted someone in the crowd. "He's cute!"

"Dollop?"

"SHUTTTTTT UPPPPPPP!" cried Mandy Zilch. Her face was red with rage. "Get the Keeper boy, you imbeciles!"

But the opportunity for a vicious battle seemed to have passed, and everyone was now more interested in talking about what had happened, and perhaps wondering what might appear next in a flash of colored light.

"What Keeper boy?" Gertie shouted, feeling the key in her pocket start to vibrate madly.

"Shut your mouth!" Mandy Zilch screeched. "Milk scum!"

"MUSH ROOM!" cried Robot Rabbit Boy.

"What boy is it they're after?" Kolt shouted to Gertie.

"She didn't say!"

"It's *me* they want," came a small voice from the hull of the pirate ship.

Kolt peered down at him. "Looks like you were almost crushed by the pirate ship!"

"Mashed fly."

"I was!" said the boy. "But thankfully all I lost was a shoe."

"That's good, but do you know why the Losers are trying to capture you?"

Then Gertie noticed Mandy Zilch was holding a magnetic cuff. "He must be a missing Keeper," she shouted before the boy could answer. "Look what the Loser girl is holding, Kolt! It's a magnetic cuff! And the Keepers' key is buzzing like crazy!"

"You're right, Gertie, he must be one of your missing Keepers. I can't believe it. A new Keeper, in the flesh!"

Gertie had forgotten about Giro with all the excitement of finding a lost Keeper. "Are we dead?" he asked, tugging lightly on her sleeve. "Is this heaven?"

"No," Gertie said, "but it's goodbye, I'm afraid, as anything that accidentally travels through time with Keepers is soon catapulted back."

"We've traveled through time? Future or past?"

"I shouldn't say," she told him, "but I can tell you that everything you've figured out about the little creatures is true."

"It is?"

Gertie nodded. "You're actually really, really clever, so keep working because the world needs your ideas."

As there was no time for lengthy explanations, she leaned in and gave Giro a hug.

"I'll miss you," he said.

"Look after those animals, especially the frog."

Then, without wasting any more time, Gertie jumped out of the gondola and sprinted toward the small figure the Losers had been trying to kidnap.

"What are you doing!" Mandy Zilch screamed at the outlaws. "Get the boy!"

"But it doesn't feel right anymore," one of the outlaws said.

"Yeah," said another. "It's like a crazy dream, where you need the toilet but can't seem to find one and eventually it starts to hurt."

"And then Jesus comes!" shouted someone from the back of the group. Everyone nodded in agreement, then resumed talking among themselves.

Just then, the pirate ship and its crew, along with Giro and his gondola, disappeared with a loud pop, leaving a few crushed Cherokee houses and a faint pink mist.

"Well, there they go!" said Kolt, who had hurried over to Sequoyah to return the syllabary. The sudden disappearance of the ships was too much for the outlaws, and they ran off into the woods.

But Mandy Zilch was not about to give up her prize. After gathering the wolves under her control into a single pack, she let them loose again. They tore across the dirt at a frightening speed toward Gertie and the young Keeper.

Just as they were about to make a leap for their victims, Robot Rabbit Boy twitched his nose three times, causing a red laser beam to shoot from one of his nostrils. The result was an enormous BOOM! and everyone was splattered by an explosion of dirt. When the smoke cleared there was a deep hole in the ground with angry wolves at the bottom of it. Unfortunately, the hole was so big that Max was now hanging on to a tree root to stop himself from falling on top of the snarling wolf pack.

"Grab my hand!" Gertie cried out, as she skidded to a stop at the edge of the pit.

"What?" Max said. "Who are you?" Just as the tree root snapped, he reached for Gertie's outstretched arm.

"Kolt!" she cried. "I can't hold him for long!"

But Kolt was already there, fiddling his key into the lock as Robot Rabbit Boy grabbed Gertie's feet to stop her slipping into the hole with the boy.

With a flash of neon green light, the four Keepers landed as a gasping tangle of bodies back on the island of Skuldark, bruised and battered but delirious with joy and relief.

They had done it. Returned two very important items, saved one of their own from a Loser kidnapping, met pirates, and all while managing to lose only one thing—Robot Rabbit Boy's fake mustache—which Kolt thought was the perfect end to the first-ever great Keeper rescue.

Part
3

25

Home Sweet Skuldark

IT TOOK A LONG time to calm the boy down. As Kolt suspected would happen, the entire memory of his previous existence was wiped out the moment they landed in the Garden of Lost Things.

"Who are you!" he kept demanding, once they'd sat him down in the cottage with a glass of warm moonberry juice. "And when can I go home?"

Kolt did his best to explain.

For Gertie, it felt like déjà vu. "You're a Keeper," she said. "I know it sounds weird, but it's your destiny—you won't be going home."

"What about my family?" the boy said.

"Do you remember who they are?" Kolt asked sympathetically. "How to find them?"

Gertie remembered that it was exactly what Kolt had said to her, almost word for word.

The boy stared at the window. A baby Slug Lamp was inching his way across a glass panel, perhaps eager to catch a glimpse of the new Keeper.

"We know it was North America," Kolt said. "Same as Gertie, just a different time."

"And I can't go back?"

"Without a memory of who your family might be," Gertie told him, "even if we went back to your time, how would you recognize them?"

The boy now seemed about to cry. "So they're lost forever?"

"Not to themselves," said Kolt, trying to find something positive to say.

The boy's head dropped, and he let out a deep sigh. "It's weird that I miss people I can't remember." Then he looked up at Gertie and Kolt. "And I have to spend the rest of my life here? Not knowing who I am?"

"Kolt heard people calling you Birdy!" Gertie pointed out.

"Birdy?" the boy said. "I don't even recognize my own name."

"But what's even weirder..." Gertie went on, "is that you probably don't even know what you look like."

"What do you mean?"

"What color are your eyes?"

The boy blinked. "You're right. I don't know."

"We're here to look after you," Kolt said kindly. "This is going to be your home."

"For how long?"

Gertie winked at Kolt. "For now," she said. "While we rescue more Keepers like yourself."

Kolt nodded. "I think it's safe to say the B.D.B.U. is fully on board, excuse the pun."

Gertie smirked. "I'll start searching the island for more keys tomorrow."

"Or the day after," Kolt said. "I thought we might have cake day tomorrow, get Birdy fully fed?"

"No, this is urgent. You bake if you want, Kolt, but I'm going on the hunt for keys."

Kolt sighed. "Well, if you're this determined, I'll prepare your aircraft in the morning, before I peel the apples and rinse the peaches."

With the sun setting over the cliffs of Skuldark, Kolt mentioned that they might want to get some sleep.

Kolt took Birdy down steep steps to the Sock Drawer, kicking a robot hand out of the way. His bedroom was through a small door at the back of the room, behind the many racks of clothes and accessories. It was smaller than Gertie's room, but also overlooked the Skuldarkian Sea at the back of the cottage.

When Gertie heard Kolt coming back up the steps from Birdy's new bedroom, she put the kettle on for one more cup of tea before bed.

Kolt picked up the apparently dead robot hand and put it in a glass jar. Then he threw a log on the fire and settled into one of the comfy velvet armchairs.

"Is he settled?"

"For now," Kolt said. "He was completely knackered."

When the kettle whistled, Gertie got up and made a

pot of tea. It was a nutty mélange of cinnamon, cardamom, and cloves, blended by an old woman they had met on a mission to India.

"It'll take time for him to adjust . . ." Gertie said, "obviously. But it's better than being stranded in some horrible place for the rest of your life. How much do you think we should tell him?"

"There's nothing really to tell. We know the year and the location, but nothing about who he is."

For a few moments, they both stared into the fire, going over the different moments of their adventure. Moments that were personal to them and that they would never forget.

"He won't be sleeping," Gertie said. "He'll be looking at himself in the mirror trying to figure out who he is, just like I was."

BEFORE GOING TO BED, Gertie decided to check on the new Keeper. She went down the steps to the Sock Drawer, looking out for any pesky robot hands she might trip over. Then, quietly tiptoeing past the enormous revolving globe, she arrived at a small door with a knocker shaped like a shoe.

"Birdy . . ." she whispered in case he was sleeping. "Birdy, it's me, Gertie."

"Come in," said a faint voice. The room was lit by a single lamp, and the boy's eyes were red as though he'd been crying. Gertie sat down next to him and looked around.

Birdy's bedroom had a loft bed reached by a narrow ladder with steps that lit up as you walked on them. On the far side of the room was a massive glass window from which Birdy could see miles and miles out to sea.

"I'm directly above you," she told him. "So if you ever need me in the night, just throw a shoe at the ceiling."

"Thanks, Gertie, I just wish I could remember something."

Underneath his bed was a desk, and a wooden case stuffed with books.

"Those things are books," Gertie said. "I can teach you how to read if you want."

"I know that already, but I'm more comfortable with *this* type of language." Birdy pointed to a heavy volume on his desk called *Calculus, Statistics, Algebra, Geometry, and Trigonometry for a Rainy Day.*

"Well, that's great," Gertie said, trying to sound positive. "Maybe you can teach me something?"

The boy nodded sadly. "I just wish I knew who I was. It's like something has taken a bite out of me."

Gertie knew the pain he was feeling. That gnawing sense of being incomplete. "It's like you know you've lost something precious, but you just don't know what it is."

"Or where to look for it," Birdy added.

"Just remember one thing, though," Gertie said. "Remember that you've been chosen out of thousands of other children for the task of saving the world from ignorance and chaos."

"You mean as a Keeper of Lost Things?"

"Yeah, exactly," Gertie said. "It's kind of a big deal."

26

Birdy Gets a Surprise

AFTER SEVERAL BOWLS EACH of Robot Rabbit Boy's famous fruit salad the next morning, Kolt wanted to show Birdy the beach.

"We can swim if the water's not too cold," he said.

Gertie stood up from the table. She couldn't believe it.

"Swimming?" she said. "When there are missing Keepers to rescue? I thought you were going to refuel the Spitfire so I could hunt for more keys?"

"Well, um, yes, certainly . . ." Kolt said, nodding, "but the beach might be a good place to start—and it's much easier digging in sand. . . ."

Gertie nodded, then looked at Birdy. "Fine," she said, "I'll bring shovels. Maybe later I'll do a sweep of the island in my aircraft."

‹‹ • • • ››

AFTER BREAKFAST, KOLT FOUND some towels and packed sandwiches, three small shovels, buckets, a yellow ball, a jar of lemon curd for Robot Rabbit Boy, and three ice-cold bottles of moonberry juice.

"Remember!" Gertie reminded them. "Any kind of glowing could be a buried key."

As they left the cottage, the path took them past the Spitfire at the entrance to Turweston Passage.

Birdy was impressed with the enormous machine.

"It's beautiful," he marveled, then asked how it could possibly conform to Newton's Laws of Motion, being so heavy.

"Er, I'm not sure, but you can sit in the cockpit if you want."

"The what?"

"C'mon," Gertie said, "we can do it later—we've got keys to find now."

"Dollops of fly . . ." said Robot Rabbit Boy, thoughtfully.

Kolt led them back through a far corner of the Garden of Lost Things, between an old fairground ride called "The Ghost Train" and weather-beaten statues of men and women that were half human and half horse.

As they neared the cliff edge, they passed two wells. One, Kolt said, could be used to draw water if the pump system failed. The other looked very old and was beginning to crumble. It had bars over the top and several padlocks preventing the bars' removal.

"Steer clear of this one, Keepers," Kolt warned them.

"Eggcup?" said Robot Rabbit Boy, distracted by two butterflies that were chasing each other.

A sign read:

SECURE ALL KEYS
BEFORE APPROACHING

USE WITH *EXTREME* CAUTION

"The Well of No Return!" Kolt said. "A last resort if ever I saw one. . . ."

"A what?" Gertie said.

"A plan Z."

"Huh?"

"When we've run out of every conceivable option . . ."

Birdy was curious about the well and asked why it was so dangerous.

"Because," Kolt explained, "whatever goes down that hole never, ever comes back to Skuldark."

Birdy looked through the bars into darkness. "Where does it go?"

"Some place in history," Kolt said.

"So what if we threw a stone down there?"

"Then it might bonk someone on the head in Scotland of 1376, or smash someone's bedroom window in Western Australia, 1998, or plop into a prehistoric sea before humans were even around."

"So you've never used it?" Gertie asked, looking in.

"I have been tempted once or twice," Kolt said, "to toss a little peach cake down there, then imagine it being enjoyed by someone, somewhere. . . ."

At the edge of the garden, the path dropped steeply to stone steps that zigzagged along the cliff.

"Hold the rope handrails! And try not to look down, it'll make you dizzy."

When they had descended halfway to the beach, Gertie could smell the sea, and taste salt on her lips.

"How are you getting on with Mrs. Pumble's book, by the way, Gertie?" Kolt said.

"Not very well," Gertie admitted. "I've been so busy, but I'm at the part where Mrs. Pumble is about to find out the truth. I'm afraid if I know how she did it, I'll do the same thing." She turned to Birdy. "That is, try and get back to where I came from."

Kolt laughed knowingly. "Very wise, Gertie. I would skip over that part if I were you—if you wish to avoid the same fate."

Birdy was more than curious. "There's a way to get back to where we're from in the world?"

"Maybe," Gertie said. "Mrs. Pumble, an old Keeper, found a way, but then decided it was better on Skuldark as a Keeper of Lost Things. I'll tell you more later."

When the path finally ended, Gertie's legs were aching, but they were now on one of Skuldark's only sandy beaches.

Along the sand were items that had washed up from the deep ocean. Giant clams, a ship's wheel standing upright, even the seaweed-strewn shell of a big blue car. Far down the beach, they could even make out the rib cage of some ancient creature, picked clean by nibbling crabs, then bleached white by the sun and salt water. It was so big they could all have sat down inside of it, and pretended they were in a skeleton jail.

"Don't worry, Birdy," Kolt reassured him, "those beasts live in deep water. You'll be safe swimming here."

"I feel certain we're going to find another key today," Gertie announced. "Keep a lookout for anything that glows! Listen for any kind of buzzing."

The Skuldarkian sea was calm that morning, the water clear and green. After laying out their beach towels, Birdy, Kolt, Gertie, and Robot Rabbit Boy ran about looking at the different objects, and digging under giant tree trunks of driftwood, to see what might be living there and to seek out any glowing objects.

When Birdy and Robot Rabbit Boy stopped to rest, Gertie kept going, and walked a mile or so with her eyes trained on the sand.

When the sun came out it was warm. And when Gertie returned from her walk, Kolt told them to cool off in the water.

But Birdy just stood there. "I don't know if I can swim," he said. "I can't remember anything."

"Take my hand," said Gertie. "I'll take you in, but then I should keep looking."

"Could there be keys under the sea?" Birdy asked.

Gertie thought about it. She had washed up on a beach, and so others could too.

"I should have brought some diving gear—at least a mask and some flippers," she said.

Kolt shivered. "Not sure I'd want to know what lives under the water."

"What do you mean?" Birdy asked.

"Oh, nothing! Enjoy your swim!"

Robot Rabbit Boy put out his paw and took Birdy's other hand. Then the three of them went to the water's edge. Small waves splashed over their feet (and paws), as they screamed at the shock of how cold it was.

"I thought you said it was warm!" Gertie shouted. "I can't go searching for keys in this! I'll turn into an ice cube!"

"Just be careful!"

The water was very cold and clear. Gertie was able to see the sand beneath and decided that after a quick swim and a sandwich, she would take Birdy and Robot Rabbit Boy on another long walk along the waterline, this time in the other direction. If she could cross the beach off her map of places to search, it would be a good day's work.

Once the sea was over their legs, it was hard to hold hands because of the pushing waves. Birdy let his body tip back into the water, and found he floated with ease.

"Look at me!" he said.

"Lavender butter," said Robot Rabbit Boy, his arms and legs moving rhythmically. Gertie knew from the instruction manual that all Series 7 Forever Friends had an aquatic feature, which allowed them to survive in almost every water environment, including tropical swamps and polar ice caps.

"I'm swimming!" Birdy yelled excitedly.

"Yeah," said Gertie, trying to shield herself from his splashing, "but maybe try and move your arms like this . . ."

Birdy tried it and his head went under. Robot Rabbit Boy doggy-paddled over to him. But then the young Keeper's head popped up, and he managed to keep his head out of the water and move his arms and legs at the same time.

"Well done!" shouted Kolt, unrolling his Victorian bathing suit from the wicker picnic basket.

Then, a little farther out, there was a loud hiss, and something big broke the surface of the water.

"Aaaargh!" Birdy cried.

Kolt heard the scream just as he was getting into his candy-striped swimming outfit.

"It's not that bad!" he shouted. "It was once the height of fashion!"

Then Birdy shrieked again as an eel-like creature circled him in the water.

"It's a worm!"

"With a head of fleshy holes?" Gertie said calmly.

"Yes, help! Help!"

Gertie was laughing now. "He's one of us."

Then Kolt shouted from the beach, "I think I just saw Johnny the Guard Worm!"

"Johnny the what?" Birdy cried.

"It's Johnny the Guard Worm," Gertie explained, rubbing salt water out of her eyes. "Kolt's pet, trained to catch Losers and protect Keepers."

"Who are Losers again?"

"I'll explain later," Gertie said. Kolt was now at the water's edge. Birdy watched with terrified fascination as an enormous snake-like, wormy creature writhed to the beach, then slithered out of the water to be petted by Kolt.

"He's sweet for an overgrown parasite," Gertie said. "Want to go over and pet him?"

"Er, not right now," said Birdy. "I'll stay here and try not to drown."

"Suit yourself, but if we ask *really* nicely, he might take us for a ride on his back."

Soon it was time to dry themselves off and eat the cheese and pickle sandwiches in the picnic basket. Birdy had fully recovered from meeting their pet moonberry worm, enlarged by Kolt with bags and bags of growing spice.

"Summer or winter moonberry juice?" Kolt asked, holding up two bottles.

"Winter for me," Gertie said, then explained to Birdy that berries harvested from the colder months were less fizzy, and gave a you a warm glow, as though you had just eaten a fuzzy sweater.

Kolt chuckled. "Water too cold?"

"I'm just glad that big worm is friendly," Birdy admitted. "What kind of skeleton does it have, Kolt, do you know? Or is it just muscle tissue?"

Gertie almost spat out her juice. "What a strange question!"

Birdy hung his head. "Oh, sorry."

"No, it's good . . ." Gertie reassured him, "just something I would never have thought to ask."

Kolt was about to put everyone to sleep with a lecture on how Johnny the Guard Worm was actually born inside a *moonberry* when the sky began to darken, and the waves of the sea began to rise up and then crash.

In the distance, over the far peaks and troughs of rolling waves, were faint silver threads of lightning.

"Oh dear!" said Kolt. "Looks like an urgent return."

"A what?" said Birdy, chewing on his sandwich.

"Now?" said Gertie. "When we have keys to find?"

"Remember, it's what we do, returning things to the world for the good of humankind."

"As Keepers of Lost Things, you mean?" Birdy asked.

"That's right," said Kolt. "Now, do you like books?"

"I love *some* books," Birdy admitted, "but most are boring to me."

"How about a very, very big one?" Kolt said.

"Is it boring?"

"It's many things," Kolt answered, "but boring is not one of them."

27

The Mysterious 9.8 m/s²

WHEN THEY WERE HALFWAY up the mountain staircase, it started to rain hard. The slippery stones and now sopping clothes made everyone miserable.

"Dollop mush," said Robot Rabbit Boy, his small robot rabbit legs worn out from all the steps.

"We should have put the towels on our heads," Gertie said, "the way some of those Cherokee were wearing turbans!"

Kolt slowed his pace, so that he was next to Gertie.

"I'm not sure Birdy's ready for the B.D.B.U.," Kolt told her quietly, "so I'll go up the tower alone and find out what we have to return and where."

Gertie's teeth were chattering from the chill of rain. "O-k-k-k-k-aaay."

Water dripped off the end of Kolt's nose. "Dry Robot Rabbit Boy with the hairdryer—it's under the kitchen

233

sink—then go back to your rooms and take hot showers—last thing we want is the pair of you coming down with colds."

"A-g-g-g-reed," Gertie said, relieved she wasn't going to have to climb the tower steps after slogging up the cliff from the beach.

AFTER FOLLOWING KOLT'S INSTRUCTIONS, Gertie, Birdy, and Robot Rabbit Boy sat at the kitchen table, dry and warm, with steaming mugs of hot chocolate.

"Where's Kolt?"

"He's in the tower finding out where we have to go, and what item needs to be returned."

"What tower?"

Gertie wondered if she should explain now about *The History of Chickens*, and the B.D.B.U.'s tower cloaked with Narcissus paint. But then she remembered her own first days on Skuldark, and how each new piece of information had filled her with sudden bouts of fear—even panic. Birdy was several years younger, so she thought it best if he learned things gradually.

"It's no big deal," Gertie said. "I'll show you sometime."

Outside rain was battering the cottage. Wind lashed the windows with a howl and whistle. The next adventure was upon them. Gertie wondered if it meant another Keeper rescue, though without a new key she was worried their chances of that were slim.

"What's going on out there?" Birdy asked. "It's a storm, right?"

"It's nothing to be worried about," Gertie said, "just sort of like an alarm clock. The weather changes when there's an item for us to return."

"Who changes it?"

"That book in the tower Kolt told you about. You'll see it one day."

She wondered if it wouldn't be a good idea to leave Birdy in the cottage for this adventure. Traveling in the Time Cat (which had safely returned itself from Renaissance Italy) might have been too much of a shock. He didn't even know how to use his key yet—or the dangers of getting snatched.

Suddenly Kolt appeared from the secret passage, and *The History of Chickens* slid back into the stack by itself.

Birdy jumped out of his seat. "That book just moved!"

Kolt was gasping for breath after descending the tower steps in such a hurry.

"Chickens ... will ... do ... that ... now ... follow ... me!" He wheezed, rushing over to the trapdoor.

Brushing the rug aside with one sweep of his foot, Kolt lifted the handle of the trapdoor to reveal a steep staircase down.

Gertie needed to speak with Kolt alone, so she asked Birdy to check that his bedroom door was locked, and to make sure he had his key. Once he had gone, she turned to the old Keeper.

"You think he's ready for this?"

"Of course not, but we can't leave him here. This is a big one, Gertie!"

"What is it we're looking for exactly?"

"A bug."

"Euugh," Gertie said. "Is that all? Why hasn't it been catapulted back to Earth like all living things that come here accidentally?"

"Because it's a robot insect, not an organic, living one."

"Could it be a robot Keeper?"

Kolt sighed. "Really, Gertie?"

Then Birdy returned. "Everything okay?"

"We're about to show you something that isn't normal," Kolt warned him. "Just warning you."

"You have to trust us, Birdy," Gertie said.

"Why? What's down there? A monster?"

Robot Rabbit Boy hopped out from his bed and touched Birdy with a grubby paw. "A dollop of mashed potato."

"What's down here is everything that's ever been lost from the world," Kolt told him, grabbing his dented bowler hat off the shelf. "Remember our long conversation yesterday?"

Birdy looked suddenly worried. "I thought you were joking."

DEEPER UNDER THE COTTAGE and into the cliff they went, as lamps on the rock wall flickered to life, casting a faint glow over the four Keepers.

Soon they reached the first level with all the different vehicles for getting around under the cliff, from single-person orange submarines to wooden skis, mini-motorbikes with spiked tires for ice, and even narrow boats made from animal bones and skin.

From some secret hive in the cave, all seven Cave Sprites appeared and led Kolt over to a glass case with yellow backpacks inside.

"Oh goody!" Kolt said with genuine surprise. "So we're finally going to put these on, are we?"

The Cave Sprites bounced up and down as if they were excited too. Kolt fed his Keepers' key into the lock on the glass case, then swung open the door.

Birdy was mesmerized by the glowing balls of light. "What are those things?"

"Cave Sprites!" Gertie said. As always, Robot Rabbit Boy was waving his paws about trying to catch one. "There are seven in total, and each is the spirit of a long-dead warrior from history. Because there are seven in total, Kolt named them after days of the week."

Gertie pointed to a Cave Sprite moving much slower than the others. "That's Sunday, the oldest."

"What do they do?"

"They guide us to the bedroom with the object that needs returning—by helping us choose the quickest route through the cliff to get there."

"Cliff?" Birdy said. "As in—something people fall off?"

Gertie remembered the old rope bridge, but decided not to mention it at that exact second. It was highly unlikely they'd be doing anything quite so terrifying for a long time. Then Kolt thrust a yellow backpack into everyone's hands (and paws).

"Put these on, and for goodness' sake make sure they're tight around your chest and waist. I'm nipping back upstairs; I think I'll leave my bowler hat in the cottage for this mission," he said mysteriously.

Gertie had always wondered what these bright yellow backpacks were used for. Written in black was a strange code, 9.8 m/s^2 with an evil-looking smiley face next to it. Gertie asked Birdy if he knew what it meant.

"It's the rate of acceleration due to gravity," he said. "9.8 meters per second, *every* second, but only if there's no air resistance."

"So something falling? Wow, that's fast," Gertie said, trying to imagine moonberries being dropped from the cockpit of her Spitfire. How satisfying it would feel to see one splat on the roof of the cottage.

Birdy touched the numbers written on the yellow canvas. "The pulling force of gravity makes the object accelerate," he explained, "so the object's acceleration is increasing every second by another 9.8 meters. After 2 seconds it would be traveling at 19.6 meters per second, and after 3 seconds, falling at a rate of 29.4 meters per second."

"So . . ." Gertie said, thinking, "9.8 meters per second times 4 seconds equals 39.2, which is how fast an object would be falling after 4 seconds?"

"Yes, with the velocity always increasing until air resistance pushing back equals the force of pulling, which is maximum velocity."

Gertie nodded, trying to take it all in.

"After you left my room last night," Birdy went on, "I couldn't sleep and so read a couple of chapters on Newton and Galileo in one of those books by my bed. There was also a formula to calculate how far something has fallen, look..." Birdy took a piece of paper and pencil from his pocket, and wrote down:

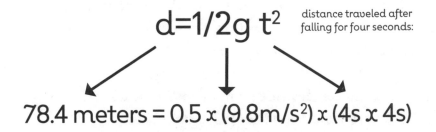

d = distance in meters
g = acceleration due to gravity
t = time in seconds

$$d = 1/2 g \, t^2$$

distance traveled after falling for four seconds:

$$78.4 \text{ meters} = 0.5 \times (9.8 m/s^2) \times (4s \times 4s)$$

"Do you really get all this math, Birdy?"

"Not really," Birdy said, "which is why I keep studying it."

"Well, I wonder why acceleration due to gravity is written on our yellow packs? They seem pretty light to me."

"Actually, light and heavy objects fall at the same rate of acceleration, 9.8 m/s^2, so a backpack full of metal would fall at the same speed as a backpack full of feathers, if they were the same mass, and there was no air resistance."

Gertie shrugged. "That's weird, then it's probably just written for decoration or something."

"Come on!" Kolt said appearing from behind a rack of skis. He led them to an old elevator in the rock face. "This will get us down to the level we need."

"I didn't think it worked," Gertie said.

"Oh, it does, trust me."

"What bedroom is it we're going to?"

"782 SE."

Gertie had never heard of a room with letters after the number, and asked what they meant.

"Southeast."

Gertie thought about it, but couldn't remember Kolt saying anything about bedrooms with directions. She was going to ask another question when there was a *ping*. A triangle above the elevator door glowed orange, and the doors slid open.

"Ever been in an elevator, Birdy?" Kolt asked.

The anxious young Keeper shook his head.

"The first ones were steam-powered, and called 'vertical railways.' This one is even more unusual than that."

They all got inside and huddled together, their yellow backpacks touching. The Cave Sprites whizzed in too, more excited than Gertie had ever seen them.

"Eggcup fly?"

"Sort of, yes . . ." Kolt admitted with a gulp.

"So which floor?" Gertie asked, reaching toward the grid of round elevator buttons.

"Doesn't matter," Kolt said, closing his eyes painfully, "any number will do."

"But which level?"

"They all take us to the same place," he said shakily, "just hit any one!"

Gertie chose to push five, but nothing happened.

She pushed it again. "It doesn't work."

"Oh, it works, just keep pushing . . ." Kolt said, wincing, "and hold on!"

"Hold on to what?"

Birdy and Robot Rabbit Boy were looking around innocently. "And why are you making that face?"

"To be honest," Kolt said, closing his eyes even tighter, "I hate this bit! I really do."

"Well," Gertie said smugly, "after that bone canoe ride we took before going to ancient China, I'm prepared for anything, anything at all."

At that exact moment, the elevator floor opened and the four Keepers tumbled silently into darkness, accelerating at a rate of $9.8m/s^2$.

28

Thermal Darts

"AAAAARRGGGGGHHHHHHHH!!!!"

"AAAAARRgggghhhhhhhh!!!!"

"EEEEEGGGGGGCUPPPPPP FFFFFLYYYY!"

"AAAAAARRggggghhhhhh!!!!"

After freefalling for several seconds in total darkness, the Keepers' yellow backpacks were triggered. From each one burst a tiny cluster of yellow smiley-face parachutes, slowing the Keepers just long enough to catch a terrific cross-draft of air, which whipped them into a side tunnel. They were no longer falling, but moving sideways through a dark passage, caught in a fast-moving air thermal that had been sucked in from several holes in the cliff face. The small smiley-face parachutes were swollen with gusting wind, like a cluster of fluorescent jellyfish, with the four Keepers dragging behind in the straps. They were moving too quickly even to scream as the parachutes whistled through the tunnel at over sixty miles per hour.

After thirty seconds or so, the tunnel opened into another vast cavern, and the rushing air weakened quickly. The four Keepers' parachutes went limp and they drifted down onto a bed of soft, springy rescue-mushrooms, which glowed the moment they were touched, lighting up the expansive chamber. All seven Cave Sprites floated down to the mess of Keepers, who were just lying on the enormous patch of fungi, wondering if they were dead, and if heaven was a fluorescent mushroom palace.

"Everybody in one piece?" Kolt said, studying his watch. "Because anything under a minute is good for thermal darts."

"Thermal what?" Gertie cried, wrestling the backpack from her shoulders. The yellow smiley faces now looked like evil shriveled Cave Sprites.

"Racing parachutes from the year 2259," Kolt said with a grin.

Birdy was lying facedown on a mushroom, barely stirring.

Gertie and Robot Rabbit Boy rushed over and tried to sit him up. After a moment he opened his eyes, which were swirling like spirals.

"There's something wrong with Birdy!" Gertie called out.

But Kolt seemed calm. "He's got mushroom-eye, I expect. He must have licked one. . . . Don't worry, it passes quickly."

Once Birdy's eyes were back to normal, Kolt told them to fold their parachutes back into the yellow packs. Then the four Keepers bounced over the glowing mushrooms, and followed the Cave Sprites into the dark mouth of another tunnel.

They chased the glowing balls around several sharp bends, then came to the end of the passageway, where a massive steel door loomed ten feet high. It was bedroom 782 SE.

"Whoa!" said Gertie. "What kind of door is this?"

"The kind that stops robots and high-tech space junk from escaping."

"What about that rocket and those escape pods in the garden?"

Kolt smiled. "Those space rockets are like the Renaissance ships we were on, Gertie, *extremely* primitive— the stuff in here is more high-tech than the Time Cat. It's where I got those Narcissus body suits. You know? The ones that make you disappear because they reflect your surroundings so perfectly?"

Gertie took out her Keepers' key and rattled it into the lock. With one turn, the door opened and a white mist escaped from the cracks.

"It's just the hygiene seal," Kolt said, ushering everyone forward. "In we go . . ."

The Cave Sprites zoomed in first, though the room was already lit by white light in the walls.

"Follow Monday!" Kolt told everyone. "She'll lead us to the item we need to return."

The floor was shiny steel and there were metal shelves with every kind of space contraption Gertie could imagine. She stopped and picked up something that looked like a steel pipe, except that its surface was mirrored.

"What's this?"

"Oh," Kolt said, turning around to examine it, "that's organic dynamite."

"Huh?"

"Just your average thermodynamic hydrogen manipulator."

Gertie put it down very, very gently.

"Don't worry, it's not dangerous here, unless you put it in your mouth of course."

"In my mouth?"

"It can change the temperature of water in a microsecond, which means that if you wanted to split a mountain, you would simply wait for it to rain, then touch any wet surface with the rod, push the snowflake button, and all the water molecules in the mountain would freeze, splitting the rock into thousands of pieces."

"Breaking a whole mountain?" asked the newest Keeper.

"Simply put, Birdy, yes. I'm sure you already knew that water expands when it freezes, and so will smash, crack, or shatter anything that tries to stop it, even solid rock, *anything*."

"So why can't I put it in my mouth?"

"Because it would freeze you, or if you pressed the flame button it would dry you into a shriveled, waterless lump, like a piece of food that fell on the floor, rolled under something, and wasn't discovered for three hundred years."

Bedroom 782 SE was twenty times the size of the Sock Drawer.

"What's that over there?" said Birdy, pointing to a golden cube with neon-colored tubes and flashing wires running along its surface.

But Kolt was too busy following the Cave Sprite. "Probably something useless—let's try and keep up with Monday, gang."

The young sprite soon led them into a scene that can only be described as an electronic nightmare—a sort of tech battlefield. Scattered across the floor were dozens and dozens and dozens of robotic hands—exactly the same ones that had been popping up all over the island of Skuldark.

Some of the hands were wriggling their fingers or tapping idly, while others were palm up and not moving at all. A few of the hands were scampering about holding wires, bumping into things, or wrestling with other robotic hands that appeared to have lost all sense of purpose.

Kolt stood with his mouth open. "What on earth is this charade! I've never seen anything like it!"

"I thought all lost limbs went to that other bedroom?" Gertie asked. "The one we visited where the arm was playing tennis, remember? It was the first night I arrived?"

"Yes, I remember," Kolt said. Then he bent down to inspect a hand. "These must be high-tech or especially dangerous to be in this bedroom. . . ."

Suddenly, one of the robot hands began charging toward Birdy. The young Keeper froze as a gray matted paw appeared from nowhere, booting the hand through the air and onto a low shelf.

"Fly eggcup fly!"

"Thanks, Robot Rabbit Boy—what a scary adventure this is!"

Kolt chuckled. "Just you wait . . ."

29

A Black Hole Muncher

BIRDY SHUDDERED. "IT GETS weirder than this?"

"Fly, butter, mush mush?"

Kolt was still examining the dead robot hand. "Looks like it perished in hand-to-hand combat."

"Ha ha," Gertie said, "please don't tell me we have to return these creepy looking things as well as the robot insect—there are hundreds!"

"Actually, the Cave Sprite seems to think it *is* one of the hands that has to go back. Maybe the robot insect is trapped inside?"

"Like a tiny pilot!"

"Let's pick up a few and have a look."

"Do we have to?" Gertie said. "Isn't there a pair of space tongs in here or something?"

"Grab the live ones by the wrist, you two. They might

be capable of crushing your bones to powder if you get too close to the fingers."

"What are they even used for?" asked Birdy.

"Didn't I tell you? Robot hands were invented in 2048 so that doctors could perform operations on people remotely."

"From far away?"

"Yes, in space actually."

"So they would send the robot hands instead of going themselves?"

"No, the hands would be built where the patient was. Then the doctor would have a 3-D image of the patient, and would perform virtual surgery, while robotic versions of the doctor's hands would be working on the *real* patient, recreating every movement exactly."

"That's impressive," said Birdy, still marveling at all the different gadgets that surrounded them. "Can we keep one?"

"Gross!" Gertie said. "No way! We already have enough upstairs, we're trying to get *rid* of them."

"The hands worked very well," Kolt went on, "unless the Wi-Fi went down mid-operation, then they would just have to make it up—which wasn't ideal as all they could do by themselves was play Rock, Paper, Scissors."

"Let's spread out," Birdy said.

As they fanned out looking for the item to return, Kolt kept talking.

"Hands were initially used as medical tools, but then companies started preprogramming them to build things,"

Kolt explained. "For instance, one hundred thousand robotic limbs could be sent by drone to the South Pole with raw materials. Then four months later, you've got a polar ice station fit for human habitation."

"Who could build so many robotic hands?"

"Other robots of course," Kolt said. "Though it takes humans to program them. Robot hands for medical use were eventually replaced by nanobots—tiny machines that perform surgery while actually inside your body."

"Did it hurt?"

"No, because nanobots are so small, a million of them would fit into a grain of sand. Though the mosquito drones are my favorite, as they were programmed to bite as many people as possible, and by doing so vaccinate them. That led to the eradication of the word's most deadly disease, malaria."

Gertie grimaced. "I wouldn't want little things in my blood, hammering around on my body parts!"

"But you wouldn't even feel them, Gertie! Imagine reading a book while having heart surgery."

"Why is this room so far from the other bedrooms?" Birdy wanted to know.

"Because some of the things in here are highly explosive and troublesome."

"Like the robot hands!" Gertie said scornfully.

"Exactly, now let's find this bug."

"What year are we visiting to return the robot insect?" Gertie asked.

"The B.D.B.U. said it was the twenty-seventh century, 2618 to be exact."

"Which country?"

"Space actually."

"Space?" said Birdy. "Wow."

Gertie surveyed the strange scene before her, as a couple robot hands wrestled like lobsters. "I suppose there are only so many games of Rock, Paper, Scissors you can play before you go insane." But then she had an idea. "Maybe we could train them to look for keys?"

"Interesting concept, and Birdy seems good at mathematics," Kolt said, looking around, "which would come in handy."

But Birdy had wandered back to the golden cube with neon wires he'd seen on the way through the room.

Suddenly he called out to them, "Come and look at this! I think I've found something!"

"Is it the robot insect?" Kolt said as they dashed to the sound of Birdy's voice. But what they found made the previous scene look like a robot-hand kindergarten. Birdy had discovered the mother lode. Fifty or sixty dead hands surrounded by cuttings of wire, metal shavings, black scorch marks, and a large gold cube wrapped with flashing neon wires and tubes.

A few of the dead robot hands were in pieces—and there were burn marks on the fingers.

The most disgusting part of all, Gertie thought, was that a few of the hands had apparently got stuck inside the golden casing when the flashing cube was welded together. Dead gold fingers stuck out from the box in mid-escape.

"I thought you should see this," Birdy said, "because there's a clock on it that seems to be counting down."

But Kolt was already reeling in horror. Gertie had never seen him so afraid.

"IT'S A BOMB!" Kolt screamed. "A BOMB, A BOMB, A BOMB, A BOMB, A BOMB, A BOMB!"

"So not the insect?" said Gertie, confused.

"What is a *bomb* exactly?" Birdy said calmly.

"LAVENDER POTATO?"

"A very, very, very, very unpleasant explosive device! But this is no ordinary bomb," Kolt cried, now frantic at the sight of what Gertie thought resembled a jewelry box gone wrong. "It's a homemade BLACK HOLE MUNCHER!"

"A what?" Gertie said.

"A bomb so powerful that it can disrupt the force of even the most intense gravitational pull—a planet killer!"

"Planet killer!" Gertie thought out loud. "But why is it on Skuldark?"

"Hard to say," Kolt said. "I truly have no idea how it got here."

"The hands must have built it!" said Birdy. "Which is why there are scraps of wire and metal pieces lying around."

Kolt surveyed the debris. "Brilliant thinking, they built it here all right, which is why some of them got stuck in the cube as it was being welded."

"But who would intentionally lose a bunch of these hands with instructions to build a bomb?" Birdy wanted to know.

"Losers!" Gertie said. "With the help of their evil super-computer, Vispoth."

Suddenly, the *gravity* of the situation began to sink in, and Gertie felt panic spread through her arms and legs like freezing water.

"Um, maybe we should see what the time is on the clock?"

They all looked together.

"Three hours and forty-five minutes," Birdy said.

"We have to get it out of here now!" barked Kolt. "I mean off Skuldark! Far away! This kind of mechanism would not only rip a hole in the cliff—it would send most of our island to the bottom of the sea!"

"This little gold box could do that?" gasped Birdy.

Kolt nodded. "The explosion would be so huge, pieces of the cottage and Fern Valley would even get propelled into space by the force of the blow."

"I never thought the Losers would actually try and kill us!" Gertie said, feeling shock and anger that her brother could be involved in such a scheme. Then she imagined Slug Lamps floating around in space like lumps of Jell-O.

"Well, the Losers wouldn't see it as murder, Gertie—to them we were simply caught in the crossfire as they tried to rid the universe of the technology that allowed them to build such a destructive device. That's Loser logic for you. It's a brilliantly devious plan, sending hands one at a time, each programmed to do a certain task."

Suddenly, on one of the robot hands, an ant crawled leisurely into the palm, as though it were out for a stroll.

"Bug!" screamed Gertie.

Kolt grabbed the hand by the wrist and turned it over. "That must be it!" But the hand wasn't dead after all. The fingers went mad with wriggling.

"Quick! Someone go and find a container we can lock this in," he said.

Birdy scrambled over to a shelf crammed with items.

He returned within a few seconds with a clear plastic tub. Kolt placed the hand inside it gently, then put the lid on.

"Look at that!" he marveled, as they stared at the robotic hand through the clear top of the tub. The limb had now gone very still, as if wondering why it was in a box. The insect was on the edge of a finger staring at them.

"I've never seen a robotic ant before," Gertie said. "It looks just like a real one."

"It's not just any robotic ant," Kolt pointed out with a nervous smile, "but the first mechanical insect that will ever go down in history as having saved Skuldark and the entire human race. If it wasn't for that little guy hitching a ride on one of the hands, we would never have come down here and found the Black Hole Muncher."

Birdy whipped a magnifying glass out of his pocket to study the robotic creature.

"Where did you get that?" Gertie asked.

"From my bedroom. It was sitting on the desk."

She turned to Kolt. "How come I didn't get one of those?"

"You got a microscope, Gertie, it's upstairs beside the fax machine."

Birdy looked at the insect through the curved glass. "Its toes are flashing blue."

Kolt was still trying to fit together the pieces of the Losers' plan. "Since Vispoth knows the location of Skuldark from when they stole the B.D.B.U., it must have programmed the hands to come here—but not the ant— that was an accident, a very lucky one for us."

Then they noticed Gertie was sniggering.

"What's so amusing?" demanded Kolt. "We're standing here with an army of evil hands, a robot ant, and a Black Hole Muncher that's going to explode in . . ." Kolt read the numbers on the countdown clock. "Three hours, thirty-nine minutes, and nine seconds—and you're laughing?"

"It's just that the Losers have been defeated this time by an ant!"

"Not yet, they haven't, not until we get this bomb somewhere it can safely explode."

"Like where?" asked Birdy.

Kolt pointed upward. "We have to go to space in the twenty-seventh century anyway, so hopefully we'll be able to find a black hole where it can detonate safely."

"With the Time Cat?" Gertie said, trying to imagine it.

"I'm afraid not, as there's no ground for the car to move on. . . ."

"Correct!" said Birdy. "It's Newton's third law, for every action, there is an equal and opposite reaction—so if you can't push on the ground, it can't push back and you can't move."

"But we can use the time machine to get us to the future, right?" Gertie wanted to know.

"Precisely, but we'll need some kind of spacecraft from down here to get us around once we arrive in 2618."

30

The End of the World (Maybe)

Kolt picked up the Black Hole Muncher and swiftly led his fellow Keepers toward a section of bedroom 782 SE where lost spacecraft were stored. From a distance, most of the ships didn't look like vehicles at all, just silver-and-gold blobs. One reminded Gertie of an oversized Slug Lamp, while another looked like an orange seashell with black spiral patterns running along the outside.

"I've got the time machine and a Keepers' key ready in my pocket," Kolt told them, "so all we need is something super-fast that's capable of manufacturing oxygen and gravity—with solar sails and maybe a hydrogen exchange booster."

"No space suits?" said Gertie, worried she was going on yet another dangerous mission without the chance to change her outfit. Kolt didn't hear or was pretending not to.

When they arrived at the space vehicle Kolt had used before, it was clear the Losers had thought through their plan very carefully. The floor was littered with more dead robot hands, along with wires, glass, shards of metal—and even giant jewels broken into thousands and thousands of pieces. Kolt stared in disbelief at the glittering fragments. "Without diamonds," he sighed, "there's no way to control our use of the speed of light—these spaceships are space junk."

"Didn't you tell me once that the Tunnels of Bodwin lead to space?" Gertie asked.

"Yes, but that's space around Skuldark, not space around Earth in the twenty-seventh century."

Kolt carefully put down the Black Hole Muncher and picked through the useless debris that the robot hands had ripped from the spaceships and destroyed.

"It's no good," he said. "We're done for, I can't fix this, I don't have the tech knowledge."

"We can't give up," said Birdy. "I want to find out who I am. I can't get blown up on my second day here."

Then Gertie had a suggestion. "Could Johnny the Guard Worm tow the bomb out to deep sea and let it explode there?"

"It would rain fish for a week!" Kolt said. "We need to find it a black hole to chew on. A Black Hole Muncher is designed to break apart a mass to lessen its gravitational pull."

"So the explosion is big?"

"Massive!" said Kolt.

"Vispoth!" Gertie nodded. "Only a genius of a computer could have come up with such a plan."

"Why didn't it stick to making hot chocolate!?" snapped Kolt. "WHY!"

"What's chocolate?" asked Birdy. "I've completely forgotton."

Kolt's expression suddenly turned from fear to fierce determination. "We *must* find a way to return the lost robot ant and get this bomb into space—otherwise Birdy will never try my cocoa nib pie with cinnamon crust and custard cream."

Then Gertie remembered something.

"The Russian space rocket in the garden!"

"That tin can! It's falling apart, we'd never make it. . . ."

"But we don't have to blast up into space," Birdy reminded them. "Just travel through time and appear there, right? Surely one of those rockets could withstand a bit of floating?"

Kolt grimaced. "Well, I suppose there's a tiny, tiny chance that it might work."

"How tiny?"

Kolt thought for a moment. "Smaller than the robotic ant's blue flashing toenail when it was a baby."

"Seriously?"

"How should I know?" Kolt said. "You haven't seen the state of that rocket. It's rusted through!"

"It's still a chance," said Birdy, holding his magnifying glass to an egg-shaped piece of metal on the floor.

"Eggcup mush dollop butter lavender potato, mashed."

"You're right, Robot Rabbit Boy, this is all we've got," Kolt said reluctantly. "So let's do it—let's get this Muncher back into space where it belongs—but let's take as many of these trouble-making hands with us as we can so they can't build anything else . . . just to be on the safe side."

"We can stuff them into the yellow backpacks," said Birdy.

"Eek! We have to touch them?" Gertie said. "Can't I carry the bomb instead?"

"No!"

"Can I just pick up the dead ones then?"

Kolt gave her a stern look. "The dead ones can stay behind, it's the live ones we need to get rid of. And if we survive this," he told them, "and that's a big 'if,' then I'm going to come back down here and set growler traps for the ones we can't take."

A SHORT TIME LATER, with as many of the live robot hands as they could carry wriggling about in the yellow backpacks, the worn-out Keepers began climbing the round, metal staircase that would take them up to ground level. Gertie wasn't thrilled with the prospect of having to climb yet another set of steps, as they must have been miles and miles from the cottage. She was still exhausted from their afternoon ascent in the rain from the beach. And she could feel the hands scrabbling around in her backpack.

"This is so gross!" she said. "I'm okay with most things, but wriggling robot hands really freak me out."

"Maybe this is all some kind of dream," Birdy told her, "though I would certainly miss you if I woke up."

"I thought it was a dream too when I first arrived," Gertie said, "but then I woke up and was still here."

"Weird," Birdy said, struggling under the weight of robot hands in his backpack.

THEY FINALLY ARRIVED AT a large metal door. Kolt opened it with his Keepers' key and they went through into a dark room.

"I don't believe it!" Gertie said, looking around at the fireplace, the long table, and the tapestry on the wall. Kolt lit some candles, and light filled the room. They had come through the door that said EXIT ONLY, and were back in the Gate Keepers' Lodge near the Line of Stones.

When George came flying out of her hole, it gave Birdy quite a fright. She stood up on her back legs and squeaked quickly at Kolt.

"Yes, yes," he explained. "This is indeed a new Keeper. His name is Birdy—but he's not yours I'm afraid, though you've done an excellent job of tidying up."

George squeaked angrily.

"When you saw him it got your hopes up?"

The mouse nodded.

"Well, we can't discuss it now, George, we need to get a bomb into Earth space in the year 2618, so . . ."

George squeaked.

"You want to come with us?"

The mouse pulled down both her eyelids.

"You're bored here?"

George nodded *yes*, that she was, indeed, extremely bored.

"But . . ." Kolt said, "this is a life-or-death mission!"

George squeaked again, and saluted Kolt and the other Keepers.

"I know you're brave . . . how about once we get rid of this bomb we'll come and get you. Maybe you can live in the cottage with us as a house mouse, at least until we find you a new Gate Keeper?"

George clapped her paws together with excitement.

"That is . . ." Kolt whispered to Gertie and Birdy, "if we make it back."

ONCE THEY HAD CLIMBED the steps to the secret stone doorway, Gertie peeked out to make sure there were no tapirs, then gave the other Keepers the all-clear.

In the fresh air, they tore off their heavy yellow backpacks and collapsed onto a patch of rough grass and weeds, sweating and exhausted. Gertie felt her body relax after shedding the weight, and the wind was soothing and cool on her warm skin.

"Everyone breathe!" Kolt said, sucking down mouthfuls of cool Skuldarkian wind. "Brrreeeeaaaathe."

"What now?" Gertie said. "That bomb clock is still ticking and we're almost a day's walk from the cottage—we'll blow up by the time we get back to the garden."

"It could always be worse," Kolt said, staring at the bomb, and the small plastic tub with the hand and the insect in it.

But then it got worse.

"Look!" cried Birdy. The robot hands had torn through the yellow fabric of the backpacks and were escaping into the tall grass where they would be impossible to find.

"Oh no!" shouted Kolt. "We can't let them escape; they'll go right back to bedroom 782 SE and make another bomb!"

Everyone got up and chased after the despicable limbs. But no matter how quickly the exhausted Keepers ran, they couldn't keep up with the mischievous hands. Soon, they all lay on the grass, doubled over with exhaustion.

Gertie was starting to feel afraid now. She couldn't think of one single thing that might save them from the Black Hole Muncher's explosive wrath. Within a few hours, they would either be dead, or lost somewhere in time without a home to return to.

She wondered if the Losers had finally succeeded in their quest to destroy the Keepers of Lost Things. And to think that her own brother might have been a part of it. She thought they had been making progress by rescuing a Keeper, and felt certain they could rescue more. But they had all underestimated the Losers. They'd managed to bring Birdy here, but he was going to die. They were supposed to be the Keepers of Lost Things, the guardians of objects. . . . *Wait that's it!* Gertie thought, interrupting herself.

"Kolt, Kolt!"

The old Keeper sat up quickly.

"The Guardians of Skuldark you were telling me about! Remember the moth who guided us when Robot Rabbit Boy was lost? Those creatures who come together to protect our island. Can they help us? How do we call them?"

"Gertie, that's it! They're our ticket home!" he said. "There's only one way to summon them. Quick, everyone, on your feet, take out your Keepers' keys!"

They did as instructed, except Robot Rabbit Boy, who didn't have one and seemed embarrassed.

"Mush . . . room?"

"Share mine!" Gertie said, and he reached out a paw so they were holding it together.

"Now listen carefully," Kolt instructed, "if you look directly into the barrel, you'll see a small hole. Follow what I do," he said, and raised the key slowly to his lips. "Blow into the hole in the key!"

Gertie, Birdy, Kolt, and Robot Rabbit Boy exhaled with great force through the tiny hole in the keys.

The sound was tremendous, as though every bird in the world had begun to sing at the same moment. Gertie wanted to cover her ears it was so loud, such a mess of whistles and chirps.

"Catch your breath!" Kolt shouted. "But keep blowing!"

The "Music of the Guardians" call wrapped around the island, soon heard by every living creature, from the biggest to the smallest—even those spirit animals composed of light and shadow, ancient creatures as old as time itself.

When Kolt stopped blowing, the other Keepers lowered their keys too, panting for breath.

"What . . . was . . . that?" asked Birdy.

Kolt smiled. "You're about to find out. Now, prepare yourselves, for what you are about to see may shock you."

31

The Guardians of Skuldark

"THAT SOUND WE MADE was a distress call to the Guardians of Skuldark."

"Who are they?" asked Birdy.

"All creatures on Skuldark possess some magical ability," Kolt explained, "but there is one every generation who is chosen to be the Guardian, either for its strength, speed, agility, intelligence—or even good judgment."

"And we just summoned them!" Gertie said proudly, noticing a faint rumbling under her feet.

"Brace yourselves!" Kolt said, as the air vibrated with a low buzz, accompanied by the sounds of snapping tree branches from far across the prairie, in the depths of Fern Valley.

"What's that thudding?" said Birdy, his eyes growing with alarm. Everyone spread their feet for balance as the ground trembled.

Within a few moments, dark lumps appeared on the horizon.

"Here they come," Kolt said.

"What will happen when they get here?" Gertie wanted to know.

"Er, I have no idea. I've never summoned them before, and to be honest, had my doubts it would even work."

Then they heard a high-pitched buzzing, as though a giant swarm of flies were approaching.

"Attercoppes?" said Gertie, as the noise intensified.

"Attercoppes, tapirs, every living thing!" Kolt cried. "But don't worry, when the Guardians are summoned, it is for the good of the island—and creatures normally dangerous to Keepers will do no harm, as we unite against a common enemy!"

Then the ground in front of them actually tore open as a brown, hairy dog-like creature with the head of a horse and bright red glowing eyes appeared from the earth. After shaking the soil off, it stood there shooting a string-like tongue in and out of its mouth, staring at the four Keepers.

Kolt bowed. "Welcome, Orispian Tunneler!"

Then from the sky came a dark figure, which hovered over their heads. It was a spider the size of a cat, with buzzing black leathery wings and glossy eyes moving in all directions. In the distance, high up in the sky, Attercoppes from every hive on the island hovered in close ranks, awaiting their queen's command.

"Greetings to you, queen of the arachnids, ferocious

Attercoppe," Kolt said, nodding in homage. Gertie gulped, and decided to bow too—just to be on the safe side.

Then a familiar sight came thundering toward them across the grassy plain, its hooves tearing up the soft earth, its white mane bouncing with each gyrating muscle.

"Noble Tapir," Kolt shouted, raising his arms in greeting.

Then another animal broke up through the ground beside the hairy dog-like one. It was a clear earthworm, but inside its transparent ringed skin was actual fire.

"Warm blessings, Night Blazer, ancient ancestor to all creatures of luminosity."

Then an innocent-looking yellow bird landed on Birdy's shoulder.

"My old friend," said Kolt, "the Northern-Spotted Blade." Gertie looked at the bird closely, noticing knife-like yellow feathers that extended past its body and were dotted with red specks she hoped weren't blood.

Birdy turned to smile, and the bird chirped and ruffled its wings.

Then a larger-than-usual Slug Lamp appeared. Robot Rabbit Boy stepped forward personally to welcome it.

"Lavender mush room butter cup eggs!"

The Slug Lamp seemed to understand what he meant and wriggled its sluggy body.

Soon, the four Keepers of Lost Things were surrounded by creatures of all colors, sizes, habits, and moods—Gertie even saw one of the white dodo birds she had befriended that very first morning on Skuldark.

Kolt turned to his fellow Keepers. "Don't be afraid," he said, "but there are also invisible animals here, and even a creature made entirely of gas called a Psss-Psss-Psss, which eats its victims from the inside after being inhaled."

With all the Guardians present, Kolt raised his arms to address the group. Gertie had never heard him take on such a commanding tone. She started to realize how powerful a Keeper Kolt was—even if most of the time he played the fool.

"Skuldarkians . . . thank you . . ." he said, "for heeding the Guardians' music, the ancient song to bind beast of land to creatures of air, magic mist to unseen mite, dutiful Keeper to the shadow jackdaws of Ravens' Peak. I salute each one of you in this moment of much-needed friendship, when our home is threatened with annihilation."

"How do they know what Kolt is saying?" Birdy whispered. Gertie explained that the language of Skuldark was understood by every living creature, though understanding the animals themselves took a bit of practice.

Kolt told the Guardians they had to get across the island to the cottage on the cliff as quickly as possible, along with the Black Hole Muncher, the plastic tub with the robot ant, and the robot hands they had brought—which must be found at all costs. That wasn't all. Gertie listened as Kolt went on to say that until the Keepers returned to Skuldark from this mission, the noble creatures must guard every entrance to the secret passages of their worlds, from the Tunnels of Bodwin to the moon shadows that form doorways on the snow.

"And should we NOT return, my friends," Kolt went on, holding up his Keepers' key, "then any person or creature who arrives not in possession of this object, this ancient talisman of our sacred home, you must ravage, stamp, suffocate, and sting, until new Keepers come and order is restored."

"Smush fly," whispered Robot Rabbit Boy, gazing down at the Slug Lamp, who blinked one eye in understanding.

ONCE KOLT HAD FINISHED his call to arms, there was a great buzzing, shuffling of hooves, and flapping of wings as the many creatures moved in all different directions in a bid to fulfill their sacred tasks.

"That seemed to go well," Kolt said cheerfully as they watched Attercoppes descend upon the fields in search of the escaped robot hands.

"You sounded great," Gertie told him. "Totally convincing."

"Are you being sarcastic?"

"No! It was a good speech."

"Well, thanks. Do you remember hearing it before?"

"No, how could I?"

"Because I sort of copied it from the insect pirate movie."

"What's the plan now?" Birdy interrupted, noticing the digital clock on the bomb still counting down.

"The Guardians will choose which of you they will carry across the island to the Garden of Lost Things," Kolt explained. "Let's meet up at the rockets when we get there.

Just remember to hold on tight, and put all your trust in our noble friends, no matter which route they take to get us home."

"Which route?" Birdy said. "Isn't there only one quickest way?"

"You'll see . . ." said Kolt, as a tapir came right up to him. Kolt grabbed a few strands of the creature's ropey mane, and pulled himself onto the animal's back.

Birdy was chosen by the Orispian Tunneler, who embraced the young Keeper in its furry, dog-like paws, then disappeared quickly into the earth with the boy firmly in its grasp.

Robot Rabbit Boy couldn't have been happier when he discovered his Guardian to be the Queen of Slug Lamps. Robot Rabbit Boy got on her back, and within seconds they inched off quickly.

With the other Keepers already returning to the cottage, Gertie thought she'd been forgotten. But then there was a great billowing of air behind her, and she turned to see a gigantic white moth with a furry body the size of a sheep, with wings the length of her Spitfire. The insect's eyes were round and black—two shiny balls in which Gertie could see herself reflected. Rising up from its head were long antennae, like two feathers, that sensed even the tiniest vibrations in the air.

The giant moth rolled its body to one side so that Gertie could climb onto its back. It was very soft, and she held on by gripping thick tufts of moth fur. With a single flap of its powdery wings, they were in the air, fluttering high over the plains until they were caught by a current of wind that took them sailing toward the cottage.

Although Gertie had been up in a 1940s Spitfire airplane and a 1920s Halton Mayfly, flying on the back of a living creature was a completely different experience. It was as though her heart was joined to the creature's heart. They were united in trust, gliding over an ocean of blowing trees and meadows. Gertie wanted to pet the creature, even try and speak to it—but the force of the wind was so immense, she was afraid of rolling off its back and falling to earth.

The moth used its wings for balance, fluttering only when it needed to keep them in the current of air. The creature's body was warm beneath the fur, and the higher they went, the tighter Gertie held on—even using her legs to grip the insect's body as if it were a giant cushion.

After a few minutes, Gertie could see the tower where the B.D.B.U. lived. They came down slowly in circles near the Spitfire on Turweston Passage, and hovered over the ground near the tree of scarves. Gertie let go and slid through the thick fur, tumbling a few feet to the grass with a bump.

The creature continued beating its wings, watching Gertie through its black bulbous eyes. "Thank you, moth!" she shouted, and the creature waved its comblike antennae. And then, with a tremendous beating of its wings, it ascended into a gust of wind and disappeared over the cliff.

But when Gertie turned toward the cottage, she got a horrible shock. It seemed to be moving. She blinked hard and looked again. The walls and the roof were literally *moving*.

32

The Battle to Save the Cottage

HUNDREDS AND HUNDREDS OF robot hands covered the cottage, and were picking it apart. Gertie could hear them scuttling and snapping bits off as they tried to pull the house down, piece by piece. In the distance, she could see her friends bashing at them with things from the garden. Kolt was holding an oar, while Birdy had some kind of medieval lance. Robot Rabbit Boy was hurling moonberries, which were just bouncing off. But this gave Gertie an idea.

About five or six minutes later, as the robot hands were lifting off an entire section of roof, there was an almighty thrumming in the sky—like a thousand angry lawn mowers. Kolt, Birdy, and Robot Rabbit Boy turned quickly to see a fighter aircraft diving toward the cottage—all Rolls-Royce Merlin engines roaring like thunder.

From the cockpit of the aircraft, Gertie could see her

friends jumping up and down. The aircraft rattled and shook with the speed of her dive. When she was within a hundred yards, Gertie checked her altitude and airspeed, then pushed hard on the firing button. The Browning machine guns screamed as over a hundred frozen moonberries crackled through the air, exploding upon impact. Any robot hands caught by a direct hit were smashed to pieces, while the others were splattered with winter moonberry juice, which instantly fried their circuits.

Gertie passed over the cliff, climbed steadily, then banked her aircraft to come round for another pass. Kolt, Robot Rabbit Boy, and Birdy were now waving their hands and paws in the air, cheering her on. Gertie lined up the cottage in her sights, then slowed her airspeed and let rip with another barrage of frozen moonberries, pummeling the robot hands and flooding their electronic brains with every Keeper's favorite fizzy drink.

After a fifth run, and then a sixth, Gertie saw the high-tech limbs on one of the walls scramble down to the grass in a bid to get away. Gertie dove upon the cottage from a different direction, cutting off their escape, then firing mercilessly upon the nasty things. Bits of thumb and finger flew into the air. The remaining limbs then turned and scrambled off the cliff to avoid being obliterated by the deadly rain of fruit.

When Gertie noticed she was running low on fuel, she opened her glass hatch against the rushing wind and waved to her friends. When she noticed the gold, flashing Black Hole Muncher at Kolt's feet, she brought her aircraft around for an immediate landing.

The three other Keepers rushed over as she touched down on Turweston Passage. Birdy was most excited. Not only had Gertie saved their home from robot limbs, but he had seen the flying machine in action.

"I never imagined frozen moonberries could be so useful!" Kolt said. "That was the best food fight I've ever seen."

The cottage was literally dripping with moonberry juice.

"Sorry about the mess, Kolt."

"Mush."

"Oh, I wouldn't worry about that, the Slug Lamps have already started licking it off—their tongues will be purple for the next year."

As they hurried back to the garden, Kolt showed Gertie how they had imprisoned a few dozen robot hands in some old lobster cages. Some of the limbs had formed fists and were banging against the bars to be let out.

"This Russian rocket ship is our only chance now," Kolt said as they rushed over to it. "But the problem is all the rivets are rusted through, which means the moment we arrive in space, it'll fall apart, and we'll just be floating there."

"Won't we have space suits on?" Gertie said, remembering that she'd seen them in a case at the back of the Sock Drawer.

"Yes, but they don't have much oxygen."

Gertie checked the tub. Inside, the insect was happily perched on a robot finger, napping.

"We'll just have to hold our breaths then," she said, but secretly hoped Birdy might think of something. "Whom are we returning the ant to?"

"A Doctor Brady, who lives on some space station."

"Who is Doctor Brady?"

"No idea...except I do remember there was a Brady who invented pollination drones to replace honey bees killed by pesticides."

"Is there a chance the space station is the Losers' headquarters?"

"Oh dear, I hadn't thought of that," Kolt said, "but it makes sense, if it's where the hands have been coming from."

"My brother might be there!"

"Whatever *that's* worth..." Kolt said.

Gertie knew he was right. This might have been her brother's idea. She didn't know. She felt further from him than she ever had and it scared her.

"Listen," Kolt said, "returning the ant and getting rid of these annoying hands is easy—it's the bomb that's our real dilemma."

"Because we need a black hole," said Birdy.

"Not only a black hole," said Kolt. "I'm afraid there's more."

"What now?"

"Dollop butter."

"We also need a spaceship that can get us out of the black hole's gravitational pull, as we don't want to get pulled in...."

"How strong is the force of attraction?" asked Birdy.

"Quite strong."

"Like how strong?" Gertie wanted to know.

"It's sort of the strongest force in the known universe times a million."

They all spun around with grave expressions to the rusting tin-can spaceship, which Gertie thought looked like an expensive garbage can that had been rolled down a mountain and then left to decay in a pit of slime.

"Maybe I could try and use Newton's laws, to calculate the pull of a black hole?" Birdy said, noticing some faded charts and diagrams on the sides of the rocket ship. He pointed them out and they all went for a closer look. When Gertie leaned in to examine some dirt on one of the diagrams, three aluminum panels fell to the grass with a clatter.

"How is it going to resist the gravitational pull of a black hole if it can't even resist the force of us looking at it!" Gertie said.

"Wait a minute . . ." said Birdy, who was still studying the faded charts, "these are Newton's three Laws of Motion, and there's an equation that represents Newton's Law of Universal Gravitation . . . plus some kind of formula for something called the speed of light from a guy called Einstein, which is $3.0 \times 10^8 \, \text{m/s} \ldots$"

"I returned his slippers once, old Albert Einstein. He gave me half his sandwich and a glass of milk. Such a nice man. Did you know he could play the violin?"

"Focus!" Gertie cried. "What about Skuldarkian seawater? To give us the thrust we would need."

"Couldn't hurt to try," Kolt said. "I'll fill up the rocket's tanks. Gertie, go to the Sock Drawer and bring back four space suits, please, and hurry. Robot Rabbit Boy, stand guard on those lobster traps!"

"Lavender!"

"Birdy, come with me inside this rocket. We're going to power it up with Skuldarkian seawater and get you working with the onboard computer."

"Okay," said Birdy. "But what's a computer?"

"Ooh, well, just imagine a picture that can change every few seconds, and that's connected to a nonhuman brain with the ability to calculate things quickly with total precision, but without any emotion whatsoever."

"But how is Birdy going to help us if this is the first computer he's ever used?" Gertie said, still looking at the dilapidated wreck of their spacecraft.

"Are you still here?" Kolt snapped.

"Are we really going to travel through time and into space in this bucket?"

"It was your idea!" Kolt said. "Now please go and get the space suits while Birdy and I tap into this old Soviet computer and get the thing functioning again. If the mainframe has an artificial intelligence option in the form of a remote transmitter, we might even be able to reprogram the robot hands we trapped. . . ."

"Reprogram them to do what?" Birdy and Gertie asked together.

"To hold this piece of space junk together so I can put my key in the time machine and we can disappear in a cosmic mist, travel to the twenty-seventh century, and save humanity, *again*."

33

The Oppenheimer-Bruno Biosphere

WITH ABOUT NINETY MINUTES left on the Black Hole Muncher before it exploded, there was no time for Birdy and Kolt to go searching for the rocket's manuals in the maze of bedrooms under the cottage.

Kolt poured forty gallons of Skuldarkian seawater into the fuel cell, and the old rocket ship came alive with flickering light panels and a banging from the engine—which Kolt said was the old space-timing belt. With the interior computer powered up, Birdy went to work. Their only hope was for Birdy to use his existing knowledge of math and physics and look for patterns in the faded chart of numbers on the rocket ship's old panels, then try different passwords to unlock the computer's operating system.

The bomb clock now read sixty-eight minutes and fourteen seconds.

"I can't guess the password!" Birdy said.

"Try *Chicken Kiev*," said Kolt.

But it didn't work.

"How about *Tetris* then?"

"Zilch."

"*Snow*?"

"Nothing."

"Well, how about *Rachmaninoff*?"

"What if we just try *password*?" Birdy suggested.

Kolt scoffed. "Don't be ridiculous, no one is going to use *password* as their password." But when Birdy tried it, the computer made a pleasant ding and Birdy entered the mainframe.

"Must be some kind of scientist humor!" Kolt said. On the screen was an electronic drawing of the rocket itself, and in one corner a robot hand.

"Look," said Kolt, "the computer has remotely picked up the robot hands' frequency."

Birdy moved the cursor with an old control wheel, and then Kolt showed him how to click on the hand icon. Once inside the robot limb's brain, Birdy figured out the pattern of code, then reprogrammed the hands to hold the ship together, with each hand grasping a main panel.

Kolt was stunned. "So we can open the lobster cages? They won't run away?"

"I don't know," Birdy said. "But I've done my best."

Kolt gave the signal and Robot Rabbit Boy flipped up the latches, one by one. Immediately, the horrible things began scampering toward the rocket, as Birdy had programmed them to do.

When Gertie got back with the space suits, Kolt gushed with praise for the new Keeper. "Birdy has hacked into the ship's computer and the robot hands' mainframe, reprogramming them to hold the ship together."

"I really like computers!" Birdy said. "It's like having a pet super brain."

"Eggcup."

"That's nice!" Gertie said. "But how long before the bomb goes off?"

"Butter fly."

"Sixty-one minutes now!" Kolt gasped. "That's just over an hour to travel through time into space, return a robot ant, potentially outsmart the Losers, find a black hole, locate a new ship to escape the black hole's gravitational pull, have lunch, get rid of the most powerful bomb ever made, and make it back—I don't suppose you remembered to get Bubble Wrap, did you, Gertie?"

"No!" Gertie snapped. "Did you even tell me to get Bubble Wrap?"

"What's Bubble Wrap?" asked Birdy.

"A dollop of mashed potato?"

"Well, there's no time now! We have to go!" said Kolt.

The robot hands were in place, holding the space rocket together. Kolt carefully carried in the bomb. Then the four Keepers climbed into their space suits, and got into the old vinyl seats of the rocket.

Thankfully, Gertie had managed to locate a baby space suit for Robot Rabbit Boy, who was perhaps wondering why only *his* helmet was decorated with teddy bears floating in zero gravity beside asteroids made of fruit and birthday cake slices.

"Don't lower your helmet visors until I put my key in the time machine," Kolt instructed. "You don't want to start the flow of oxygen until we're seconds away from our destination—which is a space station the Losers might be using as a hideaway, or it might be deep space if they've laid yet another trap for us."

"What are these Losers like?" Birdy said. "I'm worried."

"They're more pathetic than scary," Gertie said. "Though I don't think I've ever seen their leader, Cava Calla Thrax."

Then she turned to check that they had the box with the robot ant, and that the Black Hole Muncher was safely strapped to a cargo frame at the back of the rocket ship.

"Now everybody link up," Kolt said seriously, "and close your helmets. This is going to be the most dangerous mission we've ever undertaken—so summon every ounce of your courage. We've got less than an hour to save our home and get rid of this stupid bomb."

"And robot ant."

"Mush room."

The Keepers checked and double-checked the straps of their launch seats, then joined arms. Kolt fed his key into the time machine. With a quick pop, several jerks, and a lingering green mist, they disappeared from the Garden of

Lost Things, leaving behind a rash of empty lobster cages, a damaged cottage covered in fruit juice, and a light patch of grass under the rocket ship, home to earthworms, cliff ants, and a family of long-legged spiders.

When Gertie opened her eyes, she had a pounding headache and felt like throwing up. She was also looking through a dirty spaceship window at a tiny blue speck in the distance.

"Is that . . . ?"

"Earth 2618," Kolt said, the inside of his glass visor misting up. "Don't talk, Gertie—uses oxygen!" Then he looked out the window.

"No . . . sign . . . space . . . station . . . you?"

The others went to look, but it was just stars.

Then an enormous panel from the spaceship floated past the window with a robot hand still clinging to it. Gertie looked behind her to check the cargo. The bomb was still safely strapped down with no signs of damage—but the plastic lid had come off the tub, freeing the hand and lost insect, which were both floating about the cabin. The ant was now sitting up very straight in the palm of the robot hand, like some miniature insect god.

When Kolt noticed what had happened, he unstrapped himself, and floated out of his seat.

"Blast!" he yelled inside his helmet, swimming his arms and legs without going anywhere.

Birdy opened the front of his visor slowly, sending Kolt into paroxysms of panic. "EXHALE! EXHALE!" he cried to the young Keeper, waiting for the swelling to begin as water in Birdy's body began to vaporize in the vacuum of space. But Birdy just smiled. Kolt opened his visor too with a look of pure delight.

"You pressurized the cabin! How?"

"I asked Robot Rabbit Boy to seal the cracks with crushed moonberries I knew would freeze into a sealing paste in the vacuum of space," Birdy said.

"Brilliant!" said Gertie. "You're going to be a great Keeper." Then she sniffed. "Space smells like . . . burnt metal, weird!"

Kolt was more than impressed with Birdy's thinking ahead. "I've been a Keeper a long time, and it didn't even occur to me that moonberries would be useful in outer space."

Birdy looked confused. "I thought that's why they were called moonberries?"

"Ha ha, very funny," Kolt said, taking deep breaths of the metallic air while trying to glide over to the floating hand with the ant on it. "Any rocket power?"

"None," Birdy said. "And the robot hands will only last another seventeen minutes before they cease to function."

"If only we'd given them gloves! There are so many just laying around in the Sock Drawer, I'm sick of looking at them." Kolt sighed.

"What about the bomb?" asked Gertie. "If we can only survive in this old ship for another seventeen minutes, is that long enough to get rid of it?"

"We need a nice round, juicy black hole," said Kolt,

"and a sparkly new spacecraft with a mini-refrigerator and massage seats, and of course a space station to return the mechanical insect...."

They all looked at the creature, which was just sitting there rubbing his face with his tiny feet, perhaps wanting to look presentable after realizing they were trying to take him home.

Suddenly the old spacecraft's radio crackled to life.

"This is Oppenheimer-Bruno Biosphere Station I-8-PP, please identity yourselves, over."

Gertie pointed to the radio excitedly. "We're not alone up here after all!"

"Which is good news?" Birdy asked apprehensively.

"Great news!" cried Kolt. "This is the space station where we're supposed to be." He pushed a black button and spoke clearly into the microphone.

"Hello I-8-PP! We're the Skuldark Express ... Ant Station Rocket Power Moonberry, requesting assistance, over!"

"Roger that, Skuldark-Ant Station-Moonberry, but we have no record of your flight path, and can't find you on 4-D database, confirm assistance level, over."

"Well ... our spaceship is held together by robot hands and smashed fruit—so assistance level pretty high, over."

The radio went silent.

"We're not sure we understand your position, Ant Station, over?" said the perplexed voice. "You said *fruits*, over?"

"No, fruit, singular, moonbe—"

Then Gertie interrupted. "Listen—we've got fifteen

minutes before our spaceship breaks apart and we all die and it's over, over."

"Roger that, we're going to pull you in now, release any hold lock, over."

"Pull us in? Over?"

"Confirmed. Station dock 483 opening now, over."

"Er, where are you exactly, over?" Kolt asked.

There was a silence again, which meant Kolt had asked something that would have been obvious to real astronauts.

"Have you looked out your rear window, over?"

The three Keepers released their harnesses and floated to the back of the ship. Through a grubby round window, they gasped at the sight of the enormous Oppenheimer-Bruno Biosphere Station I-8-PP, which looked like eighteen sports stadiums, each with a glass dome. At the top of each rounded dome were enormous silver panels Kolt said were solar sails—or photon nets, bright and blazing hot as they harvested light particles from the sun.

"We're saved!" cried Kolt.

"For now . . ." Gertie sighed. "Should we tell them there's a giant bomb on board?"

Kolt thought for a moment. "I wouldn't . . . maybe let's drop it into the conversation later over lunch or something."

"But we only have fifty-one minutes left!" Birdy reminded them, rather desperately.

"Hmmm, that's not long at all, is it; let's hope it's buffet style, as a whole sit-down thing might . . ."

"Kolt!" Gertie said. "Focus!"

"Yes, of course." He blushed. "No munching until we've gotten rid of the Muncher."

They all stared at the mammoth space station as their tin-can spacecraft moved slowly toward the dock, pulled in by a beam of blue light.

"What are all those weird glass domes?" asked Gertie.

"It's a biosphere station," said Kolt. "A re-creation of certain ecosystems on Earth that allow people to live with the air and light they need. This is probably a prototype, a test model, because the first commercial one was a thousand times larger—so this would be considered a baby."

Kolt said the four biggest glass domes were probably rain forest, wetland, grassland, and ocean reef.

"They'll have all kinds of life in them," Kolt went on. "A mixture of plants and insects to create the right balance of gasses for breathing, and the recycling of waste of course, and the production of two hydrogen atoms and one oxygen atom, to form a covalent bond known as water, H_2O."

"There are names for the particles that make up gasses!" said Birdy. "I remember now!"

"If you think that's impressive, wait until you see my collection of periodic tables," bragged Kolt.

Gertie rolled her eyes. "How about we put nerd-fest on hold for the next . . ." She floated back to look at the bomb's digital clock. ". . . forty-seven minutes."

"Yes, yes, good thinking," Kolt said.

"Any idea who these space people are? Losers maybe?" asked Gertie.

"Probably not Losers," Kolt said, "but be on your guard."

"Could the ant be from one of the glass domes—maybe the rain forest?" added Birdy.

"Exactly," said Kolt, "it has to be. Once we dock, keep your eyes open for any sign of *Doll Head*. Hopefully we'll find this Doctor Brady."

"Mush room," said Robot Rabbit Boy, who all this time had been staring at the robot ant.

"Maybe we should split up?" Gertie suggested as they entered the bright blue docking mouth. "Birdy and I will return the ant, while you and Robot Rabbit Boy get information about the nearest black hole."

"Good idea," Kolt said. "The captain will probably want to see us, as we're not registered as visitors."

"What about the robot hands?" Gertie said. "Will they start causing trouble once we're docked?"

"Not likely," Birdy said seriously. "They'll never regain normal function."

Gertie pretended to look upset. "You mean you killed them?"

Birdy's cheeks flushed red. "Well, er, I, er . . ."

Gertie grinned. "I'm only joking!"

They landed with a clunk on the docking platform, and several of the hands dropped to the deck of the space station. The panels they had been holding fell outward, leaving three gaping holes in the spaceship.

The biosphere technicians who'd been sent down to the docking platform just stared.

"Hello," Gertie said. "We like your domes."

"Eggcup fly, eggcup dollop."

Then Gertie heard a splat and looked down. The crushed moonberries had melted, and were dropping in blobs from the cracks of their spaceship.

One of the technicians, a tall man in glasses, was wearing a white lab coat and holding an electronic pad. He wrote things on it with his finger. Long dreadlocks of hair cascaded down his back.

"Doctor Echlin," he said, stepping over a purple puddle to extend his hand. "Call me Ishmael."

"Have we met before?" laughed Kolt nervously, stepping from the wreckage of their collapsing space rocket. "That name sounds quite familiar."

While the appearance of Robot Rabbit Boy didn't surprise the space station crew, Dr. Echlin and his fellow scientists stared in disbelief at what to them was a spaceship older than the oldest ones in any of the museums on Earth (or the famous museum on the Earth-extension-moon Alpha, also known as MeeMA for short).

"If it's okay with you," Kolt said, "we'll leave our ship here to, um, cool down, and come back for our very important cargo a bit later."

"What type of cargo?" Dr. Echlin asked.

"Um, well . . ." said Kolt, covering his mouth, "that would be a COUGH COUGH COUGH, excuse me, I have a dry throat . . . too much talking in space I suspect . . ."

The technicians looked at each other.

Gertie nudged Birdy, who was leaning against one of the ship's crooked panels. "Look inside," she whispered to him, "and see how long it says we have on the bomb clock."

"I just looked a minute ago," Birdy said. "Forty-two minutes. And by the way, why would they put a clock on it? Seems like a waste of time to me."

"Good one," Gertie said. "Waste of *time.*"

Dr. Echlin cleared *his* throat so that all the Keepers were paying attention. "The captain wants to see you immediately."

Then Gertie had an idea. "Oh!" she cried. "Look!" Everyone looked. On the floor, still sitting in the palm of his host hand, was the ant.

"An insect!" she said. "Could it have come from a forest under one of the glass domes?"

"Oh my!" cried Dr. Echlin. "This is a clear breach of protocol. I don't know how, but it must have escaped its biosphere." He turned to one of the technicians standing with him. "Doctor Brady, get this precious creature back into its dome world, check its vitals, and send the forest techs to my office immediately."

"Wow, Doctor Brady, can I go with you?" Birdy blurted out, still trying to follow Gertie's plan.

"Um, why?" Dr. Echlin questioned.

"Because he's a doctor," Kolt interjected. "I know he might look young, but this child is the famous Doctor Seuss."

Dr. Echlin scratched his chin. "That name does sound familiar to me. Has he written any books?"

"Many," said Kolt. Birdy nodded and tried to look doctorish.

"Well, if Doctor Brady doesn't mind," Dr. Echlin said.

Dr. Brady seemed friendly. "I'd actually appreciate the company!"

"Fine, but the captain wants to see the rest of you pronto," Dr. Echlin went on.

Gertie nodded to Birdy that it was okay for him to go alone. She figured he could oversee the return of the ant by himself, and keep a lookout for Losers.

Dr. Echlin led the three other Keepers away from the wreckage of their ship to a floating white couch.

"Please get on the courtesy cushion," Dr. Echlin instructed.

Gertie whispered into Kolt's ear, "We should ask the captain where the nearest black hole is!"

Kolt nodded. "Let's meet the captain first."

"Wow!" Gertie said, as the levitating furniture began to massage her back. "This is the most comfortable couch ever...."

"Yeah..." Kolt said, rubbing at one of the cushions, "but I don't like the fabric at all. Imagine trying to get stains out of this!"

34

Space Muffins

THE COUCH WHISKED THEM silently through bright glass hallways and mirrored doors. When they arrived at the entrance to the captain's navigation suite, the floating piece of furniture slowed down. Soft music played through the cushions as the three Keepers were sprayed with a citrus "welcome mist."

The captain's lounge was a glass bubble, a giant blister that looked out at the dazzling pinpricks of distant suns. At the center of the room was a table of food and several more comfortable white couches, all floating. The only control panel in the room was attached to the wall near the doors. It glowed neon pink.

"Look at all that food!" Kolt said. "If you'd told me yesterday I'd be lunching in space with a giant bomb about to go off in half an hour I'd have thought you were mad, absolutely mad."

"We should focus," Gertie said, "so that doesn't happen."

The captain was a powerfully built woman with shoulder-length hair and a serious face.

She seemed more curious than happy to see them, and waved off the citrus "welcome mist" that sprayed as she entered the lounge herself. She sat opposite them on a separate floating couch and stared for a long time before finally forcing a smile.

"Why don't you just talk . . ." she said with a vaguely German accent, "because I would not know where to begin."

"Well, we're from Earth," Kolt said.

The captain gasped.

"Originally!" Kolt said. "I mean, sort of . . . as humans once were, cave men, I mean cave *people*, Captain."

The captain then turned to Gertie. "How exactly did you make it to mid-space in the thing you were flying?"

Gertie thought it might not be a good idea to explain the time travel, frozen moonberries, Losers' robot hands, or the bomb they had brought with them. So she just smiled and made up a white lie.

"We're part of a space club . . ." she said.

"That's right." Kolt nodded. "Stellar enthusiasts."

"We found the old rocket, and decided to try and fix it up and go into space."

"I can't believe it actually got you this far. There are no cells for liquid nitrogen or liquid oxygen. What fuel did you burn?"

"Hmmm, yes," Kolt said. "The fuel situation was serious, a bit scary actually, ha ha."

"Doctor Echlin told me over ear-com that you have cargo?"

"Mashed potato mush room," said Robot Rabbit Boy.

"Vegetables?" said the captain.

"That's right," said Gertie, "for space-club members to eat on the journey into space."

The captain leaned forward with a menacing grin. "You do know you were on an insane suicide mission?"

Kolt looked past her at the muffins on the food table. "Well, it wouldn't be the first time."

"A dollop of butter."

"What would you have done if we weren't here?" said the captain with genuine curiosity.

"Perished!" Kolt said, still looking at the muffin table. "Victims of our own cosmic hunger."

Then the captain's watch beeped. "Hold on, please . . ." she said, raising her wrist to whisper something.

Although she *thought* she was speaking a language her visitors wouldn't understand, the power of Skuldarkian allowed the three Keepers to comprehend perfectly the captain's next words.

"Doctor Echlin, these people are total lunatics—though probably harmless. The rabbit droid seems to be quite interesting, and reminds me of an antique Series 9 Forever Friend I had as a girl. Anyway, let's feed them and transport them back to Earth-Mater or Alpha Moon, where they can be examined by psychologists. Why don't you have Doctor

Brady and Doctor Beaverbrook film-log their ship for suspicious items and beam the file to Space Guard Council? Just in case there's some fallout with protocol, we'll be spared a kick in the butt by the stiffs from FFC."

The captain laughed at whatever her colleague's response was, then lowered her sleeve. "Sorry about that," she said. "Routine matters, I'm sure you understand."

It was suddenly obvious to Kolt and Gertie they needed to speak privately, to decide what to do before the bomb was found. As a ploy to exchange a few words without being heard, Kolt asked the captain if he might visit the food table.

"By all means," she said. "It's all healthy, grown right here, and prepared by the famous chefs of I-8-PP."

Gertie followed Kolt to the buffet and stared at the various things to eat.

Predictably, Kolt went for the enormous muffin. There was even a pot of blueberry jam for Robot Rabbit Boy.

"No matter how much danger we find ourselves in," Kolt said in a hushed tone, "isn't it funny how there's always a meal? Remember China? And Venice? And . . ."

"Kolt, what are we going to do about the bomb!?"

Kolt cut his muffin in two pieces. "Oh yes, *that*."

"Maybe we should tell her?" said Gertie.

"She'd freak out."

"I know, but it's better than getting blown up," Gertie told him.

"I suppose so, and it's not like she would kill us or anything. They don't seem to be crazed Losers, just a bunch of scientists."

"Then where are the Losers?"

Kolt shrugged. "They might have left ages ago, who knows."

Gertie wondered how Birdy was getting on, returning the ant to the place where the robot hand had most likely been made.

"So it's settled," Gertie said. "We tell her before they find it in the rocket ship?"

Kolt nodded, his mouth already stuffed with space muffin.

35

Gareth Milk Is Found

THREE MILES ACROSS THE station, the forest biosphere where the robot ant belonged was in serious danger of breaching further safety regulations. It had been mismanaged for the past year by a crew of biologists who had slowly grown to despise science. The endless data and testing had ruined their minds and left them with great bitterness.

So one day, when they received 3-D spam in their email accounts from a group known as the Losers, they found themselves *very* interested in the tagline.

MURDER KILLS, WEAPONS DESTROY,
SCIENCE IS BORING, AM I RIGHT?

After becoming members of this Earth club called THE LOSERS, the scientists were soon under their command,

and placing orders for robot hand parts from factory moon 76. Once they were built, codes sent from Vispoth were uploaded to their mainframes. Each hand was programmed to complete a particular task. Then it was ejected into space through the Nanobot Osmosis Glass (N.O.G.) of the great dome. Once in space, Vispoth created a time funnel direct to Skuldark, based on space-time coordinates the Losers had used when stealing the B.D.B.U. several months before. There, on the Island of Lost Things, the terrible hands did their work.

Like the bad scientists they were, the crew of space Losers didn't ask *why* they were building robot hands and then ejecting them, they just followed orders.

To check on operations and send regular reports, Thrax had dispatched one of their gang—a Loser by the name of Gareth Milk.

When Birdy and Dr. Brady arrived by magnetic monorail, the two Loser scientists were lying around munching on chips, with no idea they were about to meet one of their most hated enemies—a Keeper known as Birdy.

"What do you want, *Brady*?" sneered a Loser scientist with a bushy beard when he saw his colleague.

"He's come to see his insect family," a woman in a green lab coat laughed. "Looks like he's brought a specimen for us to try and step on."

They all looked at Birdy. "A new type of pest!" the bearded Loser chuckled.

Dr. Brady smiled awkwardly.

The third forest-dome scientist, whose credentials had been forged by Vispoth, was sitting at his desk in a virtual reality helmet. He was playing a game and waving his arms in the air—shooting birds that no one else could see or hear. He didn't even see Dr. Brady and Birdy pass their messy workstations and disappear through some plastic flaps into the forest dome.

"One day," Dr. Brady said, "we'll be able to create hundred-thousand-acre forests here in space that can just grow and grow for thousands of years. That is, if we can learn how to keep the robotic ants from escaping."

Birdy wondered if he had ever seen anything like it before. If he had ever been familiar with space, or if this was something that had happened beyond his own time.

"But won't the glass break?" Birdy wanted to know. "When the trees get taller?"

"No, because it's N.O.G., Nanobot Osmosis Glass, which is glass not made from sand but constructed from nanobots—tiny computers that can change their forms."

"Oh," said Birdy, "so the glass is actually millions of tiny robots squeezed together that have the ability to look clear?"

"Transparency is most certainly the greatest miracle."

"So as the forest grows . . ." Birdy thought out loud, "so too will the glass?"

"That's right," the scientist went on, "and if a meteor hits it, the nanobots can bounce it away using magnetic repulsion. There's an equation for that if you'd like to see it."

Birdy's face lit up. "I would love to! But I should really get back to my friends, I mean, fellow doctors."

They released the robot ant, and watched it crawl away to a nearby clump of moss. Then they left the forest dome and its fresh odor of trees to return through the workstation where the three biologists were still lounging about. The woman and bearded man were now drinking fizzy orange liquid from bottles while the third Loser, Gareth Milk, was just finishing his video game.

Suddenly, Birdy caught sight of something moving on the table, something wriggling. It was a robot finger. Then on another desk were a wrist joint, steel wire, and several aluminum knuckles.

"Did you see that fly escaping just then?" Birdy said, pointing upward. Dr. Brady and the two biologists all looked. Birdy swept his hand over a desk, dropping a dead thumb and other tiny robot parts into his pocket as a way to prove the robot hands *had* been coming from space station I-8-PP. He wondered then if the mean technicians could be Losers.

BACK IN THE CAPTAIN'S lounge, Gertie and Kolt had decided that before they confessed everything to the captain, they would try to get information about the nearest black hole. The clock was still counting down. It would soon be a matter of minutes.

"Wow . . . look at that," Kolt said loudly in the direction of the captain. He was pointing to a chocolate chip sticking out of his muffin. "Reminds me of an edible black hole!"

The captain strained her neck to look at Kolt's plate, but was unimpressed by the lump of protruding chocolate.

"Black holes are so weird," Gertie added. "Lucky we didn't fall into one on the way here!"

The captain smiled at this. "It's not likely," she said. "You don't fall into them, you're sucked in, and we're incredibly far from the nearest one."

"So, er, where would that be?" Kolt asked. "Just out of interest."

"In the Chestnut Cluster, beyond the moons of Ellie and Simple Bear," said the captain, rolling her eyes over the table of things to eat.

"Is it a big black hole?" Kolt asked.

"Oh yes," said the captain. "It's one of the biggest, baddest black holes in the observable universe."

"Shame we couldn't see it," Kolt said, "being members of a space club an' all."

"See it!" barked the captain. "If you got anywhere near it you'd be dragged in!"

"It's that powerful, eh?" Gertie marveled.

"Not even light can escape its mammoth gravitational pull," said the captain. "That's why it's called a *black hole*."

"Be nice to get up close though," Gertie added, chewing on a spinach leaf, "and actually feel the power."

The captain eyed the three Keepers suspiciously—especially Robot Rabbit Boy, who was now licking sticky jam from his paws.

Just then, Dr. Brady and Birdy entered in a shower of citrus "welcome mist."

"The ant has been returned, Captain, and here's the last member of their crew, Doctor Seuss."

The captain looked at him. "What kind of space club was it you said you belonged to?"

"Space club?" Birdy said. "You mean Keepers of Lost Things?"

The captain raised her sleeve to talk, but then thought better of it.

"Will you excuse myself and Doctor Brady for a few minutes?"

After they had gone, Birdy rushed over to Kolt and Gertie at the buffet table.

"Guess what?!" he said, eager to spill the contents of his pockets.

Kolt was slicing a gluten-free, vegan, soy-free, cruelty-free blueberry muffin in half.

"Keepers of Lost Things?" he said. "Gertie told them we were part of a space club!"

"Don't worry about that now," said Birdy emptying his pockets of all the things he'd swiped from the workstation table. A few of the tinier bits bounced onto Kolt's plate.

"The robot hands really were built here!" the newest Keeper exclaimed.

"Well, it doesn't matter," Gertie said darkly, "because I think we're about to be arrested, and then we're going to get blown up."

"Well, we can't be arrested," said Kolt, stuffing muffin into his mouth. "I'mstilleatingmyspacelunch."

"Gertie is right, we probably only have fifteen minutes before the Black Hole Muncher blows!"

"Fear not . . ." Kolt said, crumbs tumbling from his mouth. "I have a brilliant plan."

He took two bags of spices from a pocket deep in his space suit and held them out.

"Behold," he said, "the magic power of herbs and spices."

Gertie and Birdy looked at one another.

"One of these bags contains growing spice," Kolt went on, "the other, shrinking spice."

"How do you know which is which?" asked Birdy.

"I just know . . ." Kolt said, eyeballing the young mathematician.

"Then why," Gertie asked, "were you only two inches high when we met for the first time?"

"Well, it was dark," Kolt protested. "I couldn't see the bags properly. Anyway, listen—you two are going to eat some *growing* spice, then when you're both big, you can overpower the crew and force them to fly us to the nearest black hole, which we know is in the Chestnut Cluster beyond the moons of thingy and whatever. Then we'll release the Muncher, finish what's left of the buffet on this table, and go home to Skuldark, heroes!"

"But won't the space station get caught in the black hole's massive gravitational pull and be crushed to something smaller than a Cave Sprite?" Gertie said.

Kolt nodded. "Yes. That's the only major weakness of my plan."

Gertie had another idea. "I think we should tell the captain the whole story, and she can decide. She's the expert, after all, a *real* astronaut."

Suddenly from the corridor they heard shouting, and people running. Kolt panicked.

"Quick!" he cried, fiddling with one of the spice bags. "Eat, eat, eat!"

The captain appeared with several angry-looking scientists in a cloud of citrus "welcome mist." Kolt tried to think of something to say, but suddenly realized he'd mixed up the spice packets, as Gertie and Birdy were now shrinking instead of growing.

"Help!" Gertie cried, getting smaller and smaller.

"Don't worry," boomed Kolt's voice. "It'll wear off in about ten minutes!"

"What? What? What?"

"It could always be worse!"

36

The Hungry Sheep

WHEN THEY WERE ONLY an inch high, Kolt scooped up Gertie and Birdy and put them on the plate next to his uneaten half of blueberry muffin. But it was soon clear they'd ingested far too much shrinking spice, and continued to get smaller until they were quite invisible to both the naked eye—and eyes with clothes on.

By this point Robot Rabbit Boy was in a panic at the sight of Gertie and Birdy's sudden shrinkage, and was determined to follow them no matter what the cost. He lunged for a spice bag that had fallen on the floor, then licked out the entire contents in one flick of his rabbit tongue.

As the captain and her crew advanced on Kolt bearing electro light-rods and carrying the Black Hole Muncher, the spice Robot Rabbit Boy had gobbled up started taking effect. But instead of shrinking like Gertie and Birdy, he began to do the opposite.

At first it was only his head. But then his ears ballooned and knocked an entire cake off the food table as he got bigger and bigger and bigger.

The moment the cake splattered all over the floor, a buzzer went off on the other side of the lounge. A small door opened in the wall to release a live sheep whose job was to clean up edible spills—thereby reducing food waste and human energy output.

The captain and her crew cowered in fear as Robot Rabbit Boy was becoming so enormous he almost touched the ceiling of the N.O.G. dome.

"EGGCUP!

"EGGCUP!

"EGGCUP!

"EGGCUP!!!"

Everyone covered their ears at the head-splitting thunder of Robot Rabbit Boy's voice—everyone except Gertie and Birdy, that is. They were stranded on the side of a mountain that was actually a crumb. They were so tiny that Kolt, Robot Rabbit Boy, the captain, and her crew seemed like they were miles away, and Robot Rabbit Boy's voice was just a deep vibration that caused their muffin mountain to shake violently.

However, wandering about calmly under the table, completely undeterred by the giant rabbit, tiny children, and a bomb about to go off, was the dutiful, highly trained live cleaning sheep. The creature had already begun chomping on bits of the fallen cake—when he began to smell his most favorite food of all time—gluten-free, vegan, cruelty-free, soy-free, organic, non-GMO blueberry muffins.

With the humans distracted by a rabbit monster, the sheep carefully came up on one side of the table. Then he looked around once more to make sure he wasn't being watched. It was forbidden for a cleaning sheep to eat anything that hadn't fallen on the floor. But muffins were muffins. And so with the coast clear, the cleaning sheep homed in on where the half muffin lay innocently on the plate, minding its own business.

As Robot Rabbit Boy's head was pushing on the flexible N.O.G. ceiling, the sheep took one last look around, curled his tongue up one side of the buffet table, and tried to slurp the moist muffin-half into his mouth. But it was farther away than he thought, and his first attempt left him muffinless.

For Gertie and Birdy, the sheep's tongue was like the sky turning bright pink suddenly, then the air became sticky and tropical. They realized it was life or death, and darted into one of the many giant dough caverns, inlaid with jagged blueberry boulders.

After running in, they realized that to a tiny person, a muffin was nothing but a sweet, dark maze—a breakfast treat made up mostly of air.

The second slurp of the sheep's tongue was like a soggy earthquake. Giant bubbles of slime rained down upon the muffin mountain and oozed into the cavern, making them go deeper and deeper into the sugary darkness to avoid being sucked up.

At the continued growth of the rabbit, the captain and her crew gave up. They dropped their light-rods and the Black Hole Muncher, then escaped from the room in a spray of watermelon "farewell mist," scarpering toward the emergency pods. The pods would propel them back to Earth Station 4 in the event of the biosphere's destruction—which they never thought would come at the hands of a space rabbit's allergic reaction to blueberry jam.

LUCKY TO HAVE ESCAPED the live cleaning sheep's tongue, Gertie and Birdy soon returned to their normal size, bursting out of their muffin cave in a shower of crumbs and landing on what appeared to be a dirty gray rug—which was Robot Rabbit Boy's foot. Since he had licked up an entire packet, he was still getting bigger and bigger.

"Kolt! What's happened?"

But Kolt (or at least his body) was under the table on his hands and knees eating cake off the floor. He looked up at them. "Baaaaaa," he said, which in sheep language meant, "I swear I didn't eat that muffin, I'm just a live cleaning product."

"What is going on?" Birdy said. "Why is Robot Rabbit Boy eighty feet high and Kolt acting like a sheep?"

"Don't know!" Gertie cried, having no idea what body-swap-bots were, and that Birdy had accidentally dropped a couple onto Kolt's muffin when emptying out his pocket.

Gertie pointed. "It's the Black Hole Muncher!"

The two Keepers sprinted over to it, only to find there were seventy-four seconds left until it blew.

Before Gertie could think of what to do, a large sheep galloped toward them.

"It's me!" the animal shouted. "Baa, baa!"

"What the!?" Gertie said. "A talking sheep?"

"No, baa, it's me, baa, Kolt, baa!"

"Why are you . . . ?"

"I don't know, baa! It has to be the work of body-swap-bots!"

"Fifty-eight seconds until it blows!" said Birdy.

"Baa, don't worry . . ." said the sheep that was really Kolt.

"Stop saying baa!" Gertie snapped angrily, wondering what it would feel like to be blown up. "And don't say, It could always be worse.'"

"I can't help saying baa, I'm a sheep, baa! We have to get

the giant Robot Rabbit Boy, baa, to use his nose laser to blast the Black Hole Muncher, baa, to, baa, to the, baa, baa . . ."

"Out with it," said Birdy. "You can do it . . ."

"Baa, baa, baa, baa" went the sheep that was Kolt, his little white throat vibrating with each cry. "Nose laser, baa, blast bomb, baa, in direction of the Chestnut Cluster, baa, baa, baa, black, baa, hole . . . baa."

"That's it!" Gertie said.

"ROBOT RABBIT BAAAA!!!!!!" they all roared together.

"LAVENDER!"

"Yes!" Gertie said. "Lavender!"

Robot Rabbit Boy bent down, completely crushing the food table and almost squashing Kolt's body, which was still on the floor gobbling up cake.

"TAKE THE BOMB! BLAST IT TO, UM, TO . . ." Gertie said, turning to the sheep that was Kolt. "Where is the Chestnut thing exactly?"

"Over there, baa!" Kolt said, moving his fluffy head.

"Where?"

"Baa, there!" he said again, motioning with his head.

Then Birdy had an idea. "Use your tail!"

The sheep that was Kolt nodded, then pointed his tail in a particular direction, which Gertie then showed to Robot Rabbit Boy by using her arms.

"We have to be quick, baa, baa," Kolt bleated frantically. "Before the growing spice wears off, baa, baa."

"DOLLOP?"

With only thirty-nine seconds left before detonation, Robot Rabbit Boy scooped up what to him was a tiny gold cube with flashing wires.

"How's he going to get it out of the dome and into space?" Gertie said. But Birdy, who had been thinking about the flexible dome glass, was already at the neon pink control panel by the door.

Birdy said something to the computer, then answered Gertie without looking away from the flashing buttons. "If the Nanobot Osmosis Glass thinks Robot Rabbit Boy is a toxin—they'll release him into space."

"How are you going to do that?"

"It's voice command," Birdy said. "So I just told the computer we have a giant rabbit with a bomb, and need to let it out. . . ."

"Will it work?"

Suddenly, Robot Rabbit Boy's head passed completely through the top of the dome glass as though through a thin layer of jelly.

Gertie, Birdy, and the sheep that was Kolt watched, barely able to breathe or baa.

With twenty-one seconds remaining, the Series 7 lifted the bomb through the flexible nanobot roof with his paw and nudged the Black Hole Muncher in the direction Gertie had shown him, which was toward the nearest black hole in the Chestnut Cluster, beyond the moons of Ellie and Simple Bear.

As the bomb drifted away, Robot Rabbit Boy gave an almighty blast from his nose laser, which was now a thousand times more powerful and shook the whole space station.

The force of the blast would have caused the bomb to explode right over the space station had it not been for the pure luck of the fireproof panel from their rocket with the robot hand still sunbathing on it. It floated just in front of the bomb, shielding the weapon from the intense heat, but propelling it to an immense speed, far greater than the speed of light. A few seconds later, from somewhere deep in the Chestnut Cluster, a black hole *almost* let out a tiny burp—but as nothing can escape the pull of a black hole, it couldn't even manage that when the Black Hole Muncher blew.

They had done it again.

The Keepers of Lost Things (whose job was *supposed* to be returning articles to eccentric geniuses in history and trying interesting foods) had saved not only the human race—but every living thing from the Chestnut Cluster to planet Earth.

Only one question remained once Robot Rabbit Boy had shrunk back down to his normal size.

Had the body-swap-bots eaten by Kolt and the sheep been set to temporary or permanent?

At least one thing was certain.

They both loved cake.

37

The Losers Come for Gareth Milk and Kolt Is Still a Sheep

Slumped on the white couch, tired but jubilant and utterly relieved, Gertie, Birdy, Robot Rabbit Boy, and the sheep that was Kolt didn't have long to catch their breath before they saw something horribly familiar swoop over the top of the glass dome.

It was *Doll Head*.

"Losers, baa!"

But Gertie's first feeling was excitement. They had destroyed the Black Hole Muncher, Skuldark was safe, Birdy had been rescued, and the robotic ant was back in the rain forest dome scurrying about on leaves.

"It's us and, baa, them now, baa," Kolt said. "The captain and her crew of scientists, baa, already got, baa, in their escape pods, baa."

Birdy seemed afraid. "Real Losers? What do they want?"

"I don't baa," Kolt bleated, "but we should try and find out, baa."

Gertie turned to the newest Keeper. "Did you recognize any of the scientists at the rain forest dome? Any seem weird to you? Loserish maybe?"

Birdy shrugged. "The forest-dome techs seemed a bit off. And there was one who didn't even look at us, he was too busy wearing some kind of helmet."

"A helmet?" Gertie said.

"Yeah, waving his arms around like he was holding invisible guns."

Kolt shot Gertie a look. "Baa! Virtual reality video games, not something you'd expect a top-level scientist to be doing, baa."

"It's true, they might be Losers," Gertie said. "And they could know where to find more kidnapped Keepers."

"But we can't baa," bleated Kolt.

"We can't what?" Gertie and Birdy said together.

"We can't go, baa, to Skuldark without my baa."

"Without your what!?"

"MY *BAA* DEE."

"That's true, but *Doll Head* is most likely starting to dock," Gertie said, looking over at the sheep in Kolt's body near the crushed buffet table, still gobbling up spilled food. "How about we race over to the rain forest dome and confront the Losers face-to-face?"

"Mush butter."

"Great," Kolt protested. "This is just great, baa. The one

time I get to meet my archenemy, baa, Cava Calla Thrax, and I'm a sheep with cake stuck to its baa."

"Stop being vain!" Gertie ordered, then broke into a grin. "On second thought, he might try and turn you into a sweater."

"Ha ha, baa," the sheep that was Kolt said, stamping one hoof.

"How long before those body-swap-bot things wear off?" asked Birdy.

"I don't baa."

"Well then, we have no choice," Gertie pointed out. "We have to get over there now before they escape in *Doll Head* with whatever they have come for—maybe another bomb."

"I know where the magnetic monorail is!" said Birdy. "I think . . ."

"Let's take these floating couch things!"

The sheep that was Kolt and Robot Rabbit Boy remained on their couch while Gertie and Birdy ran across the room to another one.

They held on, barking out instructions to the giant cushions to take them to the rain forest dome.

As they were squirted with watermelon "farewell mist" on the way out, Gertie and Birdy punched the cushions on their couch. "Faster! Faster!"

From behind they could hear their fellow Keepers trying to do the same. "Mush mush," and "baa baa."

The two couches were now flying through the abandoned space station so quickly that Gertie's couch lost one of the bigger cushions. It flew up and tumbled back through the air, hitting the sheep that was Kolt in the face, resulting in a few muffled cries that sounded like . . . baaaaaaabaaaa.

The transport furniture had not been designed for high-speed, competitive couch racing, and soon bits were flying off left and right. Some of the passageways were so narrow that Gertie and Birdy had to tuck in their hands and feet so as not to get them scraped or smashed against a corner.

About halfway there, Kolt and Robot Rabbit Boy's couch must have somehow understood it was a race, and decided to take a different route, losing sight of the other Keepers.

Gertie felt she was ready for anything now—even seeing her brother face-to-face, which is exactly what was about to happen as they thundered toward the supply room outside the rain forest dome at top couch speed.

DOLL HEAD HAD ALREADY landed, and a jubilant-looking Mandy Zilch, the two lazy technicians, and Gareth Milk were loading all the robot parts from their desks into boxes to take on board the ship. It was clear they had no idea a second major defeat had just befallen them.

Suddenly, without warning, a giant couch smashed through the automatic doors and air-skidded to a stop—catapulting its occupants off the cushions into a stack of boxes. Bits of wire and robot parts went everywhere, including a robotic finger, which strangely went right into the nostril of a technician.

"Aaargh!"

"Keepers!!!" growled Mandy Zilch, as Gertie and Birdy rolled to a stop under one of the desks. "You're supposed to not exist anymore!" Then she turned to sneer at Gareth Milk.

"Don't tell me you messed this mission up as well!"

But the teenage Keeper was too shocked by the sight of his sister to reply.

"Gareth!" Gertie cried furiously. "*You* wanted to blow up Skuldark and kill us?"

"N-n-no, no," he said, taking a few steps back. "My job was to program and modify robot hands, that's all." He spun around to face Mandy Zilch. "Which I did, I promise, I did loads, like eight hundred of them . . ."

"Well, you must have done it wrong, you idiotic boy!" The circuits on one side of her head blazed with flashing lights gone wild.

"The hands were sent to blow up Skuldark?"

"Yes!" Birdy said, trying to get Gertie's attention so he could wink. "They blew it up and killed Kolt."

"They what?" Gertie said, then realized Birdy must have some kind of plan.

Gareth Milk went bright red and covered his mouth at the thought that he had killed someone. The anger Gertie had seen in him when they met in ancient China seemed to have disappeared completely. He was just a sad little boy at the mercy of bullies.

"And you," cried Mandy Zilch, suddenly recognizing Birdy from the Cherokee village, "will not escape this time!"

But then something big, white, fast, and cushiony came

hurtling into the supply room, knocking the two Loser technicians to the ground like bowling pins.

Mandy Zilch and Gareth Milk stared in shock as Robot Rabbit Boy and a fully grown sheep bounced onto the floor.

Mandy Zilch must have truly understood then what Birdy had said moments before, about Kolt being dead and the Island of Lost Things getting blown up.

"Kolt is dead? That means Skuldark is destroyed! It worked! We've won!"

"I'm not baa!" cried the sheep.

"*Yes,* Kolt *is* dead!" insisted Birdy to the sheep that was Kolt. "He died when the Black Hole Muncher went off, remember?"

"Baa?"

"You were eating cake, I mean, grass . . ."

"I baa?"

"Mush room!" whispered Robot Rabbit Boy, pulling on the sheep's fur, as though trying to alert Kolt to the fact that all this was part of Birdy's cunning plan.

"I killed Kolt!" said Gareth Milk, utterly horrified by what he thought he'd unknowingly done.

Mandy Zilch was dancing on the spot. "And you blew Skuldark up! Yes! Along with all its boring, useless, stupid creatures, and that mattress-sized comic!"

Then the sheep that was Kolt must have realized that Birdy and Gertie didn't have dust in their left eyes, but were in fact winking.

"Ooh . . . yes, baa, it was the saddest day, the worst baa in this young sheep's baa, baa, to see an entire island get baa, just like that! Baa."

"Dollops, mush, butter."

"So I suppose you want to join *us* now you have nowhere to go?" scoffed Mandy Zilch.

"You do?" said Gareth Milk, with a confused smile.

"Yes!" said Gertie. "We have nowhere to go, and with two animals to look after, we need a real home and a strong leader, not just this spaceship we accidentally found ourselves on after the explosion."

"It'll never happen," Mandy Zilch told them, "but it will be nice to see you all beg. I only wish Kolt were alive to see the end of his kind."

"Yes," Gertie said, "he was a good Keeper."

"Oh, baa!" interrupted the sheep. "He was a great one! So good at cooking, baa, baking, woodwork, baa, mechanics, welding, spice collecting, and also, baa, organizing, sewing, picking out clothes, garden work, singing, brewing moonberry juice, baa, and playing the xylophone, which he usually did in private, baa, but which he now wishes he'd shared with others, baa, as it truly was a gift, oh what a shame such a great man is baa."

"The xylophone?" Gertie said. "Is that true?"

"Oh yes, baa," said the sheep. "Kolt used to stay up late into the night hammering away on the metal rectangles with his bobble."

"What's a bobble?" asked Mandy Zilch. "And why is a sheep talking?"

"It's the thing, baa, on the end of the stick, baa."

"What stick?" asked Birdy.

"Well, baa, let's not worry about this now . . . I'm sure there's a proper name for them, but Kolt always referred to them, baa, as his bobbles."

"Ach, who cares!" roared Mandy Zilch. "Idiots!"

"So we want to join you," Gertie said again. "As the last of our kind we'll get special treatment from your leader."

"Well, you're not the last of your kind," Mandy Zilch said proudly. "We've scattered Keepers all throughout history!"

Gertie shrugged. "But they're not *real* Keepers?"

"Oh yes they are!" Mandy Zilch said. "Which is why we had to place magnetic cuffs on them, so they wouldn't disappear to Skuldark."

"I don't believe you," said Birdy. "We *are* the last now that Kolt is dead, I'm sure of it."

"Butter cup?" said Robot Rabbit Boy, pointing to himself.

"No, you're not a *real* Keeper!" said Gertie. "You're just an outdated rabbit droid who *thinks* he's a Keeper. You could never be a real one like Birdy and me."

"That's the spirit," said Mandy Zilch at Robot Rabbit Boy's humiliation. "Put fools in their place! Grind them down with cruel words so they learn . . . ha! Maybe we can find a position in the Loser ranks for you after all. . . ."

Robot Rabbit Boy's eyes dimmed to dark brown, and he dropped his head in shame, but Gertie knew she had to sound convincing for Mandy Zilch to believe she could be a Loser.

"We're the last Keepers, and as such will join the Losers at the highest ranks," said Gertie.

Birdy agreed, and pointed at Mandy Zilch. "Yeah, soon we'll be telling *you* what to do!"

"Pish! But you're *not* the last Keepers!" she went on, pulling a shiny card out of her hip pocket, then unfolding it slowly, until it was the size of a small tablecloth. The panel was dark blue on both sides, with a glowing web of lights and thin lines. White blobs drifted across the surface of the metal fabric, and reminded Gertie of small clouds.

"What's that?" she asked the smug Loser.

"It's a live pocket atlas, you idiot, proof you're not the last Keepers in the world, and therefore not special at all."

"A map?" Gertie said, staring at a dozen or so flashing orange dots.

Mandy Zilch smirked. "Each light is a Keeper of Lost Things. So while they're alive, you're not the last Keepers, and therefore *not* special."

Then the Loser turned to Birdy. "*You* were supposed to be the latest orange light," she said bitterly, "blinking at me from a place called the Black Hole of Calcutta!"

"That's very interesting, baa," the sheep that was Kolt said, "but I read that since 2093, the Black Hole of Calcutta, baa, has been a five-star hotel with three pools, a water slide, shopping, horseback riding, baa, cooking school, free airport shuttle, and a Michelin-starred restaurant, so you must be lying, baa baa. That's not a map at all, it's just aluminum foil with lights on it."

"You stupid animal," Mandy Zilch said, "you don't think Vispoth knows this? With such supreme intelligence, our super computer can tell exactly when each destination was at its worst, and that's when we dropped those sad, pathetic Keepers into their lives of misery."

Gertie wished there were some way she could remember the position of each tiny light on Zilch's live pocket atlas, but the evil Loser was already folding it back up into a shiny card. As she returned it to her hip pocket, one of the circuits on her head began to fizz and sparkle.

"It's Thrax!" she said. "He wants us back at headquarters pronto! He says it's an emergency."

"Gertie," Gareth said, reaching toward her. "I'm sorry for what happened, but I guess it was the only way. . . ."

"You still believe in the Losers' cause?"

"It's the only solution," he said. "After what I witnessed during the Information War, the only way to help people is to limit what they can learn. . . ."

"But what happened to us, Gareth?"

"What happens to any children caught in the middle of fighting? They break inside."

"But I don't feel broken," Gertie told him.

"That's because you lost your memory."

"Well, could you lose yours?"

"It doesn't matter now," Gareth said. "Skuldark is gone, and we'll always be together, working toward a simpler and brighter world, I suppose."

Gertie desperately wanted to tell him the truth—felt so

close now to winning him over. But before she could say anything else, Mandy Zilch grabbed her brother's arm and yanked him away.

"They can stay here on I-8-PP until Thrax decides what to do with them. With the B.D.B.U. in ashes, their time machine is just a piece of wood with a hole in it."

"Can I stay too?" Gareth asked.

Mandy Zilch thought for a moment. "Thrax said he wants us *all* back at headquarters for an emergency meeting, so you'd better come."

Then the half-girl-half-droid sneered at Gertie's brother. "You're probably going to be honored for the terribly wonderful things you've done, so you wouldn't want to miss that, now would you?"

"But..."

"Stop sniveling, *Doll Head* is waiting!"

"See you soon," Gareth shouted to his sister hopefully.

Gertie watched as her brother, Mandy Zilch, and the two injured Loser technicians shuffled off toward *Doll Head*.

She felt like she should run after them, try and drag her brother away from his evil Loser friends, but when she started to move, Birdy and Kolt the sheep stood in her way.

"It has to be like this," Birdy said gently. "I took a good look at that map, so we've got at least some of the information we need to try and rescue other Keepers—but if they think it's a trick then..."

"They'll find out eventually, baa," the sheep that was Kolt said. "That might even be what their emergency meeting is baa, but knowing at least a few locations will give us a chance to make a plan, and get the B.D.B.U. on board with an ongoing Keeper rescue effort, baa."

"But what about my brother?"

"He's not ready," Kolt said sympathetically.

"But he might be someday," Birdy added.

"The poor baa is a slave to all the terrible things he's seen—and so until he can get stronger than the things that have happened to him, he'll be their prisoner, which is baa, very baa."

Gertie knew they were right, and tried to stop herself from sprinting off after the Losers.

Watching *Doll Head* sail over the biosphere dome, then fizzle away in time to a flash of purple light, Gertie realized that Robot Rabbit Boy was still hunched on the floor, as if trying to make sense of what he'd been told, that he wasn't a *real* Keeper of Lost Things.

He had crawled in between some boxes, and was trembling with wet eyes.

"Robot Rabbit Boy," Gertie said, "please come over here."

The Series 7 Forever Friend got to his feet and dutifully loped over to the group of Keepers, his paws dragging on the floor, his head hung in shame.

Gertie bent down and put her hand under his chin to gently lift his head.

"Hey," she said kindly, "I *had* to say those things for them to buy Birdy's plan—but it's not true, you must know that, you're a great Keeper."

"Mashed potato . . ." Robot Rabbit Boy whispered, his voice shaking as though trying to hold back a flood of rabbit tears.

"That's right," Gertie went on, "and you're the real hero of this whole mission. You saved the entire universe. Do you have any idea what that means?"

"Butter, mashed?"

"You're probably the most important rabbit that ever lived," Birdy said.

"That's right, baa," agreed Kolt, "with quick thinking, baa, super-fast rabbit reflexes, and extreme baa, you saved *us*, the space station, the ball of rock we call baa, and every living creature on it, including Slug Lamps."

"Dollops?"

"Yes, dollops," said Gertie.

"Without you," Birdy went on, "we'd all be floating out there in tiny bits."

"Fly mush?"

"Exactly," said Gertie, "which is why I want to give you something." She took out her Keepers' key.

Two ragged, shaking paws rose slowly to accept the most sacred of all a Keeper's possessions.

"We were born Keepers," Gertie said. "But, Robot Rabbit Boy—you had a choice, and you chose the harder, more dangerous path because you wanted to keep us safe."

"Baa, baa, indeed," said Kolt. "Most pets just lie around the house trying not to poo indoors, baa—but you managed to save the universe. I'd say that's pretty special, which is why I also want to give you my baa," the eldest Keeper went on. "When I'm back in my own body of course, and it's not lost."

"If it wasn't for you and your nose laser, I would have been eaten by wolves," Birdy said truthfully. "And so I'm giving you my key too."

"You are without a doubt the most important Keeper of Lost Things there has ever been," Gertie stated officially.

At these final words, Robot Rabbit Boy looked at the keys in his paws. Then he stood up straight, trying to blink away the wetness.

"Mush fly dollop butter lavender dollop-dollop mashed fly potato eggcup dollop eggcup fly, lavender, butter, room, fly, mush, dollop of butter, mush potato, lavender, egg butter, lavender. Fly, eggcup, fly," he said poetically, "fly eggcup ... fly."

The other Keepers nodded appreciatively and gave a round of applause.

"Great, baa, speech, baa," said Kolt. "Very strong words in my opinion, though, er ... we may need to borrow back our keys from time to time ... but they're still yours of course, you can keep them in your bed, et cetera ..."

"Kolt's right," said Gertie. "Do you mind if we borrow them back right now in fact, so we can go home?"

Robot Rabbit Boy shook his head, holding out the keys to their original owners.

"Now all we need to do is rescue those missing Keepers," Gertie said.

"Baa, well, there's a bit more to it than that, baa—we'll

have to find the missing keys so the B.D.B.U. knows the time and place, baa, baa. Before we think about that, baa, can we find out where I am?"

"You're here," stated Birdy.

"As a sheep!"

"I think he means his body," Gertie said.

"Baa. I've had enough ovine fun to last a lifetime. I just hope those body-swap-bots were not set to permanent."

"But we can't stay here too long," Birdy said. "The Losers are coming back, remember?"

"I can't go home as a BAA!" Kolt said, stamping a hoof.

"Oh, stop being proud." Gertie smiled. "You can go jump around with the tapirs."

Despite being exhausted, the four Keepers of Lost Things went quickly back to the captain's area, where they found the sheep in Kolt's body sleeping off his strange adventure under the table.

Just then, Kolt's face began to shake, and with a strange flash of the eyes, the sheep let out a series of terrified sheep noises and scarpered back to its hole. A moment later, the body of an old man uncurled from beside the flattened food table and stood up.

"I'm me again!" Kolt said, wiping cream, bits of muffin, and chocolate sauce from his forehead. "I'm back! Yippee!"

Birdy helped Kolt scrape cake icing off his shoes.

Gertie stood watching, hands on her hips. "I'm glad," she said, "but we can't just leave it here."

"Leave what?"

"The sheep!"

"And why not?" asked Kolt.

"Because the Losers are coming back, and there's no crew, so they might take the space station over."

"Well, there's plenty of cake left for it to eat."

"I just don't think it's the right thing."

Robot Rabbit Boy nodded in agreement.

Kolt seemed flustered as he scooped maraschino cherries from his pockets. "Well, what's its name? Does it even have one?"

"Eggcup?"

"We can give it one," Gertie said.

"How about Max?" asked Birdy. "That name keeps coming up in my head."

"Or John?" said Kolt.

"Not John," said Gertie. "We'd get him confused with ..."

"Oh yes," Kolt realized. "Our Johnny of the sea ..."

"I actually like Max ..." Gertie said.

"Max it is then," said Kolt. "If it comes when called we take it back to Skuldark and hope the B.D.B.U. allows us to keep it, as we kept Robot Rabbit Boy and Mrs. Pumble's kitten. But if it doesn't come when we call, it'll have to stay."

"It will come," Gertie said hopefully. "Birdy, want to do the honors?"

Birdy walked forward, slapped his legs, and shouted to the hole where the cleaning sheep was hiding. "Max! Max! Good sheep! Good sheep! Max!"

The door opened a crack and a pair of frightened sheep eyes appeared.

"Good sheep!" Gertie said. "There's a good sheep!"

Slowly the animal got up and opened the door a little more with its nose.

"It's working!" said Birdy.

Kolt had his time machine and key ready to go.

"Remember, the Losers could be back any minute," he told them.

"C'mon, Max!" Birdy said, tapping his leg.

With a bowed head, and shy, hesitant eyes, the blueberry-muffin-loving cleaning sheep stepped sheepishly to the ragged band of Keepers.

"I knew it would work!" Gertie said, reaching out to pet the creature.

"We're going to look after you now," said Birdy.

"Lavender mashed," said Robot Rabbit Boy.

"Ready?" Kolt said. "There's raspberry syrup in my underpants and it's drying. . . . Link up, everyone!"

38

Home Sweet Skuldark

A WEEK LATER, THINGS were going well for the Keepers of Lost Things. Max the sheep was still in Skuldark. He had not been sent back to space by the B.D.B.U. and had found a comfortable place to nap in the hallway, halfway between the bedrooms and Robot Rabbit Boy's bed.

But the major news was that Robot Rabbit Boy had surprised them all yet again. Not by getting lost—but by recreating an exact replica of Mandy Zilch's map of missing Keepers, having used a tiny-cam function in the second toe of his right paw, to get a few seconds of footage.

One morning before anyone else was up, he went out into the garden and scorched the grass with his nose laser in the shape of continents. Then the clever Series 7 Forever Friend placed moonberries where all the little glowing dots had been. The only problem was, Slug Lamps kept zooming out to gobble them up.

Eventually, Kolt replaced each moonberry with a rock. There seemed to be sixteen Keepers in total, spread throughout the world. The only challenge was, they still didn't know *when* in time the Keepers had been put there. But everyone agreed it was a good start, and hoped the B.D.B.U. would continue to assist in the restoration of the island's Keeper population, by helping them find keys, and sending them on rescue missions.

WHEN THE COTTAGE WAS completely repaired from the damage inflicted by the robot hands and moonberry juice, the five heroes of Skuldark threw the biggest party the island had ever seen. There were fireworks from bedroom 285, noisemakers from bedroom 386, a record player and speakers from bedroom 612, Kolt's xylophone and bobble, and more cake than Max the sheep had ever seen in his entire life. Even some of the Guardians came to enjoy the eclectic range of music Gertie had chosen as DJ, and sample the many different foods Kolt had prepared for all manner of palates.

But the best part was when George the mouse, Max the sheep, and several Slug Lamps got on the dance floor with Robot Rabbit Boy, who was wearing all three Keepers' keys around his neck on a gold chain, along with the biggest, bushiest mustache ever worn by any rabbit, in the history of the universe—which was now safe, by the way, thanks to the Keepers of Lost Things, and a live cleaning sheep called Max.

Acknowledgments

The author would like to thank his agent and friend, Carrie Kania; production editor, Janet Pascal; editor, Julie Rosenberg; Alex Sanchez, editorial assistant; and Ben Schrank, president and publisher of Razorbill.

Simon Van Booy enjoys building robots, model airplanes, and R.C. vehicles. He has an impressive umbrella collection, a bowler hat, and carries a green thermos of tea everywhere. He is the bestselling author of nine books of fiction and three anthologies of philosophy. He has written for the *New York Times*, the *Financial Times*, the *Irish Times*, NPR, and the BBC. His works have been translated into many languages and optioned for film. In 2013, he founded Writers for Children, a project that helps young people build confidence in their writing abilities.